KATIE OPENS HER HEART

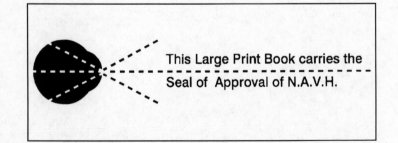

This Large Print Book carries the Seal of Approval of N.A.V.H.

KATIE OPENS
HER HEART

JERRY S. EICHER

THORNDIKE PRESS
A part of Gale, Cengage Learning

GALE
CENGAGE Learning®

Detroit • New York • San Francisco • New Haven, Conn • Waterville, Maine • London

GALE
CENGAGE Learning

LIBRARY OF CONGRESS CATALOGING-IN-PUBLICATION DATA

Eicher, Jerry S.
   Katie opens her heart / by Jerry S. Eicher.
      pages ; cm. — (Thorndike Press large print Christian romance) (Emma Raber's daughter series ; #1)
   ISBN-13: 978-1-4104-5921-3 (hardcover)
   ISBN-10: 1-4104-5921-7 (hardcover)
      1. Young women—Fiction. 2. Mothers and daughters—Fiction. 3. Conflict of generations—Fiction. 4. Amish—Fiction. 5. Mennonites—Fiction. 6. Large type books. I. Title.
PS3605.I34K386 2013b
813'.6—dc23   2013008841

Published in 2013 by arrangement with Harvest House Publishers

Printed in Mexico
1 2 3 4 5 6 7 17 16 15 14 13

KATIE OPENS HER HEART

CHAPTER ONE

The early morning sun was rising over the well-kept farms of Delaware's Amish country as Katie Raber drove her buggy toward Byler's Store near Dover to begin her day's work. She squinted when she spotted an approaching buggy in the distance. The horse had its neck arched high in the air. Katie didn't have to think long before she decided who was coming toward her. Ben Stoll would be holding the reins. It was his buggy. She was sure of that. Ben was one of the best-looking Amish boys around. Blessed was any girl who was invited to ride with him in his buggy — something Katie figured she would never experience. Ben was without a doubt the catch among the community's Amish young men. A cloud crossed the sun, and Katie held the buggy lines tight as she kept her eyes glued on the approaching buggy. Perhaps she could catch a glimpse of Ben this morning. That was all she could hope for. He was from another world. Ben never spoke to her, and she only saw him at the Sunday meetings and the Amish youth gatherings *Mamm* allowed her to attend. There he would be laughing and talking with someone else — someone more suited to his taste than "plain Katie," the out-of-step daughter of the odd widow Emma Raber. Katie could walk right under Ben Stoll's nose, and he wouldn't even know a shadow had gone by.

Yah, she was Emma Raber's daughter. That's how most people in the community thought of her. She even thought of herself that way — just an extension of her *mamm.* *Mamm* was nice enough, and Emma really loved her. So, *nee,* she wasn't really complaining. But sometimes her *mamm* did unusual things, and that made Katie seem so . . . well, weird to the other young adults in the Amish community. For one thing, there would be no *rumspringa* for Katie. Everyone else she knew among the Delaware Amish would have their time to run around and try out the ways of the world. But not Katie. Emma Raber wouldn't even consider such a thing for her daughter. And the Amish youth gatherings she was allowed to attend were few and far between. *Mamm* was suspicious of even those. "Too much socializing," she had said.

She could live without *rumspringa*. Or without Ben Stoll, for that matter. So what, Katie told herself, it might even be best for her if Ben were unobtainable. He might not be all that *wunderbah* if she ever got to know him. Katie sighed. These were desperate excuses, and she knew it, but lately *Mamm*'s restrictions were becoming harder and harder to bear. She was only trying to make herself feel better. Ben was *wunderbah*. Even her friend Arlene Miller wasn't above stealing a glance at Ben — and that with her boyfriend, Nelson Graber, sitting right across from her at the Sunday night hymn singings!

Katie wondered if all the girls were as taken with Ben as she was. She was aware of everything about him. She noticed when he wore a new black suit at communion time every spring. She noticed the way his buggy shone when the sun rays bounced off the sides at the Sunday meetings. The boy must spend hours waxing the black vinyl of his buggy, she thought. And most of all, she noticed the way Ben smiled when he was happy, which seemed like most of the time. What would it be like to be the kind of girl who made Ben smile that smile? Ha! Certainly a simple, plain soul like Emma

Raber's daughter couldn't be such a girl . . . *ever.*

Katie tried to look away from the fast-approaching buggy. She was way too fascinated with the boy. If *Mamm* knew her feelings, Katie knew she'd be given a lecture the size of the state of Delaware and right at the kitchen table after supper. *Yah, Mamm* would not understand how she felt. Life had been hard for *Mamm,* especially when it came to men. Hadn't *Daett* passed away when Katie was still a young girl? The loss had been so painful for *Mamm* that she might never marry again.

The beat of horse hooves on pavement grew louder. Katie eased open her buggy door just enough to make sure that whoever was in the passing buggy could see it was her in case a greeting was forthcoming. With her hands on the reins, Katie held her breath as the buggy approached and passed without its buggy door opening even an inch. Katie saw the unmistakable outline of Ben's face through the small window. His hat was tight on his head, and his eyes were looking straight ahead. The moment passed in a flash without the smallest flicker of a hand wave through the window. And then the buggy was gone.

It was the sun in his eyes, Katie told

herself. That's why Ben hadn't slid open the buggy door or bothered to wave. But she knew better. Ben wasn't being mean. No, she just wasn't worth the effort. He had greater and better things on his mind than paying attention to Emma Raber's odd daughter. Now if she were beautiful, or charming, or funny, or even talkative at the Sunday-night hymn singings, it might be different. With such qualities, perhaps her plainness could be overcome. But all that was a dream that would never come true. She couldn't be what she wasn't.

Perhaps she should settle for Joe Helmuth from down the road. Joe walked with a limp from a hay wagon accident when he was five. He would take over his *daett*'s farm someday, but the scars from that long-ago day would never leave him. The problem was that Joe didn't pay Katie any attention either.

Well, at least thinking about Ben Stoll helped ease the pain a little, Katie decided. She was only Katie Raber, after all. The girl who could barely open her mouth without dumb words falling out all over each other. If she could only be more like the rest of the Amish girls in the community. But that could never be either, not with how *Mamm* felt about things.

Katie slapped the reins against her horse as her thoughts swirled through her mind. She couldn't remember much about *Daett*. He'd been gone since she was three years old. She could remember happy times though. Going to the barn with him when they did the evening chores. But that was so long ago. If she only had a *daett*, Katie decided, life would be different. If *Mamm* married again, Katie figured both of them would be better accepted in the community and *Mamm* might change her ways. The most obvious possibility was widower Jesse Mast. And he'd come calling on *Mamm* again just the other evening. *Mamm* hadn't said anything about the visit, but Jesse had surely spoken of marriage.

Yah, Mamm should marry again, Katie decided. *Mamm*'s sorrow over losing her husband was still written on her face after all these years. Was it not high time things changed? *Yah,* and Katie would pray about the matter.

Da Hah must already be thinking the same thing if He was sending *Mamm* a suitor in the person of Jesse Mast. So why couldn't *Mamm* see this and accept Jesse's offer of marriage? Was she turning him down because he wasn't much to look at? *Yah,* he was a little rough around the edges. But it wasn't like *Mamm* to be so concerned with outward appearance. She went more by a person's kind heart than how he looked on the outside. Perhaps it was the fact that Jesse's *frau,* Millie, had died and left him with a family of five children. Was that why *Mamm* objected? She didn't want her household increased so dramatically?

Nee, Katie decided that couldn't be the reason either. *Mamm* didn't mind hard work. And if a large family was the problem, she should have been happy after turning down Jesse. Instead, *Mamm* had walked around the house with the lines on her face running deeper than ever. So why had she turned Jesse down? That was assuming *Mamm* had turned him down. The proposal of marriage was just a guess on Katie's part, but she was sure she was right. It couldn't have been anything else. The two had talked for a long time while sitting on the porch swing. Afterward, Jesse had stood in the yard for a few moments longer, still speaking with *Mamm.* He'd held his hat in his hand, the sweat ring in his hair still apparent from where the hat had been pressed tightly on his head. Then Jesse had walked back to his buggy, his head bowed. Even Jesse's horse, Lucy, had looked depressed as they drove down the lane.

Katie had been ready to ask *Mamm* what Jesse wanted, but one look at her face caused her to change her mind. *Mamm* looked troubled and yet, at the same time, ready to give someone a piece of her mind. A question from Katie could easily have resulted in another lecture she didn't want to hear. A lecture about being satisfied with one's lot in life and not reaching for the stars. That was the standard lecture *Mamm* always gave when Katie dared complain about attending more of the Amish youth gatherings.

"You don't know how nice you have it," *Mamm* would say. "We have enough to eat, a roof over our heads, and horses to drive us to work and church. What more could we ask for?"

Well, Katie thought, there was plenty more to ask for. All kinds of things a young woman could want. Things that were out there just waiting to enrich one's life — and, happily, things that were not forbidden by the *Ordnung.* Like liking a boy. Like some-day loving a man who would love her back and consider his life empty without her. Someone who's eyes would light up when he saw her. Someone who called her sweet things on Sunday nights as he sat on the couch beside her. Wasn't that what dating couples did? *Mamm* wouldn't say when Katie asked, other than muttering something about useless talking until all hours of the night.

How could such time be considered wasted? Katie wondered. It would be glory indeed to sit beside a boy — a soon-to-be man so near she could touch him. What delight it would be to hear his deep voice rumble when he spoke or feel his eyes watching her long before she looked up to meet his gaze. *Nee,* this couldn't be wasted time. It would be a touch of heaven, and the most worthwhile thing a girl could set her heart on. Especially if the boy were Ben Stoll . . .

Katie sighed. So had Jesse Mast asked for *Mamm*'s hand? Had she turned him down? She'd sent him away looking disappointed, so something was going on. And then there was that look on *Mamm*'s face in the evenings after the sun had set and the house was quiet. *Mamm* didn't like the loneliness of their house either — the hours without a man's voice being heard. She'd been silent after Jesse left that night, staring at the kitchen wall and seemingly more troubled than usual.

What could she do to help? Katie wondered. She should do something, *yah.*

15

A car passed Katie's buggy, its engine roaring. Katie forced her mind back on the road ahead. Her horse, Sparky, knew the way to Byler's Store. He should after all this time she'd worked there. But even so, he mustn't be allowed to go his own way.

Ahead of her, Bishop Jonas Miller's place was coming up. His wife, Laura, was out in the yard hanging wash on the line. Katie leaned out of the buggy to wave, and Laura paused long enough to wave back before bending again to her work. At least the older Amish folk didn't think she was strange, even with *Mamm* the way she was.

Katie settled herself in the buggy seat again. If *Mamm* married Jesse, she might have to stay home from her job at Byler's and help with the added work five children entailed. But that would be an attractive kind of work — more normal almost. And it could lead to other kinds of normalness in her life. And perhaps even to a boy sitting on the couch beside her some Sunday night after a hymn singing. *Yah,* somehow *Mamm* must be persuaded to accept Jesse's offer of marriage.

Katie turned into the parking lot at Byler's and pulled Sparky to a stop at the far end of the hitching rail that was located on one side of the store. She climbed down, unhitched the buggy, and led Sparky around to the back where he could munch at stray pieces of grass during the day. She tied him to the fence with a long rope before walking back to the buggy. She pushed both doors shut before heading to the employee entrance of the store.

CHAPTER TWO

Katie's day moved slowly. Every so often she would glance at the clock, which seemed to be stuck. Wasn't it 3:15 the last time she looked? How could it be only 3:20 now? It wasn't that Katie disliked her job. She really did enjoy seeing people — mostly the regulars who came once or twice a week. Her present customer, Beth Kallen, was one of those. Her full shopping cart would probably last only a few days with her husband and their six children — two of them teenagers.

Katie finished scanning and bagging the groceries. She waited while Beth wrote out a check. Behind Beth, the line of customers stretched into the aisle. At the register across from Katie, Arlene Troyer was also ringing up customers. Her line was just as long, and there were no other clerks to summon for help. Katie and Arlene would have to hurry, and those in line would just have to wait.

"Sorry to keep you waiting," Beth said as she handed Katie the check. "Seems like these middle-aged hands don't move very fast anymore."

"That's okay." Katie gave her a warm smile. "Shall I put these bags in your cart so you can push them out to your buggy?"

"That would be so nice of you," Beth said. "That's what I like about this place. All of you girls give such good service."

"That's what we're supposed to do," Katie said. "We don't want you all leaving us for one of those fancy chain stores in town." She left her register for a moment to put the sacks in the cart and hold open the door for Beth as she pushed the cart through.

Katie returned and gave the next customer a greeting. The man only had a pound of cheese in his hand, and he gave her a quick nod as she rang it up. At least he wasn't angry with the wait, even though he hadn't said anything. Now, if the man had been at Arlene's register, he would have taken the time to smile and say something sweet like, "My you look sunny today" or "How lovely you Amish girls are." Men were funny that way when it came to pretty girls.

Katie pushed the thought away as she

greeted the next person in line, an *Englisha* woman with a cart full of baked goods. She smiled and chatted while Katie rang up the purchases.

"I can't believe I was so fortunate today. I tell you, I arrived just as these rolls were coming out of the oven. The girl back there told me so herself. And I knew it was true because I'd seen her brush the frosting on just moments earlier. Not that I would have doubted an Amish girl's word, believe me. Honest folks they are, if ever there were honest folks walking under God's great heaven. Aren't you Amish yourself, darling?"

The woman didn't pause for Katie's answer. "I do believe you are Amish from the way you look. I was expecting non-Amish girls up here working the registers. Why, I don't know. I guess I always think of Amish girls working with baked goods and heaving hay into hay mows in barns." The woman stopped for a breath.

Katie smiled and said, "We do get off the farm once in awhile."

The woman laughed. "Of course you do! That's just my way of thinking." She waved her hand over the baked goods. "And I'm not eating all this food myself. I know I look like I could hold all of it, like I've been eating all my life, but believe me I haven't. My husband, he's thin as a rail, and we've taken up healthy eating lately. Sort of a craze he's insisted on. I hold out on one thing only — Amish baking. This stuff is *healthy,* I tell him. Look at the Amish. They live to ripe old ages, happy as clams in their plain homes. Ralph isn't convinced though. Flawed logic, he says. But that doesn't keep him from eating his share. And the children . . . Why they would carry off rolls and pies before I get them on the counter at home if they could. They should come down to Byler's themselves, but they're too busy they say. What with their jobs and all. But not too busy to stop by Mom's place and load up on goodies. They even know the days I come down here. Figure that! And this from children who don't even remember my birthday!"

The woman stopped for a breath again just as Katie bagged the last pie. The total on the register was high, but the woman never blinked as she slid her Visa through the credit card processor. Katie waited until the woman moved away from the counter before she turned to the next customer.

This one was an *Englisha* man about her age. He was tall, and his blue eyes twinkled as he smiled. Katie managed a quick smile as she ran his items over the scanner. Why was he looking at her that way? Katie wondered. Young, good-looking guys like this one never paid her any attention. Maybe he's just having a very good day.

"That was kind of funny," he said. "The way she never let you get a word in edgewise."

Katie took a moment to look up before she answered. "Oh, I didn't mind."

"You must be very patient," he said. "I find people like her interesting. Do you find people interesting?" He sounded curious.

Katie looked down and forced her hands to move, entering the amount for his sandwich manually. "Most people," she finally managed, not looking at him.

Esther Kuntz had fixed this sandwich only minutes ago at the deli counter. That would mean this boy had talked with Esther. He probably was still under the spell of her many charms. That girl could spew out words like water from the rock Moses hit with his staff. So why was this boy speaking with her, with plain Katie, who usually couldn't get an interesting sentence out if her life depended on it?

"You look like a person who is a good listener," he said with a short laugh.

Her voice barely a whisper, Katie asked,

"Will that be all?"

What a stupid thing to ask, she thought. Of course that was all he wanted. She was working the register, not the deli counter where customers often did want more. Esther would roll on the floor laughing if she saw this exchange. "No wonder you never get a date," Esther would say. "Your verbal skills are on the level of a farm horse."

"I think this will do just fine," the young man replied, acting like Katie had just said something brilliant.

Katie took his offered money. The change came to a dollar ten, and she handed it to him.

He smiled but didn't move on. "Do you work here regularly?"

"Most days." Katie's voice squeaked. "On weekdays, that is. Unless, of course, I'm sick, which is hardly ever. And sometimes on Saturdays."

"I've seen you here before," he said, eyes twinkling again. "Well, have a good day. And maybe you will listen to me chatter sometime."

"Of course. I–I'd l–love to," Katie stammered out.

The young man left then, the double doors swinging behind him. Katie stood still for a moment. Had she really spoken to an

23

Englisha boy? Had he actually noticed she existed? She turned to the next customer and began scanning her purchases. This woman didn't seem to mind her silence. She paid with cash when Katie announced the total.

As the woman left, Katie quickly glanced at Arlene. She was looking at her with a slight smile on her face. *Ugh,* Katie thought. Arlene had noticed the exchange with the *Englisha* boy. Did Arlene know him? It was possible. Arlene was in her *rumspringa,* and she seemed to know everyone in town — Amish and *Englisha.* Now there would be no end to Arlene's teasing. Thankfully the customer line was still full at both of their registers, but this was bound to change soon.

Sure enough, twenty minutes later the lines had died down. Katie knew what would happen.

Arlene glanced around, and seeing no one approaching, sneaked over to whisper to Katie. "I can't believe what I saw! You were chatting with Mark Bishop like he was your best friend."

"Who's Mark Bishop?" Katie asked, trying to keep her blush to a minimum.

Arlene rolled her eyes. "He's an *Englisha* farmer's son who lives a little ways toward

24

town. He's a looker, as I'm sure you saw. I wish he'd stop by and chat with me like that."

"He wasn't chatting with me," Katie protested.

"You could have fooled me," Arlene shot back. "And your face — it's fiery red."

"I'm . . . just warm, that's all," Katie reasoned.

Arlene didn't look convinced. "I do declare. Who would have thought it? Where have you been, Katie? And you're not even in your *rumspringa*! What will your *mamm* say?"

"She will say nothing," Katie said, "because there's nothing to say. That boy went through my register line like a lot of people have today. That's all there is to it."

Arlene shook her head. "You're not fooling me, Katie. I heard what he said. 'And maybe you can listen to me chatter sometime.' And you said, 'I'd love to.' I've never heard that from you before."

"You're overreacting," Katie retorted.

A customer walked up to her register with his purchases. Arlene glanced back at her own register, and when she saw no one in line, she stayed to bag the man's items.

When the man left, Arlene began again.

"Did Mark say anything more that I didn't hear?"

"*Nee,* of course not! You ought to know by now I don't know how to talk to boys. Especially *Englisha* boys. I was so astounded he was speaking with me. Really . . . it didn't mean a thing."

"I'm not so sure. I know lots of girls — Amish ones included, who would love to get even a 'hi' from Mark Bishop. You've been changing, and I guess I haven't been paying attention. You go, girl!"

Nothing has changed in the least. Ben Stoll wouldn't even give me a wave this morning, Katie almost said. Instead she pressed her lips together. There was no sense adding fuel to Arlene's over-active mind. Arlene might think she'd received some attention from Ben before and was looking for more. That wasn't possible. Katie was still Emma Raber's daughter. That wasn't changing anytime soon. Or if it did, it certainly wouldn't happen in a moment of time while tending a cash register at Byler's.

"You have a customer," Katie whispered.

Arlene hurried away. She was soon back, though, to help bag groceries for the customer Katie was waiting on. Arlene obviously was waiting to continue their conversation.

"He didn't even know my name," Katie said, anticipating Arlene's curiosity. "And he had to ask whether I work here regularly. He doesn't know me."

"Well, you've never lied to me, so I guess I have to believe you," Arlene allowed. She returned to her register. "I'll be keeping an eye on you though."

And she would, Katie knew. And now she was going to turn red every time an *Englisha* boy her age came through her register line. What if another one paid her attention today? Arlene would never let her live it down! Katie forced herself to think about something else. She had worse things to worry about than an *Englisha* boy paying her attention. That had been a once-in-a-blue-moon happening.

"Hi." A man's voice broke into her thoughts and Katie jumped.

"Nice day outside," he continued.

Katie's eyes flew up, taking in his face. He was young and smiling, and his hand was pushing a sandwich and drink forward.

"Oh! I'm sorry." Katie drew in a quick breath. "Is this all you have?" Of course it was all he had, Katie thought, her mind racing. What a dunce she was. She was still nervous from the encounter with the other *Englisha* boy. Surely this one would soon

27

move on.

"Yep!" the boy said. "Just had to grab something quick for lunch. I was told the sandwiches here are really good."

Katie scanned his items. The world was indeed coming to an end. Two *Englisha* boys paying her attention on the same day? What had she done to garner this?

"Thank you," Katie said quietly as she took the boy's money, her eyes avoiding his face.

"You're Amish, aren't you?" he asked.

Katie nodded, afraid to speak up as she handed him his change.

"Well then, have a nice day," the boy said with a smile.

Katie managed a smile in return as the blood pounded in her head. "I hope you enjoy the sandwich," she said, wishing she hadn't as soon as the words were out of her mouth.

"Thanks, I will!" he said, waving over his shoulder.

Katie dared glance toward Arlene's register. Perhaps by some miracle Arlene had missed this encounter. After all, the boy hadn't lingered that long. But Arlene was staring across the aisle with her mouth open. She'd heard everything.

CHAPTER THREE

When their shifts ended at four o'clock, Katie led the way out of Byler's, Arlene walking closely behind her. Now that the workday had ended, Arlene was obviously itching to launch into a lecture of some sort about the attention Katie had received from the two *Englisha* boys.

The two girls reached the fence where Sparky was tied, and Katie paused as Esther came out of Byler's behind them. Esther waved and climbed into her dark-blue Corvette and, with the engine roaring, sped out the driveway. Once the sound died away, Katie turned to Arlene. "I know what you're going to say. And you might as well save your breath. I don't want to hear it."

Arlene glared. "You've been trying to shut me up about this, Katie. So I know there's something to it or you wouldn't try so hard to avoid talking about it. What do you think? That I'm stupid?"

"*Nee,* of course not," Katie said, trying to smile. "You're a lot smarter than I am."

"I don't know about that," Arlene said. "But I'm beginning to think you're more devious than I thought you were — after what I saw today."

"It was nothing," Katie declared. "Those two boys were pure accidents. I had nothing to do with it."

Arlene laughed. "Two *Englisha* boys giving off smiles and practicing good graces around you, Katie? How do you expect me to believe you're innocent? You *must* have done something they interpreted as flirting."

Katie's face turned red. "Me? Flirting?" She almost burst out laughing. Instead she simply said, "Okay, so you don't believe me. But I know who I am — and I am *not* a flirt!"

Arlene studied Katie for a moment. "So you're telling me you don't know those boys? That you're still not in *rumspringa?*"

"Do I look like that sort of girl?" Katie met Arlene's searching gaze.

Arlene sighed. "I didn't think so. But you're not answering my question, Katie."

"I've never met them before." Katie faced Arlene squarely. "Honest promise, cross my heart. I'm not disobeying *Mamm* or sneaking out without her knowledge. Nor am I flirting. Now, does that satisfy you?"

Arlene's face was intent for a moment. "I don't know."

Katie threw up her hands. "Okay! So be it. I really need to get home. I have chores to do."

Arlene ignored Katie and continued. "If you're telling the truth about not flirting, then maybe you're just changing. And maybe you don't realize it."

"You've lost your mind," Katie said. "I'll never change. I am who I am."

Arlene smiled. "No offense, but I think a change would do you good. Your *mamm*'s mostly to blame for this. You do know that, don't you?"

"*Mamm* is wonderful!" Katie said just as quickly. "She does the best she can."

"I didn't say she doesn't," Arlene said with a shrug. "But you know how it is. She avoids people and has you doing it too. I guess some things can't be helped."

Katie turned to Sparky. This conversation had gone on long enough. Arlene was stirring up feelings that were best left buried. Things were the way they were. No boys noticed her, let along *Englisha* boys. Today was a fluke and nothing more.

"Truth is, the boys coming through By-

31

ler's have been looking at you for some time," Arlene said. "You just never saw it until today when those two guys spoke up."

Katie looked at Arlene. What she was saying wasn't possible.

"The *Englisha* boys," Arlene insisted, "they're seeing you change."

"I don't believe it," Katie said.

Arlene shrugged. "Suit yourself. You *are* changing, Katie. That's what's happening. A little late, but . . ." With that, Arlene turned to go.

Katie stood frozen beside her horse. Sparky nudged her and Katie came back to the present. As she untied him, led him over to the buggy, and hitched him up, she thought about what Arlene had said. If her words were true, if by some miracle she was becoming attractive to *Englisha* boys, it was a bit upsetting. This wasn't supposed to happen. Her thoughts about romance had always centered on Amish boys, especially Ben Stoll. And even he'd been just a fantasy. She could never win the love of someone like him.

Katie climbed into the buggy as she thought about Ben. If Arlene was right . . . if *Englisha* guys were noticing her, then was it possible Ben might also? Well, she'd just have to wait and see. Something *gut* was happening, it just wasn't what she'd expected. But that was life, wasn't it? You took what came your way and made sense out of it — with *Da Hah*'s help, of course. Katie drove the buggy out on the road and turned toward home. Before long *Mamm* would be wondering why she'd been delayed. Byler's Store usually didn't ask her to work late, so that wouldn't be a good excuse. Well, she'd be home soon so *Mamm* might not be too worried yet.

Katie drove fast, passing Royal Farms and turning right toward the little town of Hartly. On the edge of town lay their twenty acres, which was all they had left from the hundred her *daett* had purchased years ago. After he died, *Mamm* had sold off a lot of the acreage to raise money for their survival.

Katie turned into the driveway and saw her *mamm* standing beside the old barn looking down the road toward her. *Ach,* so she *had* been worried, Katie noted. But it would have made things worse if she'd hurried away and refused to speak with Arlene. She didn't need rumors circulating about her. Rumors *Mamm* would hear. Rumors claiming she cavorted with *Englisha* boys. Rumors far, far from the truth.

Mamm had her hands clasped in front of her as Katie pulled to a stop.

When Katie climbed down from the buggy *Mamm* started to take the tugs off on the far side. She didn't say anything.

"*Mamm* . . ." Katie broke the silence. The subject might as well be addressed. "I'm sorry I was a little late, but Arlene wanted to talk with me after we got off work."

Mamm still said nothing.

"It was important," Katie added. "Arlene had a misunderstanding she needed to straighten out with me."

"You had me worried," *Mamm* said, finally looking up. "I won't say I wasn't. There are so many dangers out there, Katie. And you're still a young woman driving the roads alone. I wish you wouldn't sometimes. I declare, if we didn't need the money so badly, I'd keep you home with me all the time."

"But *Mamm!*" Katie protested. "I love my job. And it gets me out where I can see other people — the rest of the world, so to speak."

"That's another thing that bothers me," *Mamm* said, her face stern. "What kind of influence is working at Byler's having on you, Katie? I've noticed a change in you lately. I've been meaning to say something about it. And Arlene is in her *rumspringa.*

That can't be having a good influence on you."

Leading Sparky forward while *Mamm* held the buggy shafts, Katie's heart was pounding. Was Arlene right? Had *Mamm* also noticed the mysterious changes the *Englisha* boys were seeing?

"What kind of a change are you talking about?" Katie asked, her voice shaking.

"I don't know," *Mamm* said, studying her for a moment. "Sometimes I think I see the world creeping into your life, Katie. I don't know how to describe it. It must have something to do with Byler's though, because you never were like this before."

"*Nee*, there's nothing at Byler's that influences me in a bad way," Katie said, hoping her words were true.

"You're exposed to a lot of temptations there," *Mamm* persisted. "You see *Englisha* people all day long. And you see the fancy cars they drive. You see all the money they have to spend and the worldly clothing they wear. Is that what's changing you, Katie?"

"I'm not changing in that way, *Mamm*!" Katie exclaimed, stopping so fast the reins jerked Sparky to a stop.

"Maybe not," *Mamm* said, taking Sparky from Katie. "I'm glad to hear there are no worldly thoughts moving around in that head of yours. Go into the house and change. I'll take care of Sparky."

Mamm led Sparky off while Katie stood there and stared after her *mamm*. Only when *Mamm* looked over her shoulder did Katie walk toward the house. Once inside, she went upstairs and changed into a choring dress. She joined *Mamm* in the barn ten minutes later.

Mamm didn't offer any further comments about changes, so Katie wondered if she dared mention Jesse Mast and his intentions. But the words had to be said or something was going to burst inside her.

Katie sat down to milk one of their two cows. She adjusted the three-legged stool before pushing the milk bucket under Molly's udder. Behind her, *Mamm* threw down a bale of hay from the loft. A cloud of dust rose, spreading across the barn floor. The beams of sunlight through the open barn door shone through the settling dust. At least there was still peace in the world, compared to the turmoil of her day, Katie thought as a smile crept across her face.

Moments later the peace that had descended over their chore time was disturbed by the sound of buggy wheels coming down the driveway. *Mamm* had said nothing about someone coming. Half standing, Katie peered out the barn door. Molly protested, and Katie lunged for the bucket of milk, jerking it out of the way before the cow's hind foot came forward.

Katie sat down again. Whoever this was, she'd just have to wait and see. *Mamm* wouldn't want her stopping halfway through the milking just to see who had driven in the driveway. And *Mamm* certainly wouldn't want milk spilled on the barn floor. *Mamm* came down the hayloft opening, and Katie relaxed.

"Did I hear someone drive in?" *Mamm* asked.

Katie nodded.

Mamm walked to the barn door and looked out. Her face tightened.

Katie turned her head, trying to see through the door to catch a glimpse of who it was. There was no one in her line of vision.

Mamm was still standing at the barn door, making no effort to walk out to the visitor's buggy.

"*Gut* evening," a deep, male voice said from near the barn's front doors.

Katie jumped. Jesse Mast. He had returned.

"*Gut* evening," *Mamm* replied.

Katie ducked her head behind Molly. Was

Da Hah sending them help already? She was certain He was. Surely *Mamm* would also see the wisdom of accepting Jesse's advances. Their needs were obvious enough for everyone to see.

CHAPTER FOUR

When Jesse left an hour later, *Mamm* set out a meager supper of warmed, leftover meat casserole and fresh peaches. Then she disappeared into her bedroom.

Katie waited beside the kitchen table, ready to sit down and begin eating alone if *Mamm* didn't come back soon. It was understandable that *Mamm* would be disturbed over Jesse's visit — if, indeed, he had come to ask *Mamm* to be his *frau*. No doubt becoming another man's *frau* after being married to *Daett* would cause anyone to have ruffled thoughts. But *Mamm* would accept Jesse's proposal. She simply had to!

Jesse and *Mamm* had talked while *Mamm* finished the chores — with a little help from him. Then they'd talked for a long time out by his buggy. Katie hadn't been able to catch a glimpse of Jesse's face before he left, but *Mamm* had looked quite stern afterward. Still, it was a *gut* thing this had happened

— and just at the right time. Now Katie wouldn't have to bring up the subject.

She sat down and bowed her head in prayer. Hearing the bedroom door squeak on its hinges, Katie paused and looked up. Her *mamm* was coming. She waited until *Mamm* was seated before bowing her head again. They prayed in silence, with *Mamm* keeping her head down for long moments after Katie had lifted hers.

"Mamm?" Katie reached over to touch her arm. "I'm sorry it's so hard for you, but I'm glad to see that Jesse is coming over. It's time, *Mamm.*"

Mamm's head flew up. "How do you know what he came over for? Has someone told you something?"

Katie met *Mamm*'s gaze. *"Nee,* but I can guess. I think he's seeking your hand in marriage."

A look of embarrassment crossed *Mamm*'s face. "It's a shame and a disgrace, I say, when these things have to be done right out in the open where the eyes of the young can see them."

"I'm not that young, *Mamm,*" Katie corrected. "I'm an adult now."

Mamm leaned closer. "You heard something at Byler's? Is this how you know what Jesse is after?"

40

Katie shook her head. "I only know because it's the perfectly normal thing to do, *Mamm.* You lost *Daett* years ago, and Jesse lost his wife last year. Of course he wants another *frau,* and you would make a decent match for him. And I want a *daett.*"

Mamm frowned. "I still don't think you should know so much about these things. Jesse might have come over because he wanted to borrow something."

"But he didn't, did he? Oh *Mamm!*" Katie allowed her excitement to well up. "Have you said *yah* to Jesse's offer? I know we will be absolutely happy as a family. What with Jesse's five children . . . Oh! I can't believe this might be really happening!"

Mamm added lima beans to her plate. Still frowning, she said, "I'm sorry to disappoint you, but it's *not* happening. I've told Jesse both times he was here that I will not agree to his calling on me. And there certainly will be no wedding."

"But *Mamm!*" Katie wailed. "Why not? We need a man around the house. I've never really had a *daett,* not like the other children did growing up. It's still not too late."

"I've said *nee* to Jesse Mast." *Mamm* set her lips in a tight line. "We're doing fine alone, just like we always have. I'm not changing that."

41

"But, *Mamm,* everything changes!" Katie made no attempt to hide her desperation.

"Not in our world it doesn't, Katie. And it doesn't in the world of our people. I will have you think about that long and hard."

"*Mamm,* our people marry all the time!" Katie persisted. "That's the right kind of change."

"There's no use arguing," *Mamm* said. "I'm not marrying Jesse. And I'm troubled that you're so interested in the subject all of a sudden. You never were before."

"Maybe I am changing," Katie shot back. She couldn't believe the words had burst out of her mouth, but they had.

Mamm looked shocked and silence settled over the table. Then she said, "Just as I suspected. This comes from working at that store."

"Please, *Mamm,*" Katie coaxed. "I can't help it if changes occur. *Da Hah* made us the way we are."

"He didn't make us without the ability to make choices," *Mamm* said. "And we have to make the right ones. Marrying Jesse is not the right one for me or for you."

"So there is someone out there you like then? You're just objecting to Jesse person-ally?"

"This has nothing to do with Jesse,"

Mamm said. "I'm not marrying again. And I think it would be best if you didn't think of boys either."

"But why?" Katie gasped.

"Because . . ." *Mamm* gave Katie a sharp glance. "Because you'll avoid a world of hurt, that's why."

Katie struggled to gather her composure. They finished eating, bowed their heads in another moment of prayer, and then Katie stood to clear the table.

Mamm washed the dishes and Katie dried them. As she was drying the last saucer, *Mamm* cleared her throat. "I guess I owe you an explanation, Katie. I didn't realize you were changing as fast as you are. It seems like only yesterday you were a little girl. And now you're turning into a young woman. I guess I haven't noticed."

"It's only natural to grow up," Katie said. "But I'll always be the same person. You don't have to explain anything to me."

"But I want to." *Mamm* took Katie's hand and led her into the living room. *Mamm* let go and wiped her hands on her apron as they sat on the couch. "I'm just trying to find the right words. I've never done this before."

Katie waited, not moving at all. What great and awful secret was *Mamm* preparing to tell her? Was it something that would change her life forever? Not likely. *Mamm* was more interested in keeping things the same than changing anything.

Mamm cleared her throat. "See, Katie, I loved a boy once — a long time ago. I won't tell you his name because you might run across him sometime. I don't want you to feel awkward or say something that might embarrass him. He was a good-looking boy — in fact, the best-looking boy in the community. At least I thought so, and a lot of other girls did too. I suppose many of us had dreams of turning his eye. But I didn't do a very good job of keeping my secret, so the other girls teased me."

Katie took a deep breath, listening intently. *Mamm* had never talked like this to her before.

"Of course," *Mamm* continued, "he was way above me. I should have known better, but I thought all things were possible with the great love I had in my heart for him. I dreamed of the day he would smile in my direction. And then one summer evening at the youth gathering he did. I thought I would faint from the joy in my heart."

Katie said nothing as she stared at her *mamm.*

"He even spoke words to me that night

that gave me hope," *Mamm* continued. "I, of course, was too blind in my happiness to realize he'd probably said the same things to other girls before me. In my innocence, I built great hopes out of that little molehill. And when the mountain was at its greatest — when I really knew I loved him the way a woman loves the man she marries — well, it was then that he started taking another girl home from the Sunday-night hymn singing."

"*Mamm,* I never knew this." Katie took her *mamm*'s hand in hers.

Mamm's fingers were cold. She gazed out the living room window, a faraway look in her eyes.

"What happened?" Katie asked.

Mamm shook her head before continuing. "Everyone knew how I felt. At least all the girls my age did. They'd known all along what he would do. So when he left me for another girl, it was hard to face them. It was hard to pretend I was enjoying myself around them when most of them knew my heart was broken. For the next couple of years I must have said *nee* to at least three other boys who asked me home. Even after the way he treated me, I kept hoping my dream love would come true and he would come back to me. It was only at his wedding, when I sat there and heard him promise to love another girl for the rest of his life, that I gave up and allowed my love for him to die."

Katie sighed, her fingers tight on her *mamm*'s hand.

"Don't worry, Katie." *Mamm* tried to smile. "Not long after the wedding, I accepted your *daett*'s offer to take me home. We were married the next year."

"But, *Mamm,* you still loved someone else."

"Not really. It doesn't quite work that way. At least not for our people. The other love had died, and love for your *daett* grew in its place. Not quickly though. It came to full fruition after you were born, I think. And when I finally could admit to myself that my love for your *daett* was real, he . . . died."

"I'm so sorry, *Mamm* . . ." Katie said.

Mamm took a hanky from her apron and wiped her eyes. "Now do you see why I don't want anything to do with marriage? I don't think my heart can take anything more. And as for you, I couldn't bear to ever see you hurt like I was. It's better, Katie, if we just stay the way we are. You and me together."

Katie stared ahead, her hands in her lap now.

"Can you understand a little bit?" *Mamm* stroked Katie's arm. "That's why I couldn't have been happier with the way things were going, Katie. Nobody seemed to be paying much attention to you — boys, that is. I tried to keep things that way by dressing you decent but plainer than most and keeping you from joining the *rumspringa* crowd. You grew so slowly, it was like *Da Hah* was helping me. Now when I see you starting to mature, to change, I can't bear it. I feel you're slipping away from me. You're no longer the little girl I once held in my arms. Yet I hope you will always be the one who stirs joy in my heart."

"Oh, *Mamm*!" Katie cried, throwing her arms around her *mamm*'s neck. "You mustn't talk like that."

"It's true, isn't it? You want a boy to be interested in you, don't you? You're just like me at that age. I can't bear to see you hurt like I was."

Katie looked away.

"I thought so." *Mamm* touched her arm. "I guess it can't be helped, but I know it will only lead to sorrow and heartache."

Katie said nothing as the face of Ben Stoll swam in front of her eyes.

"Is there one particular boy?" *Mamm* asked.

When Katie didn't answer, *Mamm* pressed on. "Who is he, Katie?"

"Ben Stoll," Katie choked out before bursting into tears.

"Oh my poor little girl!" *Mamm* pulled Katie close. "What does *Da Hah* have against me that He would visit us twice with this affliction?"

"It's not your fault," Katie said between sobs.

"It is *all* my fault," *Mamm* said. "Every last bit of this. I do hope you're not making the fool out of yourself that I did. Does anyone know about this?"

"I don't think so."

"Then you must never show it," *Mamm* said. "Forget the boy — as quickly as you can. He is nothing to you, Katie. He will never be anything to you. Ben is far, far above us . . . above you."

Katie sobbed, muffling her cries with the couch pillow.

Mamm held her hand. "Pride is a terrible thing, Katie. I hope you know that. The devil fell when he looked up to God and wanted to be lifted up to His high and mighty seat. We must never be like that, Katie. We must accept the station *Da Hah* has given us. If you must love, find a decent boy to long after. Still, I would protect you even from that, but I know I can't forbid it. Ben Stoll is not for you, Katie. He never was and never will be. You need to believe me."

"I believe you," Katie managed to get out. "I so wish I could stop liking Ben, but I can't. I think about him often. I can't seem to stop."

Mamm wiped her own tears and then prayed, "Oh dear *Hah,* please don't visit this pain upon my daughter. Have not I repented many times for any wrongs I may have done? Please, *Hah,* please . . ."

When she stopped praying, Katie gave *Mamm* a quick hug.

They sat in silence. And then *Mamm* finally said, "It's getting late. We best go to bed now."

Katie nodded, getting to her feet. "I'll try to forget about boys . . . about Ben."

Mamm gave Katie's hand a quick squeeze.

Once she was in her room, Katie burst into tears again. Now she knew for sure. Katie Raber really was Emma Raber's daughter in more ways than she'd imagined. And *Mamm* was never going to remarry. There would never be real change in her life. Not that way. Katie paced the floor, whispering short prayers, her face turned toward the ceiling. "Help me, dear *Hah.* I don't know what I should do."

No answer came, but peace soon arrived, settling on Katie's heart first and then reflected in her face. *Da Hah* would take care of *Mamm* and her. She didn't know how, but things would turn out right. She must not give in to despair and lose hope, no matter how dark the way became.

CHAPTER FIVE

Emma listened to the muffled sounds of her daughter crying upstairs. She dabbed at her own eyes. She should have gone up to comfort the girl, but there was little that could be done. She wasn't the one who could supply comfort anyway. If Ezra were still alive, he would know what needed saying to Katie. He always did in his calm, reasoned way. Ezra wasn't a minister, but he'd reached into her heart that first winter together, speaking words that had touched her deeply.

"It's time to start living again, Emma," Ezra had said. "Spring's coming soon, and *Da Hah* touches even the human heart in His seasons." Then he had taken her into his arms and said, "You know I love you, Emma. I will always hold you very close."

She had been so numb, so frozen inside, not unlike the snow-covered fields outside the living room window. Ezra had been a *gut* husband from the start. He knew how to work. The cupboards were well stocked with flour, butter, eggs, and anything else Emma mentioned she might need. Ezra kept the stack of wood in the basement dry, and the old furnace never was in danger of giving out.

It was her heart that had refused to move . . . let alone grow. Every time she tried, memories of Daniel would come flooding back, drowning out Ezra's face. She would sit silent as tears ran down her face even as she looked at Ezra sitting across the room during those first long, winter evenings.

Memories would return of Daniel talking with someone at the youth gatherings. She'd hear his laugh when he finished a joke. She'd hear his voice pealing across the gathered Amish young people until everyone either moved closer to hear his next words or wished to.

Yah, she had told Katie tonight that her longing for Daniel Kauffman had died on his wedding day when he'd taken Miriam Esh as his wife. That hadn't been a lie. But what she hadn't told Katie was what else had died — her heart . . . and seemingly her very desire to breathe. There was another thing she hadn't told Katie. The story of her mad dash out of the services right after Daniel and Miriam had said their vows. The gathered congregation was shocked as she recklessly drove her buggy right past Daniel and his new bride as they came out of the house. There was no mistaking the despair revealed through her actions — sorrow mingled with a flagrant disappointment and disrespect for whom Daniel had chosen to be his *frau.*

After that fiasco, she should have waited awhile before allowing Ezra to take her home from the hymn singing — at least until things had grown clearer in her heart and mind. But Ezra hadn't seemed to mind the dimness of her affections for him or her questionable reputation that hung over her since her display of hurt and anger on Daniel and Miriam's wedding day.

How could she have loved a man like Daniel Kauffman? How could she have acted so impulsively? Perhaps it would have been better if Daniel had never paid her attention. She'd been a common girl — just like Katie had turned out to be. The girl nobody noticed. Her mistake was that she'd reached high, thinking she could capture Daniel's heart. And once she'd reached toward it, it was as if her hand could not be drawn back. She was like a child whose hand was caught in a cookie jar. She couldn't blame Daniel. Her actions were all her own.

The kindness of her few friends had kept her from saying or showing more. Her feelings of gratitude toward them had played a large part in her quick *yah* that night when Ezra had approached her. She'd been standing beside her brother's buggy, and Ezra had walked up, motioning for her to follow him aside for a moment.

There, in the shadows of the barn, he'd asked, "May I take you home next Sunday night, Emma? I know this may seem a little sudden, but I'd love to do that."

And she had nodded, her *kapp* barely moving as Ezra smiled in the dim light. And once again there had seemed no turning back, even when she knew her heart wasn't responding to Ezra's advances. On the outside she said the right things. In her cynical moments she figured his acceptance of her came because they were both older and he felt he was running out of options. At other times she wondered if this man really thought she would come around. She decided he must have great faith to marry her with the risk that she wouldn't ever love him in return.

Ezra had been reading *The Budget* on that

winter evening after their wedding. The snow was blowing outside. She'd made him popcorn because that was what a *gut frau* did. All evening she'd been trying not to remember Daniel's face seated in the men's section that Sunday morning at the church service. Though Daniel now lived in another district, he'd decided to visit on the spur of the moment. Emma had gasped when she noticed him in the room. Immediately the thought came to her: What if Daniel wants to see me again? What if that was the real reason for his visit?

It was an awful thought. One forbidden by a holy *Hah* and by decent and righteous people. But there it was, coming into her mind so quickly and uncontrollably. At church she might have succeeded in paying the thought no mind, but while she was making popcorn for Ezra that night it had been unleashed in full fury.

She wanted so to love Ezra. He was worthy of even more love than a common, average girl like her could give. But she couldn't get her heart to squeeze out even a little positive emotion. Every time she tried, her love for Daniel was there, staking first claim. Ezra had to have noticed her distress in the days that followed that evening because he said so many nice things to her that weren't necessary.

"We were meant for each other," he said, coming up to slip a hand around her waist while she washed the dishes.

"You're all I ever dreamed of in a *frau*," he said one night after supper.

She'd nearly broken down in tears and told him everything. Thankfully he was satisfied with a kiss, and he had apparently taken her blushing face as proof of her growing love for him.

He was a simple man, Ezra was. Just the kind of husband she needed. And this only made things worse. She knew she was dooming any love that might rise in her heart for him. Someday Ezra would find out the truth, she feared, and his heart would seal up against her forever.

Strangely, assistance had come from an unexpected quarter. It was as if *Da Hah* had mercy at the last minute when she thought she could no longer stand the pain. The green leaves had been sprouting on the trees and the first cheerful robin was hopping in the yard when help arrived. She'd been looking out of the living room window, watching Ezra work in the field, when knowledge stirred within her. She was with child — with Ezra's child.

For the first time, the love that was theirs

alone entered her heart. She'd laughed out loud at the joy of it, and with it came the realization that she now had with Ezra what she'd never had with Daniel. *Da Hah* had visited them with a great blessing.

Daniel had always been a dream, a vision she'd looked upon from afar but never touched. Ezra, on the other hand, was real. She could love such a man exactly because he wasn't Daniel. Emma had run out of the house that day with her white apron flapping over her shoulder. She'd startled the horses, so Ezra had to hang on tight to the reins before he could bring them to a stop. When he'd stared at her with a puzzled look, she had grabbed him around the neck to kiss his cheek. He turned red and looked across the fields toward the neighbor's house to make sure no one was watching.

"What is it?" he had finally asked, at a loss for more to say.

"I think I'm with child!" Emma had said.

Ezra had smiled, his cheeks turning even redder. "That's *gut*! That's how it should be."

"*Yah,* I know." She'd ducked her head and then ran back to the house. Ezra was still staring after her when she stole a glance over her shoulder.

That night the joy was still in her heart,

and she had baked his favorite dessert — minced apple pie. Not one thought of Daniel had raced through her mind. Her love . . . her heart . . . now belonged to Ezra alone.

And so the joy had remained the rest of the spring and on into summer as her body swelled. Katie had been born that October, but not before fear had also arrived to haunt the edges of Emma's mind. She turned to worrying that with the coming of the cold winter the joy of her love for Ezra would be driven away by the chill and the ice. What if it could leave as easily as it had come in the spring?

Again it was Katie who had driven the darkness away. At Katie's first cry, the flush of love enveloped Emma. Surely this joy could go on, and on, and on — and it had. So long as Katie was near, so was joy. At age one, it was Katie kicking her feet on the blanket beside the woodstove that distracted Ezra even from his beloved *Budget.* At age three, it was Katie who welcomed Ezra in from the fields. Her shrieks of delight sending a smile across his face when he appeared in the kitchen doorway.

Katie became the center of their home. Was this why there had never been other children? Emma had wanted more, but a person could not make *Da Hah*'s will happen just by desiring something. She'd desired more of this happiness but wanted nothing to threaten what they had. Had she, perhaps, brought trouble into their lives? Had *Da Hah*'s displeasure grown strong against her because of her selfishness?

In the midst of their happiness, Ezra had been taken. So suddenly. So completely. And she'd been left alone with Katie. And the years had rolled on. Silent years. Empty . . . yet with Katie still providing a measure of joy in the house.

But now Katie was changing. Was becoming what she, Emma, had been all those years ago. It was now Katie who was reaching high where no common woman ought to reach. Emma's sins had come full circle. Katie, the one who had brought such blessings, was now bringing back the pain of the past. All while her *mamm* hadn't been paying attention, expecting life to go on like always.

And now this business with Jesse Mast. Apparently with Katie in sympathy to his plight. How like Katie to see only joy everywhere. But joy wasn't guaranteed. It came only for a moment and was soon snatched away. Dreams couldn't keep joy alive. Ezra had proven that. And now she would have to teach this to Katie — must make her understand. Katie must not disturb the life they now lived lest something even worse come upon them both.

Emma stood and paced the floor. Everything was quiet upstairs. *Katie must be sleeping.* Perhaps tomorrow they could speak more of this matter. Katie would have to accept things the way they were, that's all there was to it. Emma stood by the living room window and looked out at the falling darkness. Off in the distance a dim lantern light flickered in a window and then went out as she watched. *Katie must never be allowed to experience the sorrow and pain I've lived with for so long. Never.*

CHAPTER SIX

The following morning, Jesse Mast awoke before the alarm went off. His body was still weary after the night's sleep, but he pulled himself out of bed and pushed aside the dark curtains. He studied the dawn-streaked sky, wondering why he was so tired. When Millie was alive, he'd gone to bed much later than he had last night, and yet he'd awakened refreshed and ready to face the day. Now that she was gone, it seemed the cancer had taken so much more than just Millie. It had also taken his strength, his hope, and even his desire to get out of bed in the morning.

Yet the farm needed care. Crops didn't stop growing just because a man's *frau* died. The cows still gave their milk. Everything went on as before. Except a man's heart — his heart — now had a hole in it that grew larger each day. Am I desperate? Jesse wondered. Was he grasping for straws in pursuing the widow Emma as his *frau*? He'd been so certain *Da Hah* was leading him as he visited her that first time. Emma was also *gut* looking, especially if she'd take better care of herself and smile once in awhile. Perhaps that was part of the mystery and allure that drew him. That and thinking of *Da Hah*'s will. But the fact that she was *gut* looking was not without its appeal. He had to be honest about that.

Jesse stared at the brightening sky and thought of Emma. She'd grown up in the community, and he'd known her all his life. Until recently, he'd never paid her much attention. He had been a happily married man. From his memories of their growing-up years, Emma had always been the quiet girl. There had been no scandal that he remembered, though there had been those stories floating around that Emma's heart had been set on Daniel Kauffman. But then she'd married Ezra. And that had been none of his concern. Emma meant little to him back then. His eyes were set on Millie, the community's dashing girl. He'd won her hand even with the stiff competition from several other, far-more dashing men.

Jesse smiled thinking about his younger days. They were pleasant memories, and he should think on them more often . . . even with the pain that had followed. All the young folks in the community had been of the dashing sort in those days. But perhaps that only seemed to be true now that middle age was setting in. He was still young really — in his early forties. But he felt old. Farm work could do that to a man. Make him feel weary before his time, wrinkling his skin and lining his face.

Yet it was *Da Hah*'s best way of living. Had not *Da Hah* sent Adam out of the garden to till the soil and fight the thorns and thistles? Indeed He had. And though many men did other work that was perhaps just as worthy, there was no labor more satisfying than working the soil. Why, a man's touch could make land that had been cursed grow again. What higher calling in life was there?

Was this perhaps why he was interested in Emma Raber? She had been withering away for years now, living alone with her daughter. Wasn't it time Emma's life blossomed again? The thought caused his gaze on the dawning sky to grow more intense. *Nee,* that might not be a very *gut* reason to court a woman. And it sure would be taking a lot upon himself, trying do work that only *Da Hah* could do. But had *Da Hah* not commanded men to lay their hands to the plow and not look back? He had indeed. And so far Jesse had no plans to look back when it came to Emma. He planned to wed the woman. She needed help, that was plain to see. But that wasn't his only reason for pursuing her. He also found her attractive in a unique sort of way. Emma might even be beautiful if she were happy again. Plus, they shared a similar loss, did they not? They had both lost partners they loved. Emma had loved Ezra like he had loved Millie. Of this he was sure.

And another thing was also certain. Emma believed in taking care of herself. In the end he might fail in his pursuit of her. And if he did, there were always other options available. Homer Troyer's widow, Ruth, had recently made clear her interest in him. Her attentions had begun with warm smiles at church services. They would soon progress to other forms if he didn't miss his guess. Ruth hadn't yet begun bringing food over, but she would think of that well-known female maneuver soon. Marrying Ruth didn't greatly appeal to him though. She'd lost Homer last year to cancer, soon after Jesse had lost Millie. But Jesse still didn't feel like he had that much in common with her. Not like he had with Emma anyway.

Ruth was teaching school this year. Homer

had left her with no children after all those years. If Jesse took Ruth as his *frau,* there would be no additional children to bring into his family. That made no difference one way or the other to him. He simply wanted to wed Emma. He'd approached her twice now and been rebuffed. Emma's two refusals should have been enough to send any man running, but he wasn't ready to give up. He'd felt this pursuit was *Da Hah*'s will, and being rebuffed was no reason to change his course. Besides, Emma didn't seem to have her heart in her *nees.* He would have to find out for sure as time went on. For now there was no turning back.

His pursuit of Emma wouldn't remain a secret for long. The news would make its rounds at the women's quiltings, and their "relationship" would be discussed after church while the tables were being served. He would live through the shame, Jesse told himself, when the community questioned his wisdom.

"Did you hear that Jesse's been to visit the widow Emma Raber twice now?" someone would ask.

"Yah," the other would say. "And she turned him down both times. I can't believe Emma would do that. It's not like she gets many offers. And Jesse is such a *gut* catch,

you know."

Jesse turned away from the window. Perhaps they wouldn't say the part about him being a *gut* catch, but something close to it. Because he was, if the truth were told. He wasn't the best man in the community, of course, but he was the most eligible widower at the moment. And he'd won Millie's hand. That took some doing, didn't it? That made Emma's refusals all the more puzzling.

Jesse looked at his clothing scattered beside the bed. There would be plenty of time to think about this later. For now, the day was well underway, and he had no time to wool-gather about his prospects for a *frau*. He dressed and went out, shutting the bedroom door behind him. He made his way to the living room and lit the kerosene lamp. Then he walked over to holler up the stairs, "Time to get up, children! The sun is rising." Moments passed in silence so he hollered again. Faint thumps followed and Jesse smiled. They were good children, all of them. *Gut* like Millie had been *gut*. Jesse named them off in his mind as he pulled on his outer coat in the washroom. Leroy was the oldest at twenty years of age. He was already thinking of taking a girl home from the Sunday-night hymn singing, even though he was much too young for such things. Jesse paused to think. He'd been twenty when he first took Millie home, and that hadn't seemed too young back then. It was funny how things changed when one became older.

Willis, the next boy, was strong for his eighteen years, still growing but hopefully stopping soon. He would be the tallest of them all.

Mabel had the heaviest load. At sixteen, she shouldn't have the responsibility of the household on her shoulders. In part, it was for her sake that he needed to find another *frau.* It wasn't right that such a young girl should have to bake, sew, and wash for six people. *Yah,* his sisters came over to help when they could, but both Sarah and Barbara had growing households of their own.

Jesse set the kerosene lamp on the kitchen table as his thoughts drifted back to his children. Carolyn was twelve years old and helped out a lot. But with her the same problem existed as with Mabel, only worse. Carolyn was even younger than Mabel, and there was no *mamm* around to tell the girls where the line lay between work and too much work.

If the girls carried a lazy streak, he wouldn't worry so much. But neither were lazy, especially Carolyn. He'd seen her on washday carrying hampers of wet clothes out to the line by herself. Loads that were too heavy for the back of a sixteen-year-old girl, let alone a twelve-year-old. He should speak with Mabel about the matter, but that wasn't fair either. Mabel shouldn't be burdened with such things. She had enough to do.

He needed a *mamm* for them. Surely Emma could be made to understand this. He had tried to explain the matter to her on his two visits, but his words had been like water running off a duck's back. A thought ran through his head. Surely Emma didn't expect to be courted again? Perhaps he shouldn't have gone over and stated his proposal right out like he had. But she was Emma Raber — a widow — and surely she wasn't given to schoolgirl fantasies about love. Emma would hardly expect the coy looks young people gave each other or the long buggy rides home on Sunday evenings. For both of them life had moved far beyond that. He pushed those thoughts away.

Jesse lit the gas lantern in the washroom and took it with him out the door. As he let the screen door slam, he heard the first steps of children coming down the stairs behind him. A familiar and welcome sound it was. Just like this place . . . home. The home where his love for his family had grown. This emotion he felt for his children and the feelings he had for Millie when she was alive were all here with him right now.

I could have the same thing with Emma . . . if she would only cooperate. *Yah,* they could have a home again — the two of them . . . Emma and Katie. His children would learn to love Emma as their own *mamm* and Katie as their sister. At least they would over time. Right now the two children who knew about his visits to Emma's place weren't that excited about the idea. Leroy and Mabel had figured out what he was up to. He supposed Willis and Carolyn didn't care either way. Children often weren't happy when the surviving parent remarried, but they would come around.

Thankfully, Joel, his youngest at age six, seemed hardly to notice, let alone care. At the moment he was still allowed to stay in bed while the others got up early. Joel slept until breakfast, when he had to get up for school. But soon the time would come for assigning chores other than his job of feeding the chickens in the afternoon. Jesse had been putting that moment off. Perhaps because he hated to see his youngest child grow up. Yet it wasn't fair to hold the boy back. And that's what he was doing. He might as well be honest. Joel needed more responsibility regardless of how painful the experience was for his *daett.*

Emma could help with that too, Jesse thought. In fact, they all needed Emma more than Emma needed them. Was that perhaps Emma's reason for not accepting his offer? Six children in the house would be a big change after having only Katie around. Emma was a hard worker from the looks of her place. She couldn't be afraid of the additional workload. Look at how things were kept up at her place. Nothing fancy, but everything was clean and the house had been repainted white last year. Emma and Katie had done the work themselves. It took a *gut* kind of woman to take on such a large project. Emma could have asked for help, but she hadn't. And that must come from her own thinking because Ezra and Emma used to host frolics and silo-fillings at their place. Obviously since Ezra had passed Emma had drawn into herself. Funny how everyone just accepted that fact without doing much about it. But he supposed no one could be held to blame. Emma gave off that kind of air, saying without actually saying it, "Don't bother me, and I'll be okay."

Jesse pushed open the barn door. He entered and hung the gas lantern from a nail in the ceiling. The cows bellowed in the barnyard. They were already pushing against the sturdy door. Jesse went into the milk house. He found the milking buckets in the darkness and carried them to the door. He set them down and spread feed in the trough before undoing the outside door latch.

He stood aside and watched the cows scramble across the concrete floor to the stanchions. Their necks clanged against the metal clamps as they thrust their heads through the openings to get at the feed. Jesse walked along, closing each latch with a flick of his hand. A few of the cows lifted their heads to look at him. The others were too busy eating to notice.

Behind him the barn door opened, and Leroy and Willis walked in. *"Gut* morning, *Daett,"* Leroy said, grabbing a milk bucket without waiting for a response. Willis, the slower riser, shook his head a few times, his eyes still full of sleep. He looked around for a moment before taking a bucket.

Willis will grow into a *gut* farmer someday, Jesse thought. As would Leroy. They were both steady and dependable boys. Willis took the time to look before he jumped into something. Leroy scolded Willis often for his moments of indecision, but it wasn't like that at all. Willis's hesitations were marks of wisdom that shouldn't be quenched.

Praise must be given out carefully, Jesse believed. Willis might be better off not knowing his *gut* qualities too soon. But he was thankful for both of his older boys. Out of all the children, they seemed bothered the least by the lack of a *mamm* in the house. Still . . . Jesse picked up his bucket. Emma would also be *gut* for Leroy and Willis.

CHAPTER SEVEN

After the chores were finished that morning, Jesse sat at the kitchen table waiting while Mabel brought over the plate of eggs. Leroy and Willis were still washing up, the noises of their splashing coming through the washroom door. They soon stepped inside, their hair still wet across their foreheads.

"Don't come into my kitchen dripping water all over the place!" Mabel ordered, throwing them each a towel. "Dry yourselves off first."

Leroy grinned and said, "What's up with this? Giving us orders like we're little boys? I declare! Mabel's acting more like a boss each and every day." The boys dried themselves with the towels and took their places on the back bench at the table.

Jesse gently chided, "Mabel does the best she can, and we should be thankful for all her hard work."

"There! Let that be a lesson!" Mabel seized upon the help her *daett* had given and glared at her brothers.

"I think the boys should listen to Mabel," Carolyn announced from her place beside the stove as she picked the last of the bacon from the frying pan.

Jesse laughed. "Okay, that's enough. I must say that Mabel and Carolyn do their share of the work around here."

Broad smiles spread across the girls' faces.

"Come, let's sit down!" Mabel took Carolyn's hand after she'd set the plateful of bacon on the table. "The food's ready."

"And it's more than *gut* enough," Jesse said. "Both of you have done very well with the work around the house since *Mamm* died. And you are all — including the boys — growing into decent, hard-working children. *Mamm* would be very happy to see this if she were still with us."

Mabel and Carolyn had sober looks on their faces. Jesse waited. He allowed the silence to stretch into long moments. It did them all *gut* to occasionally reflect on Millie's passing and on the future. When the two older boys shuffled their feet a bit, Jesse knew it was time to move on to prayer.

On the back bench, Leroy and Willis had their heads up, looking first at him and then at the food on the table.

The boys were hungrier after the early morning chores than he was, Jesse noted.

Leroy cleared his throat.

Jesse bowed his head and mumbled, "Let's pray." He gave them a few seconds to bow their heads. "Great God in heaven, we thank You this morning again, first of all for this food that You have so graciously given us and for our night's rest from which we have all awakened unharmed. Give us grace this day so that we might live right. Give us mercy through the blood of Your Son who covers any transgressions we have made in the weaknesses of our flesh. Forgive us our sins as we forgive those who sin against us. Give grace to our family at this time and in the days ahead. And may our hearts always be turned toward Your face. May we seek to walk in obedience to Your Word. In the name of the Father, and the Son, and the Holy Spirit, we ask this. Amen."

Leroy grabbed the plate of eggs before Jesse even opened his eyes. For a moment words of rebuke hovered on Jesse's lips, but he pushed them back. This morning was not the time for hard words. Rather, it was a time for overlooking faults and thinking of the *gut* things still to come. It was time, he thought, to mention Emma to the children.

Mabel was watching her brother out of the corner of her eye, disapproval written all over her face.

Jesse smiled, shaking his head at her.

Mabel gave a little sigh of disgust before she took a piece of toast and passed the plate on to Carolyn.

Jesse held his fork in his hand, filling his own plate when the eggs came around. He soon cleared his throat. No one looked up but he began anyway. "I suppose some of you are wondering where I went last night. And perhaps the night the other week when I was gone for an hour or so."

"I already know," Leroy announced, not looking up from his plate.

"So do I," Mabel said.

Neither Carolyn or Willis offered a comment. Little Joel didn't even look up from his plate.

"I was visiting the widow Emma Raber," Jesse continued. Saying the words felt *gut.*

"What did you want with Emma Raber?" Carolyn stared at him.

"That's what I'd like to know," Leroy muttered.

Jesse gave him a sharp, sideways glance. He'd suspected Leroy entertained a negative opinion of Emma, but the boy didn't need to express his thoughts so freely in

76

front of the others.

"I don't like the woman," Mabel said, speaking right out plain. "She's not like *Mamm* at all."

Jesse opened his mouth and closed it again without saying anything. This was not going well.

"Do you really want to marry Emma Raber?" Willis's face was filled with astonishment. "I've never heard one *gut* thing about her."

Jesse took a deep breath. Where these strong feelings were coming from, he couldn't imagine. He'd expected some objections, but he obviously misjudged his children's receptivity. But now that he'd brought the subject up, it was better to deal with it in the open rather than sweep it under the living room rug, so to speak.

"I wasn't expecting all of you to have such strong feelings about this." Jesse kept his voice even. "But I guess you do have the right to speak your minds since I hope Emma will someday be your new *mamm.*"

"She has agreed to this?" Mabel said after she gasped. "*Daett,* how can you marry so quickly after *Mamm*'s passing? And to such a weird woman?"

"*Yah,* really weird," Leroy agreed. "I get chill bumps just driving past their place.

And that daughter of hers . . ."

"Her name's Katie," Willis offered, apparently trying to be helpful.

"*Yah.* Katie, that's the one," Leroy said. "And, Willis, don't tell me you've been making eyes at her or I'll disown you as a brother."

"I have not!" Willis retorted. "She's way too old for me."

"Children, children!" Jesse interrupted. What was he to tell them? They would have to be persuaded Emma was a good woman. Scolding would get him nowhere. He had to exercise patience and understanding. Of course, this idea was kind of sudden for them. And any new *mamm* would no doubt be a hard adjustment for all of them in some ways. Since he wasn't saying anything, the children all looked at him, even little Joel. They were waiting for him to say something more. The problem was that he didn't know how to go on.

"Who is this Emma?" Little Joel was the first to break the silence. His smiling face shone over his plate of eggs and bacon.

Jesse smiled back. At least he had one child on his side.

"She's a widow woman," Jesse said. "She lost her husband the same way we lost *Mamm,* only it's the other way around."

Joel pondered the information.

"Would you like Emma for your new *mamm*?" Jesse asked.

"I don't know," Joel said. "Would she be like *Mamm* was?"

Silence settled on the room again as they all looked at their *daett*. Leroy even stopped chewing.

What should he say, Jesse wondered.

Willis spoke up. "I think we should let *Daett* do what he wants about . . ."

Mabel answered before all the words were out of Willis's mouth. "I think *Daett* should answer Joel's question. I would like to know myself. Does he think he can find another *mamm* like we had?"

Jesse swallowed hard before speaking. "No other woman will be like your *mamm*, Mabel. But a new *mamm* can still be a *gut mamm* all the same. And I think Emma is the woman *Da Hah* wants me to marry."

"Do you think I'm not doing a *gut* enough job with the housework?" Mabel asked. "Is that why you want to marry again?"

"*Nee.*" Jesse smiled. "I just told both you and Carolyn what a *gut* job you're doing. But you shouldn't be working this hard. And you should be thinking about normal girl things instead of doing all this housework."

Mabel didn't look convinced. "Emma's horribly strange, and I don't like her."

"Emma Raber is never going to be anything like *Mamm.*" Carolyn had tears brimming in her eyes.

Jesse stroked his beard, his breakfast forgotten. This hadn't been a *gut* idea, he decided, bringing the subject up during breakfast. Millie would have known it wasn't, but Millie wasn't here any longer. If anything brought out his need for a *frau* in the house, this conversation surely was doing so. Taking a deep breath, he tried again. "Emma would not be like *Mamm,* I agree. But we would grow to love her as time goes by. I feel in my heart that I can, and I believe you also can. Perhaps not like we loved *Mamm* because nothing can ever be like that, but in a different way, a special way. I believe Emma and her daughter can find places in our hearts."

"I don't think I can stand that woman in my house!" Mabel declared, not looking at her *daett.*

"I can understand how you feel." Jesse tried to say calm. "All our hearts were torn by *Mamm*'s passing. But you children shouldn't have to bear all the extra work. You're too young for that. Mabel, you're only sixteen, and a sixteen-year-old shouldn't have to plan meals for the whole family, manage washdays, and oversee her younger sister and brother. It's too much to ask of you, and I'm sorry that I've had to. So far I haven't had a choice, but I'm hoping Emma will change that."

"I still don't like it!" Mabel clearly wasn't backing down an inch.

"You don't have to make such a fit," Willis spoke up. "It's disturbing my breakfast."

"That's because you don't think further than your nose," Mabel shot back at him. "You can go out to the fields and get away from *Daett*'s new *frau,* but I'll have to live in the house with her, cook with her, fix supper with her, and take orders from her. She will affect my life the most. How can you do this to us, *Daett*? Wasn't it bad enough when *Da Hah* took *Mamm*? Now you plan to bring a woman in to take *Mamm*'s place?"

"Please, Mabel," Jesse said, "give the idea a chance. Emma would be a *gut mamm* for you. And have you ever spoken with Katie? She seems like a nice girl from what I've seen and heard of her. She was out helping with chores when I visited last night."

Mabel looked close to tears. "Maybe if I'd help with the outside chores you wouldn't feel the need to marry someone. But how can I? The housework is more than I can handle now."

"Stop talking this nonsense, Mabel," Leroy said. "You don't like Emma, and neither do I. But don't feel sorry for yourself. I can't stand that."

Jesse figured he had to bring the conversation back under control, but how? Should he tell them all to hush? Tell them he was going to do what he wished, what he thought was right? That would silence the children, but it wouldn't silence the pain in their eyes or the sorrow in their hearts. Perhaps it was better to allow this ruckus than to drive the pain into hiding. "I'm sorry for how much this hurts," he said after a few minutes. "You're all very dear to my heart. I could listen to your desires and not visit Emma again, but I don't believe that is the right thing to do. Why? I believe this is what *Da Hah* wants for me . . . and for you. I would like to have Emma as my *frau* and for her to be your new *mamm.* But the truth is that Emma has not yet agreed to any of this."

"Then *Da Hah* be praised!" Leroy said. "At least the woman has some sense in her head."

"Leroy!" Jesse glanced sideways at his oldest. "That's enough out of you." Expressing themselves in a time of pain was one thing, but disrespect was another. Jesse would not tolerate his children being disrespectful. That could only lead downhill until they disrespected the church, next the ministers, and finally *Da Hah* Himself.

"I'm sorry," Leroy said, dropping his head.

"Perhaps we will talk more about this later," Jesse said, pushing away from the table. "I had hoped you would be a little more understanding about this matter, but even in my disappointment I still want you to express your feelings as we work through this. Emma apparently agrees with all of you except for little Joel. But we shall see. I have not yet been persuaded in my heart that *Da Hah* isn't leading me in asking Emma to be my *frau.*" Jesse looked around the table, and they all had their eyes cast down . . . even little Joel. "Come," he said. "Let's go to the living room for the Scripture reading. It looks like we all need *Da Hah*'s Word for the days ahead."

They followed him and took their seats as he opened the big family Bible. He began reading in the book of Psalms, chapter forty. "I waited patiently for the LORD; and he inclined unto me . . ." *A verse most appropriate,* Jesse thought as he read on.

CHAPTER EIGHT

Katie finished the last of the breakfast dishes after the morning rush of chores. She pulled the plug on the drain and watched the water rush down in a small whirlpool. She looked away, her thoughts going to *Mamm* sitting in the living room. *Mamm* wouldn't be waiting to read the Scripture like other families did each morning. People simply didn't read the Scriptures out loud with no *daett* in the house. At least that's what *Mamm* claimed. It hadn't bothered Katie much before, but it did this morning. Her feelings were changing with the news of Jesse's proposal of marriage. Could it be that someday soon the Scriptures would be read aloud each morning again? The thought thrilled Katie and made her even more hopeful that *Mamm* would change her mind about Jesse's offer.

Mamm hadn't spoken all morning, other than what was necessary to get the work

84

done. But now she was getting ready to speak. Katie read the signs at breakfast. They were written on *Mamm*'s face — the tense jaw and the sorrowful look in her eyes. *Mamm* had a soft heart, but when she believed something there was little chance of persuading her otherwise. Nor was there much chance of holding back a lecture once she'd decided it must be delivered.

Not that Katie hadn't tried before. And on the subject of Jesse Mast, she felt she must. This was too important a matter to not weigh in. Perhaps *Mamm* thought this was only about her relationship with Jesse, but it wasn't. *Mamm* might think she could take away her daughter's job at Byler's and life would return to normal, but she was wrong. It was too late for that. From now on, *Mamm* would need to consider Katie's views on family matters. If not on *Mamm*'s thoughts on Jesse Mast, then at least on matters pertaining to Katie's life. It was, after all, *her* life — not *Mamm*'s or anyone else's. If she was interested in boys, *Mamm* would have to accept the fact.

At least *Mamm* didn't know she'd spoken so casually with the *Englisha* boys at Byler's. If she knew, *Mamm* would probably call on Deacon Elmer. Not that Deacon Elmer could do anything since he believed in *rumspringa*. With that choice taken from her, *Mamm* likely decided to take care of the problem on her own.

"Katie!" *Mamm* called from the living room. "I thought you were almost done with the dishes. Do you need help?"

"*Nee,* I'm done," Katie answered. "I'm coming."

"I have some things to speak with you about before you leave," *Mamm* said. "Please hurry. There's not much time."

"*Yah, Mamm.*" Katie kept her voice calm. Getting upset with *Mamm* wasn't going to help. They would have this conversation like two adults should. Like Arlene no doubt had conversations with her *mamm* and *daett.* Katie walked across the kitchen floor, pausing to straighten a chair before continuing. Perhaps she was stalling. After all, the conversation ahead probably wouldn't be a pleasant one. She took a deep breath and entered the living room.

Mamm was sitting on the couch, their large black Bible open on her lap. The Bible *Daett* used to read from. Oh, it would be so *wunderbah* to have *Daett* sitting in the living room on a morning like this, his Bible open on his lap, his deep voice filling the room as he read the sacred words.

"Please sit down," *Mamm* said. "We have

86

to talk."

Katie sat on the couch, her hands in her lap.

"Look at me, Katie. What I have to say is very important for both of us."

Katie lifted her eyes. She owed *Mamm* that much cooperation, she figured.

"I've been thinking since last night." *Mamm* smiled a bit. "I don't know why Jesse Mast is showing an interest in me or why you seem to be changing, but I don't like either one. I want things to stay the way they've been. We've been happy. I don't want to allow anything to happen that will end our happiness. On my part, I've told Jesse I'm not interested in being his *frau.* On your part, I want you to curb your interest in boys."

"What did you tell Jesse exactly?" Katie fixed her gaze on *Mamm*'s face.

"I simply told him I'm not interested in him as my husband."

"Mamm . . ." Katie sighed. "The truth is that I need a *daett* and you need a husband."

"Katie!" *Mamm* said, "How can you say that? How can you think that? Have you been unhappy with our life together and not told me?"

"It's not about whether I've been happy

or unhappy. It's about whether *Da Hah* has happiness for me in the future — and happiness for you too. Even more happiness than we've known in the past. It won't happen if we close the door to His will."

"You think you know *Da Hah*'s will more than I do? I'm your *mamm!*"

Katie sputtered, "I might know something about it because I'm open to change . . . and you're not. You act like . . . like . . . like Jesse committed a sin for wanting you as his *frau*. I think it would be *wunderbah* to have a *daett*. In fact, this might, perhaps, be among the best things that could happen to us. I think you should say *yah* and become his *frau*. After all, it's not like another man will show up anytime soon."

Mamm looked horrified. "I can't believe you're talking like this, Katie! What has happened to my little girl?"

"I'm not a little girl anymore," Katie declared. "That's what's happening to me. Why don't you open your eyes? You are, after all, my *mamm.*"

Tears sprang to *Mamm*'s eyes. "Oh, Katie, you don't know how it tears my heart apart to hear you talk like this. You're changing into someone I don't even know."

Katie looked away. "I'm sorry." She knew she shouldn't be speaking to *Mamm* this way. A few months ago — or even a few weeks ago — she wouldn't have even thought to say such words. But something *was* changing inside her, and it couldn't be stopped now.

Mamm moved closer and slipped her arm around Katie's shoulder. Katie laid her head against *Mamm*'s shoulder. They sat in silence, not moving as the old clock ticked on the living room wall. When the half-hour chime went off a few minutes later, Katie sat up. *Mamm* kept hold of her hand and whispered, "You're still my child, Katie."

"I know." Katie nodded. "But I guess you'll have to accept that your little girl is growing up."

Mamm squeezed her hand. "Growing up doesn't have to include the desire for Ben Stoll or any other boy."

"But that's not normal, *Mamm,*" Katie countered. She needed to leave for work, but she felt she had to make her *mamm* understand. "*Mamm,* I don't want to hurt you, but the truth is that I'm tired of this. I'm tired of being looked at as strange. I'm tired of people pitying me because I'm Emma Raber's daughter. Do you know that everyone calls me that? I want to be known as *Katie* Raber for a change. I want to be accepted as me, a person separate from you.

I want people — including boys — to look at me and see me not you."

Tears were in *Mamm*'s eyes again. "You're all I have, Katie. I can't lose you."

"You could have more," Katie said. "Jesse Mast is offering you a whole lot more. You could be a *mamm* to more children who need you. You're not that old. You might even have another baby in the house, not to mention the five children Jesse already has. And I would have a *daett.*" Katie took a deep breath. She must leave or she'd be late for work. These were hard truths she was saying, but they seemed to bubble up from inside of her, demanding expression.

Mamm cleared her throat. "If I lose a daughter — as it seems I am — then having a husband I don't love won't make my life any better. I'm not accepting Jesse's offer even if he comes back."

"Well, I hope he does come back," Katie insisted. "And I hope you change your mind."

"He won't be back. I told him I wasn't interested, and any decent man would have the sense to take *nee* for an answer. As for you, Katie, I wish you would feel sorry for the way you're acting."

"I can't change the way I feel."

Mamm didn't answer for a long time.

Katie was ready to speak again when *Mamm* turned toward her. "I wish you would believe me when I tell you that we have something very *wunderbah* between us. This is our home. A safe place from an evil world out there that's full of pain. We don't have to change, Katie. We don't have to experience the pain that's out there. We don't need others to be happy. But if you go running after a boy, all he will give you is heartache and suffering. And the same thing will happen to me if I accept Jesse's offer. It will not bring happiness to either of us. I had my chances at happiness, and they were taken away from me. Can you understand that, Katie?"

"I don't think *Da Hah* offers us only two chances at happiness, *Mamm.* He's offering you a third chance — but you won't take it."

Mamm seemed to tune Katie out. "You were the miracle that brought the love for your *daett* alive in my heart, Katie. You were the part of him that became a part of me. Together your *daett* and I brought new life into the world unlike any before us. *Da Hah* allowed me to see this so clearly that love came alive in my heart. Then your *daett* was taken. It seemed like *Da Hah* had something against me. Like there was a terrible sin I'd

91

done that needed paying for. Can you understand that, Katie? Can you see what might happen if I told Jesse I would marry him? What we have between us might die forever, and what comes afterward might be a whole lot worse than anything we have yet experienced."

"But, *Mamm*," Katie countered, clutching her mother's hand, "*Da Hah* could help us experience even more happiness."

Mamm shook her head. "*Nee,* Katie. I will not reach for such heights again. I am thankful *Da Hah* was once gracious to me."

"I really must go." Katie got up and moved toward the front door.

Mamm nodded but said nothing more.

Katie glanced back as she went out the door. *Mamm* was still sitting on the couch and staring out the window.

CHAPTER NINE

Thirty minutes later Katie pulled to a stop at the intersection near Royal Farm's gas station. She looked both ways before venturing ahead. As the buggy wheels hummed beneath her, Katie's mind drifted back to the tense moments at home this morning. At least *Mamm* had relented a bit and come outside to help hitch Sparky. And they had embraced before Katie had climbed inside the buggy.

Katie held on tight to the lines and thought of Ben Stoll. She pictured Ben driving into their driveway, just like Jesse had done the other evening, and then tying his horse to the hitching post. What an impossible dream. At least *Mamm* was right about that. The sooner she got rid of her silly daydreams about Ben the better. She'd been wishing she wouldn't be so obsessed with him anyway. Maybe this *kafuffle* with *Mamm* would help move her in that direction. If

Mamm had her way, Katie would never think about boys again. That was impossible! Even if her *mamm* had resolved to do that in her own life, it was unreasonable to expect her to do the same. At least *Mamm* had been married and borne a child. That made quite a difference. But to hope her daughter would never love a man or find a husband? Is that what *Mamm* was asking of her?

Mamm hadn't quite worded it that way, but from the sounds of it, she expected Katie to remain single all her life. What a depressing thought. The years stretching before her in such a condition seemed empty and cruel, to say the least. Her cozy little world with *Mamm* no longer looked safe. In fact, it looked threatening.

Katie sighed as she held the reins loosely in her lap. Why couldn't *Mamm* understand? Somehow *Da Hah* would have to open up a way to get through. *Mamm*'s way of thinking just wasn't right. They both needed a normal family life — that was for sure.

Ahead of her, Byler's Store came into view. Eventually Katie slowed down to make the turn into the driveway. When she stopped by the hitching post and climbed out, Esther Kuntz's car pulled in. Esther waved, and Katie smiled and waved back.

Before she'd unhitched Sparky, Esther's cheerful voice called out, "What a lovely day, isn't it!"

"*Yah,* it is," Katie agreed with a quick glance at Esther. Then she led Sparky to the back and tied him up. Esther was sure in an unusually good mood this morning. Katie walked toward her coworker.

"I have something I'm supposed to ask you," Esther said as the two met up and headed to the back of the store.

"You have something to ask me?"

Esther was all smiles now as she leaned toward Katie. "Roy Coblenz has invited you to his birthday party tomorrow night. How about that?"

Katie's mind raced. "Who is Roy Coblenz?"

Esther raised her eyebrows. "I thought you would know since he specifically asked me to invite you."

"I don't remember the name," Katie said. "There must be some mistake. Or are you teasing me, Esther?"

Esther laughed. "Believe me, Katie, I do like to tease. But not this time, if you know what I mean."

Katie nodded. She did know what Esther meant. Bringing false news of a boy's interest would go well beyond a tease. It would be mean.

Esther shrugged. "Are you sure you don't know Roy? He said he spoke with you when he stopped in at the store."

"Here at Byler's?" Katie questioned.

"That's what Roy said."

Katie searched her mind. There were those two boys who had noticed her — *Englisha* boys.

"He's an *Englisha* boy?" Katie asked.

"Well, he's not Amish. But he's not a heathen either," Esther said with grin. "He's Mennonite. That's how I know him . . . from church. He's blond and a little tall."

"And his name is Roy?" Katie heard a tremble in her voice.

"Yes. Roy Coblenz. So will you go? Will your mom let you?"

Katie was silent. That was a good question. After their discussion this morning, it wasn't likely.

"I don't know if she will," Katie admitted.

"Well, it's not like a date, you know. It's just an invite to a Mennonite birthday party. And besides, you're not a member of the Amish church yet, are you?"

"*Nee,* not yet," Katie replied.

"Then there's no problem," Esther said as they entered the store through the employee entrance. "I'm invited too. How about if I

96

pick you up tomorrow night?"

"Tomorrow night? Pick me up? Why would you be willing to do that?"

"I just thought you might want a ride," Esther said.

Katie's head was spinning. Maybe this was *Da Hah*'s answer to her prayer? A solution she'd never thought of?

"Come on!" Esther teased. "It's not that big a deal. I'll be glad to pick you up."

"Do you know where I live?" Katie asked.

"I think I do. Toward Hartly and on the left?"

"*Yah,* we live in the old, white farmhouse."

"See you at seven then. Don't forget."

How could I forget? Katie wondered. There would be no overlooking this news even if she wanted to. And she didn't want to! Not a bit. This was a door opened for her, was it not? An open door from *Da Hah* to help her make friends. She was certain of it now that she knew Roy was Mennonite.

Esther walked toward the deli, and Katie made her way to her cash register. As she counted out her opening money, she glanced over to see Arlene just finishing her count. The fellow store clerk returned her glance and asked, "What happened to you? You look like you've seen a ghost."

Katie nodded. "I think I did." She looked

toward the deli where Esther was putting out the meat trays.

Arlene followed Katie's glance. "Something involving Esther?"

"I was talking with Esther."

"What did Esther talk you into?" Arlene asked with a sigh. "If she's pulling some trick on you, tell me and I'll go back there to talk with her right away. You know I'm not going to stand here and watch a girl like Esther take advantage of you."

"It's not what you think," Katie managed to say. "Don't worry. I'm okay."

Arlene didn't look convinced. "I'm getting to the bottom of this later, Katie. You can depend on that."

Katie ignored Arlene and forced a smile when the manager, Mrs. Cole, walked up. She had to keep her courage up. Even with the strange turn of events she was sure everything would turn out okay. *Da Hah* was in charge.

CHAPTER TEN

It was a busy day at Byler's. During the few breaks between customers and at lunch, Arlene tried to get Katie to open up about her conversation with Esther. But for now, Katie didn't want to talk about it. She wanted to savor the invitation. Now quitting time was approaching, and Katie knew it would bring no relief from Arlene's curiosity. She sighed as the next customer in line, an old man, looked up and smiled at her.

"You look tired," he said. "Time to go home?"

"Almost," Katie replied.

"Well, don't get too tired to go out socializing with the boys tonight."

Katie forced herself to smile at his banter. If he only knew. Boys didn't socialize with her.

The man pressed on. "Some good-looking young man you're out with tonight? About as good-looking as me, eh?"

Katie laughed at the irony. Still, the situations in her life right now regarding her *mamm* and boys weren't really funny at all. Katie smiled at the man and handed him his change. "Thank you for shopping at Byler's," she said.

The man nodded. Still chuckling, he pushed his grocery cart toward the front doors.

He was enjoying his own joke immensely, Katie thought as she watched him go. She turned back to her register, suppressing a sigh and forcing a smile for the older couple next in line. "Did you find everything you need?" Katie asked as she scanned the grocery items.

"Yes, we did," the woman said. "And I must say this is the most awesome place to shop. We're so pleased that you Amish make your baked goods and crafts available to us outside folk. I know we should all live simpler lives, but this is the second best, I suppose."

"I'm glad you found everything," Katie responded as she continued scanning.

"Bonnie cleans me out every time we come here," the man grumbled. "Can you give us a little break on the prices? Perhaps do an impromptu sale day?"

Katie smiled. "I'm afraid I can't do much

about that."

"Now don't you mind Nelson one bit," Bonnie said. "He's just teasing. And I worked as hard for that money as he did, so he has nothing to complain about. And we get it all back and then some when we sit down to eat these wonderful pies and cinnamon rolls."

Nelson patted his stomach and nodded. "This is where the money goes. But I must say it goes down right smoothly, so why should I complain? Besides, you can't take the money with you, they say."

Katie announced the total, and Bonnie reached into her purse for her checkbook. Nelson moved the bagged goods to their grocery cart while his wife wrote out the check and handed it to Katie. As the couple walked away, Nelson said over his shoulder, "See you next time, young lady."

"You both have a good evening now," Katie replied. She watched them go. They seemed so normal. What a contrast to her own situation. Could she possibly find the kind of love they shared by defying *Mamm*'s wishes? It was so hard to imagine. She checked out one final customer just as the two girls on the evening shift arrived. Mrs. Cole came out from her office to oversee the transfer. She motioned the remaining two customers in Katie's line over to another register.

As Katie finished, she glanced over at Arlene, who had already reconciled her cash receipts and was getting ready to leave. Now if Mrs. Cole would find some way of keeping Arlene occupied for a few minutes until she could finish up and dash outside and get away that would be *wunderbah.* But of course that wasn't going to happen. And even if it did, Arlene would be at her again tomorrow. If Arlene waited for her, Katie decided she might as well deal with it and get it over with.

Sure enough, a few minutes later when she left, Arlene was waiting for her outside.

"You know I want to speak with you," Arlene said.

"*Yah,* I know," Katie said, nodding to an *Englisha* couple climbing out of their car. The man had a camera draped around his neck. He looked like he would love to snap her picture, especially as she neared her buggy. Well, he would just have to live without achieving his wish. She wasn't about to break more rules. Going to a Mennonite birthday party was going to be bad enough. When they arrived at their buggies, Arlene said, "Thankfully they're not taking our picture. But perhaps we should talk where they can't see us."

"We'll be out of sight over here," Katie said, catching one final glimpse of the man with the camera as she walked behind her buggy.

"Now," Arlene began, "you're going to tell me what's going on. What has Esther talked you into doing?"

Katie took a deep breath and closed her eyes. "Esther brought me an invite from a boy named Roy Coblenz. He wants me to come to his birthday party tomorrow night. He's a Mennonite like Esther is — not an *Englisha.*"

"You're going to a Mennonite youth gathering?" Arlene stared at her.

"*Yah,* and Esther offered to pick me up."

"Wow! You're going to a Mennonite party! I can't believe it." Arlene was glowing. "You've been keeping this news from me all day? I think it's *wunderbah* you're going. And here you had me all worried the other day about you consorting with *Englisha* boys. Now that would have been bad, but a Mennonite boy might just work for you. I didn't even know you knew any Mennonites that well."

Katie was a bit surprised at Arlene's attitude. But, after all, she was in her *rumspringa,* so maybe that accounted for it. "I don't," Katie said. "Apparently he saw me yesterday here at Byler's and probably needs to fill his guest list or something."

Arlene studied Katie for a few seconds. "You don't seem all that happy about it. You should though. Getting invitations to Mennonite youth gatherings is a *gut* thing. I've been to some myself. You've never been before, but I can tell you it's not a bad thing."

"It's *Mamm,*" Katie admitted. "She'll never agree to this. I'm not even allowed to do *rumspringa.*"

"Oh, I forgot about that. She's pretty strict, isn't she? Are you sure she won't budge on this?"

"I'm quite sure," Katie said.

"Well, you'll live through it," Arlene said. "Your *mamm* will understand — after some time has elapsed. Just go home and tell her that someone invited you to a birthday party and that you're going."

"It's not just that it's a Mennonite party," Katie said before moaning. "It's worse because it's a party for a boy. You don't know what that will mean to *Mamm.*"

"She'll be happy after she gets over the shock of her daughter finally growing up. All parents go through that. Mine did a few years ago, but they got over it."

"Maybe," Katie said, but she knew it wasn't true in her case. She wasn't about to say more to Arlene about *Mamm* and why she felt the way she did.

They walked around to Sparky, and Arlene helped Katie get him between the buggy shafts and hitched up. Then Katie headed home to face *Mamm*. She figured it would be one of the hardest things she'd ever do in her life.

CHAPTER ELEVEN

As Katie pulled into their lane at home, she saw *Mamm* standing beside the barn. When she drove closer, she noticed *Mamm*'s face appeared stern and her eyes were fixed on Katie's buggy. Pulling to a stop, Katie let go of the lines. Her hands trembled as she climbed down using the buggy step.

"I'm glad to see you're finally home," *Mamm* said as she came over to help unhitch.

Katie's heart pounded, but she didn't look at *Mamm*'s face. Her news about the invitation should be told soon, but her mouth was so dry nothing would come out at the moment.

"One of our cows has a huge bulge on its side," *Mamm* said, taking the tugs off on her side. "I went to the phone shack to call the vet. He should be here any minute. I certainly didn't want to be here by myself when he arrived."

"Oh!" Katie's mind whirled.

"Yah," Mamm said. "I know how you feel. We can't afford to lose a cow, nor can we afford the vet bill either. But losing the cow would be worse."

"Do you know what's causing the bulge?" Katie asked as she tried to collect her thoughts.

"*Nee,* but the swelling has gotten worse since I called the vet."

"Which cow is it?"

"Molly." *Mamm* glanced toward the barn. "Bossy looks okay to me, but you never know. I sure hope this isn't something catching."

Katie focused her attention on the task at hand — finishing her side of the unhitching. She led Sparky forward while *Mamm* held the buggy shafts. Leading the horse into the barn, Katie slid the harness off and hung it on the wall. *Mamm* released Sparky into his stall and added oats in the feed trough. As mother and daughter entered the barnyard, *Mamm* pointed toward the ailing milk cow.

Molly looked mournfully up at them as they approached, her upper left side extended with a large hump. It looked like a balloon had been stuck under her skin.

Mamm ran her hand over the bulging skin,

and Molly groaned in protest.

"It looks awful," Katie said.

From behind them they heard the sound of an *Englisha* vehicle driving down the lane.

"It's the vet!" *Mamm* said, relief on her face.

Katie stayed with Molly while *Mamm* went to greet the man. Bossy was standing by the barn door now, banging her head against the side boards and making her will to be milked known. This was a *gut* sign. Bossy must not have whatever Molly had caught.

Katie turned back to the moaning cow and stroked the long, familiar face. There was nothing she could do but supply a little comfort. "Don't go dying on us now," Katie crooned. "We need you badly."

Molly continued moaning, lifting one of her front feet to stomp the ground. Behind Katie the barn door swung open again, and *Mamm* led the vet to the sick cow.

The vet nodded to Katie, giving her a quick glance before examining Molly.

Before long *Mamm* asked, "Can you see what's wrong with her? Will we be losing her?"

"That depends," the vet replied. "I don't think this is too far advanced, thankfully. Have you been feeding these cows alfalfa? Or wheat perhaps?"

"Yah." **Mamm** sounded puzzled. "I just had all my pastures redone in alfalfa last year, but that's a *gut* thing, isn't it?"

"One would think so," the vet responded, "but not always. It depends on how much your cattle can get to other kinds of feed."

Mamm took a moment before answering. "I guess I had the cows mostly on grass the last week or so. But we give them grain when we milk."

"I'd get them off the pasture for awhile," the vet said. "This cow has a case of pasture bloat. How serious, I don't know. Let's lead her around and see how she walks."

"Bloating?" *Mamm* asked. "I don't remember any such thing happening to my father's cows."

"Your father may have kept several different types of pastures on his farm," the vet said.

"That could be," *Mamm* agreed. "I don't really remember."

The vet turned his attention back to Molly and slapped her on the backside. Molly groaned and lurched to her feet before lumbering forward a few steps. The vet studied Molly from behind and then walked around to the front. He bent down to check her mouth.

"What do you think?" *Mamm* asked.

The vet rubbed his jaw. "I was trying to decide how much of a risk we should take. If I leave without doing a rumenotomy and the cow gets much worse, I might not get back in time if you call me. Once they start to stagger or show real signs of distress, it's often too late. Do you think you could do a small emergency procedure if things go badly? It's not difficult or serious, but it would provide some relief for the cow until I can return."

"This would be a surgery, *yah*?" *Mamm*'s face looked distressed. "I don't think I wish to tackle surgery."

A hint of smile played on the vet's face. "I could show you, ma'am. It's not that difficult, and you could call me afterward to come and sew it up."

The vet must know they didn't have much money and was trying to help out, Katie decided. Could she do this surgery he spoke of? She could imagine herself with a knife held over Molly's tough hide, trembling like crazy but trying to cut her way inside. Katie shuddered and looked at *Mamm,* who still wasn't saying anything.

"It might save you a lot of expense, ma'am," the vet said. "Not to mention easing the discomfort for the cow. If I do the surgery now, all the bases are covered, but she might recover just as well by being led around the barnyard every thirty minutes or so until the gas is worked out."

"What is this surgery like?" Katie asked, finally finding her voice.

The vet turned her way. "Are you brave enough to try it, then?"

"I think so." Katie heard the sound of her voice as if it were coming from off in the distance.

"I certainly can't do surgery on a cow," *Mamm* decided. "And Katie is much too young."

The vet smiled. "It's not that hard, ma'am. I think the girl would be up to the task. But as I said, surgery may not be needed. Just keep 'er walking until the gas has run its course."

"Well . . ." *Mamm* considered the idea. "Why don't you explain this procedure to us then."

"Good." The vet ran his hand over Molly's back and pointed to her left flank. "Right here is where you would cut. I'll mark it. Take a sharp knife and cut a two-inch long incision through the skin. From there you cut through the muscle and into the 'rumen,' which is Molly's first stomach. Be ready for what will happen next. A lot of air will explode outward. Keep your face away unless you want stinky gas blown into it."

"I'll leave a syringe of local anesthetic and bandages . . . if you decide to undertake this task."

"You'll mark the spot well?" *Mamm*'s hand was shaking.

"Sure." The vet pulled a purple marker out of his pouch. He drew a line where his finger had run over earlier.

"After you make the incision," the vet continued, "you call me. I'll come out to sew her up. I hope you won't have to make the cut. I think if you lead her around the barnyard for awhile, perhaps up and down a slight slope, that will work. It's an old folk remedy, I know, but what's wrong with trying?"

"*Yah,* we will try that," *Mamm* told him. "And thank you so much."

Katie patted Molly on the nose as she moaned again.

The vet smiled. "I'm leaving our good cow here in the great care of two lovely ladies. The best of luck to you."

"Thank you," *Mamm* said as Bossy banged on the barn door behind them.

Katie waited until the vet had left, his truck tires crunching on the gravel. She led Molly out of the barnyard and toward a sloping embankment behind the barn. *Mamm* ran ahead and opened the gate.

Looking over her shoulder, Katie saw *Mamm* shut the gate and shoo Bossy in front of her until they disappeared into the barn. How would they milk Molly tonight if she was in this condition? Katie wondered. That question could be solved later. The important thing at the moment was to follow the vet's instructions.

Above Molly's left flank was the bright purple mark left by the vet's pen. It appeared more ominous the longer she looked at it. Katie pulled her eyes away, and patted Molly on the nose. "We'll not be plunging a knife into one of your stomachs if we can keep from it, Molly. I promise you. Let's you and me walk up and down this bank and see if we can get rid of those ugly gasses inside you."

Molly seemed to understand as she followed Katie up and down the embankment. The bovine let out an occasional groan. On the third trip up, Molly let out a large belch and moved her mouth around like she was chewing her cud.

"Phew!" Katie waved her hand in front of her face. "That stinks."

The smell lingered for a few minutes — a mixture of fresh grass and sour rot. Then

Molly stopped in her tracks and refused to move.

"Do you feel better?" Katie asked as she patted Molly's side. She looked at the bulge on the left flank. It still seemed about the same size, but the belch showed progress.

Katie pulled hard on the lead rope, finally getting Molly to move down the slope again. On the next walk up, another belch came. This time Katie jumped aside in time and turned her face in the other direction.

Moments later *Mamm* appeared with an empty bucket and a three-legged stool.

"How's it going?" *Mamm* asked.

"She's belching some," Katie said.

"Good!" *Mamm* said. "I so hope we don't have to cut into her."

"I know," Katie agreed, bringing Molly back to the bottom of the embankment. She held the tie rope as *Mamm,* without further ado, sat down to milk. They made a mighty strange sight if anyone saw them from the road. Katie holding the cow outside the barn while the lady of the house milked her.

Katie waited, growing more embarrassed by the minute as *Mamm* milked. She searched the road for any signs of buggies but saw none. This was another reason why they needed a man around, she thought. A man doing this wouldn't seem nearly as silly as two women doing it. After this fiasco, how could she go in for supper and tell *Mamm* about her plans for tomorrow night? That conversation would have to wait. *Mamm* had enough worries on her mind with Molly being sick. And if Molly had to have the emergency surgery sometime tonight, there was no sense adding more drama to their lives. She would speak with *Mamm* in the morning.

Molly belched again, swinging her tail.

A smile crept across *Mamm*'s face.

CHAPTER TWELVE

That night Katie awoke to the soft shaking of *Mamm*'s hand on her shoulder. She sat bolt upright, and the bedcovers went flying. The moon was shining through the upstairs window, revealing *Mamm*'s faint form standing beside the bed, kerosene lamp in hand.

"Katie!" *Mamm* whispered. "Wake up. It's time to check on Molly."

Katie climbed out of bed and followed *Mamm*. They'd talked about this last evening, so Katie had slept in her chore dress. She followed *Mamm* down to the kitchen. *Mamm* retrieved the flashlight from the top of the refrigerator. She set the lamp on the kitchen table, and they walked out into the bright moonlight.

Mamm walked ahead of Katie, leading the way to the stall where they'd left the ailing cow. After a quick look with the beam of the flashlight, she said, "The swelling is up again."

Katie rushed over to look for herself. It was true. The swelling was almost back to where it had been before the vet arrived.

"What shall we do?" *Mamm* asked. "Shall we get the knife and do the surgery the vet told us about?"

Katie ran her hand over Molly's left flank. "I'd like to try walking her again before we do any cutting."

"It's the middle of the night," *Mamm* said. "But this sort of thing comes with keeping a farm." Katie opened the stall door and slipped the rope around Molly's neck. She tugged hard. The cow moaned and stretched her neck but didn't move her legs.

"She's already over-bloated," *Mamm* said.

"Let's be quick!" Katie said. "Slap her on the backside. That might help."

Mamm whacked Molly with her hand. When that didn't work, she pushed Molly's rear, and the cow lunged to her feet.

"Come, girl!" Katie spoke in soothing tones.

Mamm ran ahead, the flashlight beam bouncing off the walls. She opened the outside barn doors. Katie arrived with Molly still moaning with every step. They stepped into the bright moonlight. Bossy raised her head from the middle of the barnyard where she was lying down. She mooed twice, the soft bellow causing Molly to lift her head higher.

"Oh no you're not. You're not staying with her," Katie said. "We're going out back again."

Mamm raced across the barnyard to push open the side gate.

Katie pulled Molly through before Bossy could get up and barge after them. Looking over her shoulder as she led Molly toward the embankment, Katie expected Bossy to already be leaning over the gate, stretching her long neck toward them.

Mamm looked back at the same time. "Get back there, you silly thing! You'll push our gate over."

Bossy jerked her head about as if she understood. She lumbered along the fence, following them for a short distance before giving up.

Katie led Molly up the embankment. *Mamm* followed behind, ready to push if necessary. Molly belched halfway up the incline and seemed to move faster after that. Katie turned Molly around at the top, and they lumbered down again.

"She's coming along," *Mamm* said when they reached the bottom. "I think I'll wait for you here."

Katie repeated the trip. On the next

round, *Mamm* took a turn. They traded off every second trip up while the other person sprawled out on the ground to rest. Katie's heart throbbed as she watched *Mamm* climb the hill in the moonlight leading Molly. Now wide awake, she considered that now might be the time to mention the birthday invitation. They'd be too tired and rushed in the morning, and the party was the next evening. *If not now then when?* she reasoned.

Molly belched again as *Mamm* turned her around at the top of the hill.

Mamm laughed. "It's working, Katie! I'm so thankful."

Moments later *Mamm* came down the embankment, the moonlight shining on her white *kapp*. Behind her, Molly was walking much faster now.

Katie took the rope. She turned to *Mamm*. "Will you walk with me this time? I have something I need to talk with you about."

"Okay."

Katie led Molly up the embankment with *Mamm* beside her.

Katie looked over at her *Mamm*'s face, the moon over her head revealing her features. "It's hard for me to bring this up now, but I have to."

"What is it?" *Mamm* asked. "Have you done something you shouldn't have?"

"Not yet," Katie said. "But I'm going to. Or, rather, it might be something you will think I shouldn't do."

Mamm didn't say anything for a few moments. She looked across the moonlit landscape. "You're going to allow Ben Stoll to bring you home from the hymn singing?" *Mamm* finally said.

"Nee," Katie responded. "It's not that. Besides Ben wouldn't ask me home from a hymn singing."

"What is it then?"

"Esther Kuntz told me I've been invited to a birthday party for Roy Coblenz, and I agreed to go."

"Who is Roy Coblenz?" *Mamm* had stopped and was staring at her.

"A Mennonite boy." She might as well admit the worst, Katie figured. Although it really would have been a lot worse if Roy were *Englisha*.

Mamm's voice cut through the darkness. "And he asked you to come to his birthday party? This Mennonite boy?"

"Well . . ." Katie tried to keep her voice calm, but the moonlit fields seemed to be going around in circles in front of her eyes, making her dizzy and unsteady.

"Well what?" *Mamm* asked.

Katie pushed the words out. "Roy asked

120

Esther to ask me. So I think it's just an ordinary kind of invitation he gave to everybody. He probably wants to fill his yard with people."

"How does he know you?"

Katie tried to move up the hill, but her head was swimming. "He spoke with me a little bit at Byler's when he was in line to pay for his groceries," Katie said. "That's all he knows about me."

Mamm face was now shadowed in the moonlight. "You know I'm not going to allow this, Katie."

Katie stopped and looked at her *mamm.* "I have to go, *Mamm.* And I want to. We can't go on living so isolated forever. It wasn't meant to be. I'm growing up. And *Da Hah* is opening this door for me. He is, *Mamm.* I know it."

"Growing up has nothing to do with this," *Mamm* said, her voice firm. "*Da Hah* causes people to grow up, but He doesn't make them attend Mennonite birthday parties. We have our own youth gatherings you can go to and that's good enough."

"But you hardly ever allow me to attend those," Katie protested.

Mamm fell silent.

"Will you allow me to attend the Amish youth gatherings if Ben Stoll brings me home on a Sunday night?"

"So you *do* have a date with Ben? And you're trying to get me to agree by making me believe there is something worse going on? Is that what you're doing, Katie?"

Katie had nothing of the sort planned, but she had to know what *Mamm* would say if she believed this was the truth. Would she agree to Ben Stoll bringing her home from an Amish hymn singing? Ben Stoll was a *gut* Amish boy, and there should be no objection. That would prove *Mamm* was only worried about the Mennonite aspect of the party. As Katie expected, *Mamm* took her silence as guilt.

Mamm didn't wait for confirmation before giving her answer. "That is also forbidden, Katie. I will not have you spending time in the company of that boy."

"What about some other Amish boy?" Katie asked. She knew the answer, but she wanted to hear *Mamm* say it.

"It's not possible that you have *two* invitations for the same night," *Mamm* said. "But even if you did, I would not allow it."

So *Mamm* really was keeping all the doors shut on her social life, Katie thought. But *Da Hah* was opening them! All she had to do was walk through them. She would have to trust Him for the wisdom about walking through and finding out where they would lead.

"You're still young, Katie. You don't understand the hurt boys can bring to your heart," *Mamm* said. "I want nothing more than to save you from the pain I've been through. That's all I'm trying to do."

Katie pulled on the rope and led Molly up and down the hill again. *Mamm* watched her go, thinking she'd won the argument. But when Katie arrived back at the bottom of the hill after a few rounds, she stopped Molly in front of *Mamm.*

"I'm sorry to disobey you, but I'm going to that birthday party, *Mamm.* And Ben Stoll didn't ask to bring me home on Sunday night. I just wanted to see what you would say about that."

Pain crossed *Mamm*'s face. "What is wrong with what we have, Katie? We love each other, don't we?"

"*Yah,* we do," Katie agreed. "And I'll never stop loving you. But I was created to love more than my *mamm.* And I didn't make myself like that, *Da Hah* did. So I guess you'll have to blame Him."

"You'll come to your senses in the morning." *Mamm* took the lead rope from Katie's hand. "I think it's time we got back to bed."

"It'll be morning before long." Katie

motioned toward the horizon where the first faint signs of dawn were streaking skyward.

Mamm looked that way but didn't move for a few seconds. "Come!" she finally said. "Molly has had enough walking for one night. If she doesn't get better soon, we'll call the vet again."

Katie ran ahead to open the barnyard gate.

Mamm spoke up as she walked through with Molly. "You're not going in to work at Byler's today, Katie. I need you at home."

"I can't do that!" Katie said as she opened the barn doors.

Mamm didn't answer as she led Molly into the barn.

The first contest of their wills had arrived, and Katie decided she needed to win. The stakes were too high not to win.

CHAPTER THIRTEEN

Emma stood on the front porch watching Katie drive down the lane. Her daughter slapped the reins hard against Sparky as she turned right onto the main road. She gave her *mamm* a little wave before she disappeared from sight. Emma returned the wave, but she couldn't shake the sadness of what had happened this morning. Her own daughter, her precious little girl, had shown a streak of rebellion. Tears formed in Emma's eyes. Not only was Katie refusing to obey, but she also couldn't wait to get away from the house. Emma made her way to the front-porch swing and sat down.

"Oh Ezra!" Emma moaned, holding her face in her hands. "Where are you when I need you? Why did *Da Hah* take you from me? She held still, as if she awaited an answer. Soon she began rocking. She lifted her feet from the wooden floor with each move forward as her thoughts drifted. With

Katie gone to work, a deep stillness lay over the farm. This morning Emma could almost see Ezra. He used to sit beside her on this very swing during the cool summer evenings. They would talk and laugh even during the time she'd been heavy with Katie. Emma could almost smell the hay on Ezra's clothing as the breeze stirred. It was enough to bring a sigh and a smile to her lips. She even remembered how things had been when Ezra had come in from the fields. His scent, after a hard day's work, would be mixed with the smell of the barn and the horses. Was *Da Hah* having mercy on her this morning? Emma wondered. Was He sending a clear memory from the past to comfort her in this sorrow of Katie's rebellion?

"Oh Ezra, I miss you so!" she cried as she began to weep again. As the memory of Ezra faded, Emma saw Katie's face. It had been so set this morning, so focused on having her way. Emma's words had meant nothing. No warning she had offered moved Katie from her determination to continue working at Byler's Store or having that Mennonite girl pick her up tonight.

In spite of Katie's rebellion, Emma knew she needed to stay strong. *But what good would even that do?* she asked herself. She'd been strong last night. She'd told Katie she couldn't go back to Byler's to work. She'd told Katie the same thing this morning, but her daughter had simply gone out to the barn, harnessed Sparky, hitched him up to the buggy, and drove off. What was a *mamm* supposed to do about that?

Surely Katie would be back tonight as usual. Surely she wouldn't go so far as to move out, would she? Was it possible she would speak to the Mennonite girl today and arrange some way of never returning home? *Nee,* that wasn't like Katie, Emma decided. But did she really know her daughter anymore?

Emma caught her breath as another thought took hold. What if Katie planned to join the Mennonite church? Emma clutched the edge of the swing. If Katie did such a thing, sorrow and loss would be unbearable. Surely that wouldn't happen. This time of defiance was rebellion pure and simple. She must not make things worse than they already were.

What had she done wrong in bringing up Katie? Children weren't supposed to turn out rebellious. She'd tried her best. Katie had always been such an obedient child — until yesterday. How could that have changed in such a short time? Oh, if she'd just seen this coming she could have prepared for it somehow.

If only Ezra were still alive. He might have seen this awful thing coming weeks ago and done something about it. But he wasn't here, so Emma might as well stop thinking about it. It was wasted effort. Katie was the one who needed her focus right now. How could she awaken Katie to the dangers that lay ahead of her?

Emma stopped the motion of the swing with her feet. She listened for any sound of Katie's horse that might linger on the morning air. There was only silence. Emma stood and went into the house. In the kitchen the dishes were dried and stacked on the counter. Katie had seen to that this morning, even in the middle of the lecture she was hearing. Fresh tears rolled down Emma's cheeks as she pictured Katie standing there, her face so stubborn as she washed dishes with all her might so she could get out of the house to get to work on time.

Katie was a *gut* girl. Emma would just have to pray more and cry out to *Da Hah* for help. He would answer! Did *Da Hah* not care for widows and orphans? *Yah,* He'd made her a widow in the first place, but He still cared for her, did He not? With that comforting hope, Emma remembered her duties for the busy day ahead. She must get to work. Today was wash day. She turned and headed for the basement. There the stillness of the room swept over her. All around her were the familiar stone walls of the old house's foundation. She'd lived here since she'd married Ezra, but today the walls seemed like they belonged to another woman's house. It was almost as if she'd never seen them before.

Emma sat down on the bottom step, put her head in her hands, and wept again. Did the house feel what she was feeling? Did it know she'd failed as a *mamm* and no longer belonged here? Was Ezra seeing her from that land on the other side and feeling a great disappointment in how she'd lost their daughter? Certainly Ezra wouldn't want Katie attending a Mennonite's birthday party. If he knew, he would have a look on his face like the clouds from the north before a great thunderstorm. Did he know? Emma trembled at the thought. Who knew the answer to that question? Clearly she had failed Ezra, she had failed Katie, and she had failed *Da Hah.*

But she must go on, Emma told herself, forcing herself to stand up. Regardless of her failures, there was work to do. Perhaps she could redeem herself yet. Katie might see the error of her ways before the evening came. Maybe some words she'd spoken this morning had more effect than she thought they did. Katie was a *gut* girl. She'd always been a *gut* girl. It simply wasn't possible she could turn so quickly and go so bad.

Was this just a phase Katie was going through? Emma had never participated in the *rumspringa,* so she'd forbidden Katie from it as well. She expected Katie to see things as she had in the past and as she did in the present. Obviously Katie didn't.

Emma walked to the washing machine and stood there for a moment before bending over to give the starter rope a strong jerk. The motor roared to life. Emma turned on the spigot and stood back to watch the water stream from the hose and into the tub. Perhaps *Da Hah* had given them a *gut* sign last night. Hadn't Molly survived? That was an encouragement, was it not? Even with the vet bill still coming, it could have been much higher if they hadn't stayed up and walked Molly. Perhaps this storm would blow over soon, and they could go on with life as it had been.

Emma loaded the washer with dirty dresses. She paused to listen. Had someone driven down the lane? With all the racket from the washing machine, Emma wasn't sure. She took a moment to glance outside the basement door, but she didn't see anyone. She returned to check on the wash before heading upstairs for another hamper of dirty clothes.

As she walked through the kitchen, a knock sounded on the front door. Emma quickly shoved the hamper underneath the kitchen table before going to answer the door. She paused at the window and noticed a familiar buggy in the driveway. Jesse's buggy. What nerve the man had, coming around again after she'd firmly sent him on his way last time.

When she opened the door, she was met with a broad smile and a hearty, "*Gut* morning! How are you today, Emma?"

If he only knew! Emma thought. But then again, it was none of his business. No doubt Jesse had all five of his children under control. He would probably scorn her efforts if he knew the problems she was having with Katie.

"We're doing okay." Emma knew her voice was tense, but the man had no reason to barge in on her like this.

"I'm glad to hear that." Jesse was still smiling. "The vet stopped by my place late last night. Some of my cows have mastitis problems so I've been working with him.

131

He told me about your bloated cow. I thought I'd stop by after chores this morning to see how you're doing with her."

"We're doing okay," Emma repeated, not moving away from the door or inviting the man in. If he thought he was going to weasel his way into her heart by offering to help with her farm troubles, he had another guess coming.

Jesse seemed unfazed by the look on her face. "Do you mind if I take a look at her? Perhaps there's some way I can help."

"I think Molly's fine," Emma said. "Katie and I walked her last evening and again very early this morning. She seems much better."

"Is Molly your smaller cow?"

He is a stubborn man, Emma thought. *I have to get rid of him somehow.* If answering his questions sends him on down the road faster, then she would do so.

"*Yah.* I have a load of wash going in the basement right now, so I really have to get back to it."

"I'll take a look at your cow then." Jesse gave her a bright smile. He didn't wait for an answer before turning and walking across the yard toward the barn.

Emma watched him go with her mouth open. The gall of the man! If this went on,

132

he would be setting the wedding date with the bishop whether she agreed to it or not. Well, that was not going to happen! Not in a hundred years of him making trips over to take care of her farm or her animals. Emma almost hollered after him to stop, but instead she picked up the hamper and continued down to the basement.

When the first load had finished, Emma peeked over the basement steps to see if Jesse was still around. If he was, she'd make a quick dash for the wash line by going around the back of the house.

But his buggy was gone.

Jesse must not have found anything wrong with Molly so everything was okay. Emma caught herself just before heaving a huge sigh of relief. She pushed the feeling away. That was exactly the reaction Jesse was trying to stir in her heart. She would not be tricked. Molly was fine before he arrived, and Molly was certainly no better off after he left.

Katie and she would make it through this hard time together. They had to. They only had each other in this harsh world.

It was then that Emma paused, hearing Katie's voice echo in her mind. The sound came clear as a bell, "You act like Jesse committed a sin for wanting you as his *frau*."

"I do not," Emma said out loud. And yet it was true. She knew it was true.

Katie's voice came again in Emma's mind, stronger this time, only it wasn't Katie any longer, it was as if Ezra was speaking.

"You could have more. Jesse Mast is offering you a whole lot more. You could be a *mamm* to more children who need you. You're not that old. You might even have another baby in the house, not to mention the five children Jesse already has."

Emma caught her breath. She wasn't dreaming, not hearing things. Katie had said those very words not that long ago. But now she could hear Ezra saying them. And *yah,* he would say them.

Had she been wrong then? Would Ezra approve of Katie's plans tonight? Not likely, but then neither would Ezra approve of what she had become.

Emma sat on the basement steps and covered her face with her hands.

CHAPTER FOURTEEN

Jesse brought his horse to a stop near the barn after driving home from Emma's place in a great rush. As he climbed out of the buggy, he saw Mabel running toward him. Her face had a worried look.

"Is something wrong?" he asked as she approached and gasped for breath.

"Joel is still not off to school," Mabel said. She paused to catch another breath. "He wouldn't put on a clean pair of pants, and I wouldn't let him go wearing his dirty ones from yesterday."

"Oh my . . ." Jesse allowed a smile to spread over his face. "Are you sure they were really that dirty?" This wasn't as bad as he feared. But then Mabel was that way sometimes — easily overwrought.

"Daett!" Mabel protested. "They had grass stains all over them. Joel doesn't know how to stay clean when he plays prisoner's base with his friends. I couldn't let him go out of

the house looking like that."

"Okay, okay." Jesse tied Lucy to the hitching post. "Let's go into the house. I'll talk to him. But tell me what happened. Joel seemed ready to leave for school when I saw him at breakfast."

"That's because he only acts stubborn when I'm alone with him," Mabel said. "Now there's going to be a scene at school when he arrives late. Can Joel stay home today? That would be better than Ruth thinking I can't take care of him."

"Now, now . . ." Jesse placed his hand on Mabel's shoulder. "It's not right that you make all these decisions on your own. You're still young yourself without having to take care of your brothers and sisters like *Mamm* would."

"Don't pity me, *Daett*," Mabel said. "Just whip Joel's behind *gut*, and perhaps he'll listen the next time I tell him what to wear."

Jesse almost laughed but held back. The vengeance in Mabel's voice wasn't *gut*. And it really wasn't funny, he supposed. Mabel was right. He too had noticed that Joel only acted up under her authority. The boy knew weakness when he saw it — as most children his age did. What Joel needed was a *mamm* — and rather quickly from the looks of things. Maybe the boy also needed a couple whacks on the behind. If nothing else, it would alleviate Mabel's despair.

When they walked into the house, Joel was sitting on the couch kicking his feet. Mabel marched up and glared at him. "See, *Daett*? Aren't those awfully dirty pants? They aren't fit for barn work, let alone for school."

"They're not that dirty!" Joel protested. "They're nice and clean."

"You should listen to your sister," Jesse said. "Especially when I'm not around. Mabel knows much more about clean clothes than you do. Now get up to your room and change. I'll be taking you to school when you're ready."

Joel hung his head and marched upstairs, obviously unhappy over this outcome.

His pants *were* dirty, Jesse noted, but he had to admit that he wouldn't have noticed or cared if Mabel hadn't pointed it out.

"You should have smacked his backside *gut*," Mabel muttered at Joel's retreating back. "I'm going to next time myself."

"*Nee*, Mabel," Jesse said. He repeated his standing instructions that Mabel wasn't to discipline her siblings. Having her spank the younger children was a bridge he didn't wish to cross.

"He doesn't get spanked enough," Mabel asserted. "He saves all his misbehaving for when you aren't around."

Mabel was probably right, Jesse figured. Children were that way. They caught on quickly regarding when they could get away with things.

"I'll talk with him on the way to school," Jesse said.

Mabel nodded and retreated to the kitchen.

Jesse looked out the window toward the back fields while he waited for Joel to come back downstairs. Leroy was busy cutting the hay pasture, and Willis was spreading manure. He should be helping with both projects, he thought. Instead he was playing *mamm* right now and suitor less than an hour ago at Emma Raber's place. Everything seemed to be turned upside down since Millie had passed. And he hadn't gotten them turned right side up again.

"Please help me, dear *Hah,*" he whispered. He heard the sound of Joel's footsteps approaching and walked over to open the stair door. He took a quick look at what Joel was wearing.

"They're clean!" Joel announced, his face beaming. "They're the cleanest ones I have."

"He has lots of clean ones!" Mabel hollered from the kitchen. "Don't let him start blaming me for his naughtiness."

138

"No one is blaming you," Jesse responded as he paused at the kitchen door. "You do much better than anyone else could hope to do, Mabel."

His daughter didn't turn around to look at him. Her hands were deep in the soapy dishwater.

Jesse hesitated. Mabel was obviously troubled about something since she didn't at least look up. But what was he supposed to do? He guessed he should ask her what was wrong. He walked up to her and slipped an arm around her thin shoulders. "I'm sorry for the load our situation is placing on you," he said. "I really do think you're doing a great job."

She looked up at him, her eyes sorrowful. "You went to see that woman again this morning, didn't you?"

"*Yah.* But it's not 'that woman,' Mabel. Her name is Emma."

Mabel rinsed the dish in her hand. "I wish you wouldn't see her, *Daett.* But I guess what happened with Joel this morning will make you want to marry her even sooner."

"Mabel, listen to me," Jesse said, his hand now on her shoulder. "You're not responsible for this household of children. You're still young yourself. You're only sixteen years old! It's time you go with Leroy and Willis

139

to the young folk gatherings. You're taking way too much responsibility on yourself."

"I'll gladly take all the responsibility on my shoulders if you don't marry that woman," Mabel said. "Emma's weird, and so is her daughter. I don't want a *mamm* like that or a sister like Katie."

Jesse took a deep breath. After the discussion with the children the other night, he had no stomach for more arguments. There should be a *mamm* here to deal with these things. If Mabel didn't begin attending the young folk gatherings, to say nothing of going through *rumspringa,* she would be considered strange herself. He didn't want his daughter to be stuck with such a label. She was a wonderful girl, and the misfortunes of his life shouldn't take such a toll on her or the other children.

"Please, *Hah,*" he whispered.

"What did you say?" Mabel asked as she looked up at him.

Jesse ignored the question. "This thing with Emma is not what you think. I want you to have as normal a life as possible. I want you to be able to be young as long as possible."

"My life is just fine," she said.

"Mabel, look at me." He waited until she glanced up. "I can't explain things to you

140

like your *mamm* did, but you're taking way too much on yourself. And it's not because you're not *gut* enough or doing a *gut* job. It's because you're not ready for such heavy responsibilities. *Yah,* you will be someday, especially when *Da Hah* gives you a husband and a family of your own. But until then, you shouldn't have to carry the full load of a family, even if they are your brothers and sisters."

Mabel's eyes looked pleadingly at him. "Don't marry that woman, *Daett.* Please? Will you promise?"

"Mabel, I can't do that." His voice was firm. "I believe *Da Hah* is in charge of this." Emma was on his mind, and he couldn't seem to let go of her. In the days ahead he would sort this all out. He would ask *Da Hah* for more wisdom to understand what he was to do. For now, he would continue what he was doing. He gave Mabel a quick hug, took Joel's hand, and went outside. Lucy stood beside the hitching rack, looking at him as if she didn't understand why she hadn't been unhitched by now.

Jesse swung Joel up into the front seat, untied Lucy, and climbed into the buggy. Pulling the reins tight, Jesse signaled to Lucy to get going. She shook her head as he guided her to the main road.

The schoolhouse lay a half mile away, well within walking distance. But it was a little too far for Joel to walk when he was already late. No doubt Jesse would cause a disturbance pulling in like this after school had begun, but that was better than leaving Joel home all day. Skipping school could get Joel's six-year-old mind to thinking he should try the same stunt tomorrow.

"Listen," he told Joel, "you're going to start obeying Mabel when she tells you to do something. I can't always be at home, I know Mabel is not *Mamm,* but she's doing the best she can to take care of us."

Joel wrinkled his face.

"Yah," Jesse continued. "All children have to obey. And sometimes they have to obey their sisters even when they have a *mamm."*

"I want a *mamm,"* Joel said, looking up at his *daett*'s face. "Can we have one soon?"

Jesse smiled. "Well, if you had a *mamm,* she might spank you for disobeying."

The delight on Joel's face disappeared. "I don't like to be spanked," he said, pouting.

"Then don't disobey and you won't be," Jesse said as they pulled into the school-yard. As the buggy bounced to a stop, the doors of the school burst open and children poured out.

Time for recess, Jesse figured. *Gut.* He

142

wouldn't be causing such a disturbance bringing Joel in late.

"Go ahead," Jesse told Joel. "Jump down and join them. You can go inside when recess is over."

Joel grinned and climbed down.

As Jesse was backing Lucy up to turn around, the plump figure of Ruth Troyer appeared in the schoolhouse doorway. She waved for Jesse to come over.

Carolyn had surely told Ruth the whole story of her stubborn little brother by now, Jesse figured. A sad tale of how they couldn't get Joel to change into clean pants this morning because their *daett* wasn't around when they needed him the most. At least Ruth didn't know where he'd been. If she did, she'd no doubt have a few things to say about fathers who courted in the daytime while neglecting their children.

It wasn't courting, he told himself. He'd gone over to see if Emma needed help with her cow. Of course, if this had resulted in courting, he wouldn't have objected. But it obviously hadn't. Emma was stubborn — about as stubborn as he was. How else could one explain his determination to win Emma's hand in the face of such clear rejection?

Well, I'd better get down and see what Ruth

wants, Jesse decided. *That would be better than sitting here arguing with myself.* He groaned under his breath. A conversation with Ruth was exactly what he didn't want this morning. But there were some things in life that couldn't be avoided. He climbed down, tied Lucy to the hitching post, and headed toward the school building.

CHAPTER FIFTEEN

As Jesse took a shortcut across the school-yard, the children ran around him playing tag. Joel had disappeared inside somewhere. He must have decided against the risk of getting dirt on his clean pants. A smile crept across Jesse's face at the thought of the lecture Mabel would give Joel if he came home tonight with fresh grass stains on his clean pants. Joel had probably figured that out and decided to go at least one day before incurring his sister's wrath again. Not to mention having to wear another clean pair of pants tomorrow. Jesse paused to allow three girls to race past him. Joel was that way. He liked order and sameness each day, even if that meant wearing dirty pants all week. A *mamm* would know if this was *gut* or not. Yes, he needed a *frau,* and his children needed a *mamm.* He would continue visiting Emma until her resistance wore down. That's all there was to it.

Ruth was still standing at the door. She was talking to someone inside as she waited for him. She turned to face him when he neared.

Jesse touched the brim of his hat. "*Gut* morning, Ruth. Did you want to speak to me?"

"*Yah,*" Ruth said, her gaze wavering for a minute. "I saw you bring Joel in, and I wondered if there was something I needed to know about his being late this morning."

"I figured Carolyn told you about our little *kafuffle* with Joel this morning," Jesse replied.

"*Yah,* Carolyn told me." Ruth's face softened. "I figured you were back in the fields working, so the girls didn't want to disturb you. I know how busy a farmer can be."

"Ah . . ." Jesse cleared his throat. "I wasn't home when Joel was making a fuss. That's why the girls couldn't get a hold of me. I'd gone to check on a neighbor's sick cow."

Ruth looked him up and down, not saying anything. Obviously she thought he had no business being away from home, neighbor's sick cow or not. "I see," she finally said. "Carolyn didn't say anything about a sick cow."

Jesse dropped his gaze to the ground

without answering. Ruth had a way of making him feel Joel's age. Should he say more? It was really none of her business where he was. And if he admitted where he'd been, tongues would start wagging. Then Emma would never agree to his marriage proposal. She might even think he was disrespecting her or trying to force her hand.

"I did know your children weren't sure where you were." Ruth was still looking at him. "That's not *gut,* Jesse. Your children should know where you're at all the time. You're the only parent they have left."

"Yah," Jesse agreed. "Leroy and Willis were home if a real emergency had come up."

"I suppose," Ruth allowed.

"How are the children doing in school?" Jesse asked. He might as well show some interest in his children's schoolwork. It might get him back in Ruth's good graces.

"Joel and Carolyn are a joy," Ruth said. "They're getting along very well with their lessons. They have a *gut daett* to thank for that, I'm sure."

"Thank you." Jesse moved back a step. Surely it was time for Ruth to begin classes again. This was getting a little too personal. Behind Ruth he saw a few children glance at the clock and then at their teacher. Ruth showed no signs of ending the conversation.

"I was wondering if there was something more I could do for Joel and Carolyn, Jesse. Although their grades are okay, Carolyn is struggling a bit with her arithmetic and could do better. Joel could use help with his reading."

That he didn't know any of this was a fact best not admitted to, Jesse decided. Ruth might consider that infraction worse than this morning's absence.

"I know how busy you are." Ruth kept going. "I'm sure they've told you — at least Carolyn would have. I can't imagine Joel saying much of anything, even if he is struggling in his studies."

Jesse took a deep breath. He was tired of being painted into a corner by this woman, even if she was his children's schoolteacher and a widow.

"I didn't know they were having trouble in their studies," he admitted. "I'll ask them this evening if they need help. I'll attend to that after supper."

For a moment Ruth's face showed displeasure. Then the beaming smile came back. "Why don't I come down after grading schoolwork? I'll see what I can do to help. It wouldn't be out of my way at all, and I'd have plenty of time before I needed to go home and prepare supper for myself."

Jesse hesitated. He hadn't expected this. He could use the help, couldn't he? And Ruth was his children's teacher, so she could jump right in where they were having problems in ways he couldn't.

Jesse cleared his throat. "I guess that would be appreciated. It's not like I have plenty of extra time. But I wouldn't expect you to do this for nothing. I mean, I could pay you a little."

"I wouldn't think of it!" Ruth was really gushing now. "Seeing Joel and Carolyn do well will be reward enough. That's how I feel about all my students."

But she wasn't offering to stop in at the home of any of the others, Jesse figured. Still . . . He glanced around for a moment. Come to think of it, he was the only single *daett* who sent children to this school.

"Then it's settled." Ruth apparently took whatever look was on his face as a positive answer. "I'll be there well before supper, so I won't interfere with your family time. I know how important that is."

Jesse was still searching for words to say when Ruth turned and marched to her desk. She rang the bell, and Jesse had to move back from the door as the children came in from outside.

Ruth waved at him, this time from her

desk. That clearly meant he was supposed to get moving. Jesse turned around, stepped outside, and pulled the door shut behind him. He shook his head as he walked to his buggy. Once there, he paused for a moment to think this situation over. How had he been talked into inviting Ruth to visit his house tonight? Jesse looked at Lucy as if she might have an answer, but the mare gazed back with a blank look. Jesse climbed into the buggy. What was done was done. If Ruth had nothing better to do, why shouldn't she come to his house to teach his children? Her marriage with Homer had produced no children. Since she had no one at home to care for, perhaps that explained her interest in teaching and her desire to help Carolyn and Joel with their education.

Jesse drove Lucy out of the schoolyard and toward home. He listened to the steady beat of horse hooves on the pavement. What if Ruth had further designs on him than were readily apparent? What if she was hoping to move their relationship in a direction he wasn't interested in with her? What if she was seeing the affection Carolyn and Joel had for her and thinking some of it was coming from their *daett*?

And hadn't he thought of Ruth as a possible *mamm* for his children not that long ago? *Yah,* he had. But he hadn't said a word about it to anyone. His children knew only of his intention to marry Emma. Perhaps Carolyn had mentioned Emma in school, letting it slip that she and Mabel didn't want Emma as their *mamm.*

Jesse sighed. Children were that way. He shouldn't blame Carolyn if she'd talked about it. Still, he wished this hadn't happened — if indeed it had. He could ask Carolyn tonight, he supposed, but why put the girl in that position? He was the one to blame, if anyone was. He should have kept his feelings to himself until Emma agreed to his proposal.

And maybe his thoughts about Ruth were all in his imagination. She could have no intention other than teaching his children out of the goodness of her heart. Jesse slapped the reins against Lucy's back and urged her on. He needed to get home and get to work. He'd wasted enough time thinking about finding a *frau.* And it was getting confusing.

Jesse sighed as he turned into his driveway. He'd been thinking so much about his children he hadn't given much thought about what he wanted or needed. It would be *wunderbah* to find love again, he admitted. He didn't really want to have a dry marriage of convenience as so many second marriages seemed to become. He had enjoyed the special love he'd had with Millie before *Da Hah* took her. Finding it again was a lot to ask. And there was no promise he would find it with Emma. Still, it was a nice thought. He certainly wasn't going to find that kind of love with Ruth. Married to Ruth, he would spend his time feeling like a little boy in the first grade who was continually lectured by his teacher. That wasn't what he had in mind. *Nee,* Emma was his best chance. Surely she would soon see things his way.

Jesse pulled up to the barn, climbed out of the buggy, unhitched Lucy, and led her through the front doorway. Opening the back gate, he slapped the mare on her backside, sending her into the barnyard. Jesse glanced toward the back field. Willis was approaching with an empty manure wagon. This time Jesse was home to help with the work. He slipped on his old boots he kept in the barn and grabbed a pitchfork just as Willis came bouncing up. The cold air made the horses look like they were blowing steam out of their nostrils.

"Sorry I've been gone so long," Jesse said as he opened the barn door.

Willis smiled and shrugged. "I saw you

were taking Joel to school. Did you get everything straightened out?"

"I hope so." Jesse threw fork loads of manure into the wagon.

Willis grunted and joined him, their pitchforks swinging in steady rhythm.

Jesse decided he might have solved some of this morning's problems, but he might also have created a whole lot more. There was no sense in worrying about it. Time would reveal the truth.

CHAPTER SIXTEEN

That evening Jesse washed up in the wash-room sink after coming in from the barn. He ran the soapy water over his beard before rinsing and then rubbing his face dry with the fresh towel hanging on the nail. Mabel must have made a quick dash out to change towels for him. Leroy and Willis were already inside, having cleaned up before he came in. They wouldn't leave a towel this dry.

Jesse sighed. Mabel tried so hard. She was *gut* at taking care of the house. But she needed to do and experience the things other sixteen-year-old girls did — new dresses, going to youth gatherings, and meeting a *wunderbah* boy whose eye she might catch and, perhaps, become his future *frau.* Instead she was taking care of him, the other children, and the household. She rarely even had time for herself.

And now he had another problem to

handle this evening. Ruth Troyer was still here. Why else would her buggy still be parked in the barnyard? Was Joel so far behind on his reading that he required more time? Even so, having Ruth in the house was more than a little uncomfortable. How would they eat supper as a family if Ruth still had one of the children in the living room studying? He didn't wish to push suppertime back. They were all hungry after their hard day's work.

Jesse stood at the washroom door listening to the sounds of his children's voices rising and falling in the kitchen. They must be waiting for supper, wondering just like he was what would happen. Jesse paused with his hand on the doorknob. Was there another voice mixed in with that of his children? He listened closely. Was Ruth in the kitchen with the children? It sounded like it. But why? Was she working with the children at the kitchen table? That wasn't probable. Mabel should have the table spread by now. Did Ruth plan to eat with them and continue lessons after supper?

Jesse pushed open the door. Mabel's cheerful face was the first one he saw. She was looking up at him from her usual place at the table. Around Mabel were all of the others, waiting patiently. The steaming meal was sitting on the table in uncovered dishes. At the end of the table, opposite his place, right where Millie had always sat, was Ruth, her face beaming. No schoolbooks were in sight.

"Daett!" Mabel jumped to her feet. "We were waiting for you! I was about ready to go check where you were. Supper's getting cold."

Jesse looked around, his mind whirling.

"Ach, of course, I'm forgetting myself." Ruth stood. "I know my being here for supper is unexpected, Jesse. But the children invited me to stay, and I couldn't resist. What a lovely family you have! And it's a lonely house I return to at nights, with not one smiling face to warm my heart. You can see, I'm sure, why I accepted."

"Yah, I guess," Jesse mumbled. What else was there to say with the eager faces of all his children looking at him? Ruth was still on her feet, waving her hand around as if she were at the schoolhouse door directing him over to speak with her. *This is my place,* Jesse told himself. *I need to seize control.*

"Your children are just the sweetest, Jesse," Ruth gushed. "You've done such a *wunderbah* job of raising them. How can you manage so much? And Mabel! She's almost grown up, I do declare. Carolyn, of course, I see in school every day, and she's also so mature. And your two oldest . . . Jesse, why I would have passed out to see such handsome men in my younger dating days."

Willis turned bright red, Jesse noticed. Well, it would serve them all right to taste a little embarrassment.

"And now they've invited me for supper." Ruth had barely stopped for breath. "I get to eat food I didn't have to fix! I do declare, it's been *years* — in fact, not since I left home to marry Homer — since anyone prepared such a meal for me. Mabel wouldn't even allow me to lift a finger to help. I sat right there in the living room and worked with little Joel and his reading lessons until a few minutes ago when Mabel hollered that supper was ready. You don't know how decent and upright a family you've raised, Jesse."

Jesse gave an inward sigh and motioned for Ruth to be seated. The woman was here, and the food was getting cold. There was only so much a man could do. He sat down, said "Let us pray," and bowed his head. "Our gracious heavenly Father, we come at this evening hour to give You thanks for Your many great and kind blessings toward us. You have given us another sunny day in which to work, and You have blessed all of us with healthy bodies and sound minds. We ask for Your mercy to soften our hearts toward the weaknesses of others, even as You give us mercy for our many shortcomings. Bless now this meal which Mabel has prepared. I know she has worked hard, as have the other children. They all seek to live lives that are pleasing to You. Be with us the rest of the evening and for the night's rest that lies before us. Keep us safe in Your arms so we may awaken to a new morning to partake again of Your grace. Amen."

"Amen," Ruth added after him, her voice seeming to echo in the kitchen.

Jesse stared at Leroy, who was grinning from his place on the back bench. The boy sobered when he saw his father looking at him. *At least he still has respect for me,* Jesse thought. But if he didn't get on his toes soon, Ruth was going to leave him as plucked as a molted hen. What had gotten into the woman? She clearly planned to take over the house first . . . and from there probably go for his heart. Right now the woman was cooing to little Joel as she measured out his mashed potatoes.

"So how much do you want, sweetie pie?"

Joel was wiggling from head to toe, his face aglow with happiness. He hadn't had this much attention in a long time, which was obviously the effect Ruth was after. Even Leroy was patiently waiting while Ruth dished out Joel's small portion. Under normal circumstances, Leroy would have lunged across the table at the first sign his food was being delayed.

"And here you are, Carolyn." Ruth passed on the dish, still cooing.

Jesse noticed that Ruth hadn't taken any potatoes for herself. She would wait until last, he figured, to make the best impression possible. And from the look on Mabel's face, the gesture hadn't gone unnoticed.

Mabel leaned across the table. "*Nee,* Ruth. You take some first. You're our visitor."

"I can easily wait till last," Ruth said, batting her eyes. "You just go on as if I weren't here. I want to make sure there's enough for everyone."

"Come on, take some," Mabel insisted, not backing down. "There's enough."

"Well, if you insist," Ruth said with a smile.

Jesse had enough of this. He grabbed the gravy bowl in front of him. "Okay, everybody, pass things around like normal. I'm hungry, and we don't have to do everything proper tonight just because we have a visitor. You know you don't act this way when we're by ourselves."

Did the children know what was going on here? *Nee*, probably not. They wouldn't see a fly if it buzzed in front of their eyes. Jesse suppressed a sigh. Perhaps his quest for Emma was wrong. Maybe he should allow Ruth to take over. There certainly would be no need of a long courting period. He wouldn't need to make fruitless trips over to another woman's place. Here was a future *frau* all packaged and ready to go. All he had to do was accept the gift.

"Come on, *Daett*! Don't look so sober," Mabel said, interrupting his thoughts. "It has been a *gut* day."

Jesse smiled a little. "*Yah,* even with the little *kafuffle* we had with Joel this morning."

"*Ach,* that," Mabel said, as if such a thing were no longer even worth considering. "I'm sure Joel learned his lesson. At least he didn't come home with grass stains on his pants today."

"How did you manage that?" Jesse asked, glancing at Joel who was still grinning.

"I didn't play outside today," Joel proclaimed. "I stayed inside so I wouldn't get my pants dirty."

"See!" Mabel patted Joel's head. "He's

160

learning fast."

Jesse laid down his spoon. "Now wait a minute. Since when is it good for little boys to stay inside during recess? Joel, you should be outside playing with the others."

"I didn't want to get my pants dirty," Joel protested. "Mabel gets angry when I do."

"Well, Mabel will just have to get upset," Jesse said. "You need to go out and play. It's not good for little boys to be inside all day."

Jesse waited, expecting Joel to glance at Mabel for approval. Instead, Joel looked over at Ruth. "You told me not to go out and play so Mabel wouldn't be angry."

Ruth smiled, stroking Joel on the head. "That's okay. You didn't do anything wrong by obeying me, Joel. I'll talk to your *daett* after supper and explain things to him. But maybe tomorrow you should go outside."

"Okay." Joel turned back to his supper. "I like to play outside even if I do get grass stains on my pants."

Ruth had the decency to turn a little red, Jesse noticed. He ignored her for the rest of the meal, although the children chatted with her. When they were finished eating, Ruth jumped up and started clearing the table.

Jesse interrupted her. "Come, Ruth. We need to talk. The girls can clean the table."

"But they've worked so hard making supper," Ruth said. "I can't just walk out and leave them with all of this."

"Please, *Daett,*" Mabel said, her eyes begging his approval. "We do need help. And I'm tired after all the fuss we had today."

Jesse thought for a moment. Were Ruth's charms already working on him like they were on the children? Something certainly was. He had no answer to give but *yah*. Mabel did deserve the help, and, truth be told, he really didn't want to speak with Ruth. He had a good idea how that conversation would go.

"Why are you tormenting me, Ruth?" he would ask. She would look shocked and proclaim she was only doing her duty.

"I'm not going to marry you," he would say. She would turn white and say she'd never meant to imply such a thing. How could he even think that of her?

"Okay," Jesse finally said out loud. "I have some chores to finish in the barn." He rose and headed out the washroom door. He was soon in the barn busying himself by throwing down hay from the mow. Some twenty minutes later he heard Ruth's buggy rattle down the lane.

Chapter Seventeen

Katie crept down from her room on the night of the Mennonite birthday party. She'd changed into her blue Sunday dress. Her hands were trembling as she paused to listen at the bottom of the stairs. *Mamm* was still in the kitchen putting away the last of the supper dishes. There were sharp clinks coming from around the corner, as if plates were being placed together carelessly. This was not going to be easy. *Mamm* hadn't smiled all evening. But neither had she delivered a lecture. Katie decided a lecture would have been easier to bear than the silence. She hesitated by the kitchen doorway. This was so heartbreaking. *Mamm* had once been her best friend in the world. Katie wanted to rush into the kitchen and take *Mamm* into her arms. But crying on *Mamm*'s shoulder wouldn't do much *gut* now.

Mamm wanted her to end this mad idea

of attending a Mennonite youth gathering on the basis of an invitation from a boy she'd only met once. Life could return to normal, *Mamm* had said, if they could go on like before. If Katie would only repent of this grave sin. But, *nee,* that wouldn't happen. Katie felt she had to go with Esther at this point.

As Katie turned away from the kitchen, *Mamm* picked up on her presence. "Katie, will you come here a minute?"

"Yah." Katie hesitated before turning back. She stood in the doorway. When *Mamm* turned, her eyes showed signs of crying. Katie decided if she didn't sit down her legs would collapse. She pulled out a chair and sat by the table. *Mamm* hardly ever cried. And here she was the one bringing *Mamm* this heavy sorrow.

Mamm approached and pulled out her chair. "Won't you consider changing your mind, Katie?" *Mamm* took Katie's hand. "All you have to do is tell that Mennonite girl you've changed your mind. I don't think *Daett* would have liked this."

"They're expecting me." Katie didn't meet *Mamm*'s eyes. It wasn't right for *Mamm* to bring up memories of *Daett* at this moment.

Mamm stroked her hand. "They have

plenty of other young people to attend their party. I only have you, Katie."

Katie sprang to her feet. "*Mamm,* I love you, but I have to do this. I don't know exactly why or what it means, but I can't go on living like we are. I want something more. I don't know what that is or if I will find it tonight at this gathering, but I have to go."

"*Nee,* you don't *have* to go. No one is forcing you." *Mamm*'s eyes searched her face.

"No, *Mamm,* it's not like that. Something inside of me is . . . well . . . changing. I can't explain it."

"You're going because some boy paid you attention." *Mamm* reached up to pull Katie back down in her chair. "Do you know how empty that will be in the end?"

Katie looked away. That she should wish to be noticed was an awful thing, but it was true. She *had* enjoyed being noticed by Roy Coblenz.

"It's true, isn't it?" *Mamm* persisted.

"*Yah,*" Katie admitted, not looking up. "Why is it wrong to want a man's love?"

"We've been through this before." *Mamm*'s voice was earnest. "This will bring you nothing but trouble, Katie. I know because I've been there."

"And you want us to go on living like we are now — just the two of us?"

Mamm nodded.

"I can't!" Katie protested. "How can I? I wasn't made to live isolated. I want someone to love. I want a husband, *Mamm.* Is that a sin? I want children. Don't you want grand-children? How can that be wrong?"

"Katie, the things you want most, you won't find with the Mennonites."

"So where am I supposed to find them? Here? The Amish boys around here don't notice me. They think of me merely as your daughter . . . or the weird girl. That won't change anytime soon. Once our people get something into their heads, you know there is no getting it out."

"Katie, Katie!" *Mamm* said. "You're talking wild things. So what if our people think we're nothing. That is *Da Hah*'s will for us. We can be happy together."

"I can no longer be happy living like this." Katie rose again. "I've already seen too much, *Mamm.* There's a world out there you're missing out on, and I don't want to live that way. *Da Hah* is helping me by open-ing doors. I have prayed about this, *Mamm.*"

Mamm shook her head. "Don't blame this on *Da Hah,* Katie. None of those things will be what you think they are once you get them. I've been there. I know."

Katie heard tires crunching on the gravel driveway.

Mamm looked up.

"I'm sorry. I have to go." Katie headed for the door.

Mamm's voice pleaded behind her. "What do you think I should do, Katie? What would keep you away from the Mennonites?"

Katie paused and turned around. "I'm not asking you to do anything, *Mamm.* Don't stay up for me. I'll be okay."

"Do you want me to marry Jesse?" *Mamm* had tears on her cheeks again. "Would that keep you here with me?"

Katie paused, her hand on the doorknob. What should she say to a question like that? She would love it if *Mamm* married Jesse. But if *Mamm* did this only to please her, that would be wrong for everyone. And she might still end up being known only as the odd widow Emma Raber's weird daughter.

"Don't go out tonight, Katie. Not before we've had a chance to talk some more about this."

Katie choked back a sob. If she waited one minute longer, she would explode into tears. *"Nee,* marrying Jesse when you don't love him won't solve anything. I've got to go,

Mamm." Katie opened the front door and rushed down the steps.

What was she doing? Katie wondered. Was she closing a door that could never be opened again? She ran across the yard toward Esther's dark-blue car. She would keep trusting *Da Hah* even though the waters were rough right now. She'd known they would be. Through the sheen of her tears, Esther's car was a blur. Katie groped for the door handle.

"Hi there!" Esther said when Katie opened the door.

"*Gut* evening." Katie slid in, trying to hide her wet face.

"Troubles?" Esther asked as she started the car.

"*Mamm* didn't want me to go tonight." *That was putting it mildly,* Katie thought. But there was no need for Esther to know the whole story.

"Oh, she'll get over it," Esther said, as if she knew about it from experience.

Katie's smile was strained. She decided to talk about something else, if for no other reason then to make this awful ache in her heart go away.

"We'll have you cheered up in no time," Esther said, gunning her car out of the driveway with a loud roar. Katie winced, thinking of *Mamm*'s reaction to the noise.

"Don't worry," Esther continued. "It will all be good. I see you've worn your Sunday dress."

Katie nodded.

"You wouldn't have had to," Esther said. "Any old thing would have been good enough for tonight. It's just a little shindig with some of Roy's friends. But better overdressed than underdressed, that's what I always say."

"I didn't know what to wear." Katie tried to keep fear from racing through her. Was she going to stand out this evening? That was all she needed on top of everything else.

Esther leaned toward Katie as they raced down the road. "Roy did check with me an hour ago to see if you were coming for sure."

"Oh . . ." Katie looked away. What did that mean? She didn't dare ask. Thankfully, Esther didn't seem to notice her discomfort. Getting teased about a boy would be one trial too much at the moment.

"Yes, it's going to be a grand evening." Esther chattered away. "A happy time among friends who accept you. That's one of the nice things about these parties. You get to see lots of people and still have time to speak with the ones you haven't seen for some time."

"I see," Katie allowed. She hung on to the armrest as Esther took a tight curve. Esther had always taken off from Byler's like she was shooting for the moon, and now Katie was experiencing what it was like to be inside a rocket.

"Are you okay?" Esther asked, taking another curve without slowing down much.

Katie forced herself to smile. There was no sense in admitting she was scared, even if she'd never ridden this fast in an *Englisha* automobile before.

"We'll be there before long," Esther told her, as if that were the concern. "Roy's place is just on the other side of Dover a bit."

Katie hung on as they approached Byler's. Someone in a buggy was coming out of the driveway, but Katie couldn't make out the face as they sped by. It was just as well. This way he or she couldn't figure out who she was either.

"So what do you and your mom do since you live by yourselves?" Esther asked, slowing down as they approached the town limits.

"Not much . . . just the usual."

"Is your mom thinking of marrying again?"

Katie stole a sideways glance at Esther and noticed a twinkle in her eye. Did Esther know about Jesse? Surely not. Such a thing couldn't have come out this quickly. Not with the few visits Jesse had made to call on *Mamm*. And how would it get to the Mennonite circle?

"I wish she would," Katie finally said. That was a safe enough answer, she figured, and perhaps Esther wouldn't dig deeper.

"It must get lonely living by yourselves," Esther said, and she sounded sympathetic. "Do you have family who lives in the area? I mean . . . you must have . . ."

"Mom's brothers all live in Lancaster," Katie said. "And we don't get up there often."

The truth was they hadn't been up there in five years or so, but Esther didn't need to know that.

"And your dad's side of the family? They come from around here, don't they?"

"Yah," Katie admitted. "And we get together sometimes. The Rabers had a reunion here in the Dover community this spring that we attended."

"That's nice." Esther slowed down even further as they encountered traffic lights. A few minutes later, she turned the car down a driveway of a well-kept farm.

Katie was still holding on to the armrest as Esther pulled to a stop by one of the huge, red barns. A long row of cars were already parked, but there were no signs of any young people.

"Here we are!" Esther announced, opening her car door. "Let's go inside and see where everyone is."

A shiver ran through Katie. How was the evening going to turn out? Was she going to enjoy herself? Would she get a glimpse of what she could be like in a world where she wasn't looked down upon or disparaged? Katie held her breath for a moment, and then she climbed out of Esther's car. That was a lot to expect or even hope for, she told herself. Yet why couldn't it happen? A few weeks ago, who would have dreamed she'd even attend a Mennonite youth gathering?

CHAPTER EIGHTEEN

Katie heard the murmur of voices growing louder as she and Esther approached the barn. The party was in progress. In the mix of the sounds rose occasional peals of laughter.

Two more cars pulled in and parked by Esther's car. Esther waved to the newcomers and went on into the barn. Katie reluctantly followed her, still not knowing what to expect from the evening.

Once inside, Katie caught her breath as she took in the sight of dozens of young people her age gathered by tables. Some of them were seated while others were standing around. A few glanced toward Katie and Esther. Katie didn't move until Esther pulled her arm. "Come on! Let's go see Roy. He'll be glad to know you're here."

Katie allowed Esther to lead her forward. At least her feet were working now. Among the crowd she saw a lone Amish face she knew. Emery Yoder was staring at her with a puzzled look on his face. He was from a district closer to Dover and rarely was at the few Amish youth gatherings Katie attended. He was having a hard time figuring out why an Amish girl was being escorted into the birthday party by a high-flying Mennonite like Esther. Well, Emory would just have to wonder. Katie wasn't going to stop and enlighten him. She tried to keep breathing as Esther pushed through a small group of young folks who nodded to them. They broke through to the other side, and Esther came to a stop before a young man who was apparently Roy. He had his back turned to them and was deep in conversation with several people.

Katie hoped no one could hear the loud beating of her heart.

Esther tapped Roy on his shoulder.

He turned around, a broad smile on his face. "Well, who have we here?" Roy teased, holding out his hand to Katie.

Katie tried to still her trembling as she took his hand.

"Katie Raber," Esther said before Katie could answer. "I invited her like you said, and here we are."

"I'm glad you could come, Katie," Roy said. "You're just in time. We have some games planned first, and then we'll eat cake and ice cream later. That's what Esther is looking forward to."

"I am not." Esther slapped Roy's arm. "You make me sound like a spoiled child."

Roy laughed and turned back to Katie. "Here, let me introduce you to some of the others. Over here is Harold Kargel, of local fame for his volleyball spikes, and his sister Margaret who is almost as good."

Roy was summoned to the kitchen just as Katie got out a "Hi" to the two youth.

"I'm glad you could come," Margaret said. "You work with Esther at Byler's, right?"

"Yah," Katie replied.

"Do you live in the Amish community near there?"

"Yah," Katie repeated.

"Why don't you ever stop in at Byler's for lunch, Harold?" Esther asked, punching him lightly in the ribs. "Are we too lowbrow for your high standards or what?"

"Maybe I like my mother's sandwiches for lunch," Harold said. "Besides, they're cheaper than Byler's."

"I could fix you up with the most scrumptious meat sandwich with your choice of cheese," Esther said. "Add coleslaw and pork and beans, and it can't be beat."

Harold laughed. "Maybe I just don't want to see you."

Esther made a face at him before smiling. The others joined in the laughter.

"Come on," Margaret whispered in Katie's ear. "Let me show you around since Esther has the boys entertained."

"If that's okay with Esther," Katie replied, glancing in Esther's direction. "She brought me."

"Esther doesn't care," Margaret assured her, leading Katie away. "Is this your first young folks gathering with us? It must be because I haven't seen you before."

"*Yah.* Roy invited me through Esther. He saw me working at Byler's."

"We don't have that large a group compared to your Amish community," Margaret said. "We're always glad when someone new shows up."

Katie opened her mouth to say that she was the one who was really thankful that Margaret was being so nice to her. But her new friend was already introducing her to another girl so the words died in her mouth.

"Katie, this is Sharon Watson," Margaret was saying. "She's a good friend of mine and a darling at making quilts. She and her mom can outwork even our experienced women without even trying."

"Now that's not a nice thing to say," Sharon countered, offering Katie a smile. "Don't pay any attention to what Margaret tells you. She exaggerates."

"You know it's true," Margaret shot back. "All the two of you have is that little sign out in the front yard, and you sell quilts faster than you can make them."

Katie stared at Sharon. Did she also live alone with her *mamm*? Sharon looked perfectly normal, so perhaps a mother and daughter could make it alone. Did she dare ask whether Sharon's *daett* had passed away?

"So what brings you here tonight, Katie?" Sharon asked.

"Roy invited me through Esther," Katie said. "Because . . . well . . . he comes through Byler's once in awhile, which is where Esther and I work."

"That's wonderful," Sharon said. "I hope you feel very welcome here."

"Thanks," Katie said, glancing at the floor.

They were being so nice. Was it put on or did they really mean it? Perhaps they gave a special welcome to all visitors? A welcome that would soon be taken away once they really knew her. But could that possibly be true? These girls seemed much too nice for that.

Margaret touched Katie's arm as the flow of young people moved toward the back of the barn. "It looks like everyone's moving out to the other barn to play volleyball. Shall we join them?"

"I love to play volleyball!" Sharon exclaimed. "What about you, Katie?"

"*Yah,* of course," Katie said as she followed the two girls through the back door and into an even larger barn where the ceiling went so high Katie had to put her head way back to see the top.

Cobwebs hung high in the air, lit up by bright lights from a string of electric flood lamps attached along the walls. Katie shivered as the thought of *Mamm* flashed through her mind. It must be dark outside by now, and *Mamm* would be waiting by the kitchen table or looking out the living room window wondering what she was doing. And here she was at a Mennonite gathering with electric lights hanging from the ceiling. *Mamm* would be so horrified she'd pass out. Katie pushed the thoughts away and turned her attention back to the two girls. She was determined to enjoy every minute of her time with them, even if it turned out they were only nice to newcomers.

Across the barn floor a boy shouted out

instructions. "Everybody get themselves to one side or the other."

"Come on!" Sharon said. "Katie, you can be on our side."

Katie hesitated and then joined the two girls on one side of the net.

Sounds of laughter rose all around her and Katie froze for a second, and then she relaxed. *Nee,* these people weren't laughing at her. No one was even staring at her. Instead, a boy was motioning everyone to their places around the net, waving his hands about. There seemed to be no rhythm or pattern to the boy's decisions, other than making sure an equal number of boys and girls ended up on both sides of the net. Katie found herself standing on the far side with boys she'd never seen before on either side of her. Sharon was also on her end, but positioned further back. Margaret had been moved to the other side to make the teams even. The boy who had directed the two teams to their places was now hollering, "Come on! Come on! Get ready to start."

A girl on the opposite side was twirling a volleyball around in her hands. She soon backed up to the far corner to give the ball a good whack.

"This is the deciding ball," the boy hollered again. "The team who gets the first point starts the game."

She knew all that, Katie thought, but they sure were starting the game fast and without a lot of fuss. On the other side of the barn, it looked like another game was also getting ready to begin. Katie pulled her eyes away and kept her gaze on the ball as it came over the net. The two boys beside her tensed up, but the arc carried the ball well over their heads.

On the bounce back, the other team sent it over to the left side of the court. Katie was sure it would be out of bounds, but a girl playing the spot chose not to take the chance. With both hands held together, she sent the ball back across. This time it returned with such force that everyone stayed away as the ball bounced out of bounds.

"Yeah! It's ours!" the boy to Katie's left hollered in triumph. He offered his hand to Katie as the server on their side prepared to start the game. "Hi! How are you tonight? Name's Bryan."

"Katie," she said, speaking over the murmur of voices around her.

"Glad to have you here." Bryan pointed to the boy on the other side of her. "That's John, the bad one. You want to watch yourself around him."

Katie laughed. Bryan was teasing, she was sure. But the fact that he'd been so nice to her caused her not to care if he was giving her a hard time. He at least had spoken to her. She could hardly believe it.

"Hi!"

Katie turned to offer her hand to John. "I'm sure you're not as bad as he makes you sound."

"I wouldn't be too sure about that," John said with a grin. "I have my moments."

The girl in the server's spot launched the ball, and the other team sent it back with force as everyone traced its flight. Katie readied herself. At the last minute she saw the ball would travel to the left, so she stepped back as Bryan stepped forward. He sent the ball flying back to the other side, where it was set up and spiked successfully.

"You don't have to be shy of us," Bryan told Katie. "You can see I didn't do too well. Just step right in and give it a try. And we're not much into counting scores. It's all about playing the game."

Katie took a deep breath and smiled. Five minutes later the ball came within her reach, and she stepped up and sent it back to the right side of the court. A girl tried to set the ball up for the front row but failed. The result was a sluggish return, which was set up and spiked by Katie's side.

"There you go!" John cheered. "That was great. Almost as good as Bryan could do."

Katie relaxed even more. This was much better than she'd expected. If *Mamm* could only see her now, perhaps she would understand. Was that possible? Had *Mamm* ever had this sort of fun? Katie's face darkened. There was no way *Mamm* would think any of this was right . . . or fun. She was, no doubt, even now weeping over her rebellious daughter. Katie shoved the dark thoughts away, concentrating on the ball as it flew back and forth over the net. She made herself listen to the happy chatter John and Bryan were keeping up. They were including her, and she didn't even have to try to fit in. It was almost as if she belonged — and had always belonged — among them.

CHAPTER NINETEEN

More than an hour later, Katie stood between Margaret and Sharon as the entire gathering sang the "Happy Birthday" song to Roy. The chorus ended with a round of applause and broad smiles as Roy blew out the candles on top of a white-frosted, stacked birthday cake. "To many more happy years!" a boy shouted, and there was another round of hand clapping.

Roy's mother gave him a big hug and then cut the cake. She motioned for a line to form in front of the table where fruit, ice cream, and two additional cakes were laid out.

What a wunderbah *group of people,* Katie thought as she stood in line with Margaret and Sharon and listened to the friendly chatter around her. As she moved nearer to the front of the line, she felt a tap on her shoulder. She turned to see Roy, a plate splattered with cake crumbs in his hand.

"Have you had a good time so far?" he asked above the noise.

Katie felt her face turning red, so she glanced away before answering. "It's been a lot of fun, Roy. Thank you for inviting me."

"You're welcome!" he said. "I hope you come to more of our gatherings."

When Katie didn't say anything, he added, "You're always welcome, you know. And Esther will be willing to pick you up, I'm sure."

"Thank you so much for everything," Katie responded, finally meeting his eyes.

He smiled before moving away to speak with someone in line behind her.

Katie took several deep breaths when Roy was gone as she tried to slow the pounding of her heart. She mustn't read too much into this, she told herself again and again. Tomorrow would come, and she would be back to the same old Katie. But right now she felt lightheaded and very happy all at the same time. *Oh, if* Mamm *could only see how much* gut *this party is doing for me! Perhaps she wouldn't be so opposed to me coming back.*

Katie wondered why she was having so much fun tonight, and yet she'd seldom enjoyed herself at Amish youth gatherings. Was she acting in a different way from what she usually did at Amish gatherings? If so, how? She certainly wasn't *trying* to act differently — it just *felt* different. And she seemed to have nothing to do with it at all.

Ahead of her Margaret had a plate in one hand and was dipping ice cream with the other. She turned to Katie. "Do you want some?"

"*Yah,* but I can get it myself," Katie said. "You don't have to wait on me."

Margaret laughed. "The dipper's sticky, so I might as well dip for you too now that my fingers are already in it."

"Okay." Katie held out her plate. "Thanks. Only one scoop, please."

Roy's mother must have noticed the stickiness problem because she came up with a washcloth. She wiped Margaret's fingers, the two women laughing the whole time. Roy's mother cleaned the dipper next, and soon the line was moving past the ice cream bucket again.

Sharon had disappeared into the crowd, but Margaret stayed close to Katie while they ate, making sure she was included in the conversation.

Katie was almost finished with her food, when Esther showed up, apparently out of nowhere. Margaret jumped up and offered Esther her chair.

"No, no!" Esther told her. "Stay sitting.

I'm only here to see if Katie's ready to go. I need to get on the road."

"Just a few more bites," Katie said as she gulped down the cold ice cream.

"You'll give the poor girl a frozen throat," Margaret protested.

Katie stood up. "I'm fine. And thanks, Margaret, for helping make this such a great evening. Will you thank Sharon for me as well? I don't know where she got to."

"Sure," Margaret said. "And you're very welcome. I'll tell Sharon you enjoyed the evening."

Esther motioned with her hand for Katie to hurry. "Over here's the place to leave your plate. And we'd better stop by and say goodbye to Roy. We can't leave the birthday boy without giving our last good wishes."

Katie stayed close to Esther as they made their way across the room. Already the crowd had begun to thin out. They spotted Roy standing near the door, shaking hands with departing guests.

"Leaving already?" he teased Esther and Katie with a grin.

"You know we have to go," Esther said. "It's already past my bedtime, and I have to work tomorrow."

"Thanks for coming," Roy said. "And you too, Katie. Stop by our youth gatherings again sometime."

"I will," Katie almost said, but she choked back the words. "Thank you for the invitation," she said instead. "It's been so nice."

When Roy turned to the person behind them, Katie took one last, quick look around the barn before following Esther outside. If this never happened again, she wanted the memory of her time here stuck in her mind so it would never be lost. She'd felt so normal and at home tonight. Roy had no idea what he'd done for her. He might think she'd done him a favor by coming to his birthday party, but it was really the other way around.

"What a night!" Esther sighed as she opened the car door. "I'll be paying for this tomorrow though. Mrs. Cole will chew me out if I can't stay awake at the deli counter."

"It was a very nice evening," Katie agreed, sliding into the passenger car seat.

Esther started the car, backed up, and pulled out onto the road.

Katie settled back in her seat and hung on to the armrest. The ride back with Esther was even scarier in the dark, Katie decided. Her friend drove like a mad woman, and the shadows seemed to dance along the side of the road as they passed. Katie prayed *Da Hah* would see fit to get them home safely.

Mamm would be sure judgment had struck if they were found dead tomorrow morning and the car was wrapped around a tree.

Fifteen minutes later, at the sight of her home place in the shadows ahead, Katie breathed a silent "Thank You, dear *Hah.*"

Esther slowed down just enough to make the turn into the driveway, bouncing the car across the ruts in the road. Coming to a halt near the hitching post, she turned to Katie with a cheerful, "Here we are, safe and sound!"

Katie reached for the door latch. "Thank you for the ride, Esther. And for inviting me to the birthday party."

Esther smiled brightly. "No problem. Let me know if you need a ride again some-time."

"I probably won't get any more birthday invitations," Katie said as she climbed out of the vehicle.

Esther shrugged. "You don't need an invitation to come to our regular gather-ings. You seemed to enjoy yourself tonight, and we enjoyed having you. Just let me know when you want to come and need a ride."

"Okay, I'll see," Katie said. She stepped back from the car and waited while Esther turned around and then roared out the driveway. Katie pivoted and walked toward the house, noticing a dim light coming from the kitchen window. She halted.

Mamm was up waiting like she said she would be. Katie forced her feet forward. She moved up the steps, through the front door, and tiptoed across the living room to peak into the kitchen. *Yah,* there was *Mamm,* her eyes closed, her head resting on her arms, which were resting on the kitchen table. The kerosene lamp was burning in front of her. How *Mamm* could be sleeping with all the noise Esther had made coming in and going out the driveway was amazing.

Should she tiptoe on upstairs and let *Mamm* wake up later? Katie didn't think too long on that question. That wouldn't be right, she decided. *Mamm* might wake up hours from now and think her daughter still hadn't come home. *Mamm* had already been through enough tonight without adding to her distress.

"*Mamm!*" she said quietly as she slipped into the chair beside her. She slid her arm around *Mamm*'s shoulder. "*Mamm,* I'm home."

Mamm awoke with a start and called out in alarm.

"It's me, *Mamm,*" Katie said again. "I'm home."

Mamm was silent. She was shivering, and she wouldn't look at Katie.

"Come," Katie said gently as she pulled on *Mamm*'s arm. Glancing up at the round clock on the kitchen wall, Katie said, "You should be in bed by now instead of waiting up for me. It's close to midnight."

"What have they done to you?" *Mamm* looked Katie over like she didn't know her.

"Nothing, *Mamm*. I'm just happy. Isn't that a *gut* thing to have happen?"

Mamm groaned and rose. "We will speak no more about this tonight. I have words to share that are best spoken in the daylight."

"I had a *wunderbah* time, and I did nothing wrong," Katie said.

"I've been praying while you were gone," *Mamm* said. "And we will have to do something about this. I don't know exactly what yet, but I can't lose you, Katie."

"You haven't lost me!" Katie tugged on *Mamm*'s arm. "If you want to sit down, I'll tell you all about my evening. Please, *Mamm*."

Mamm sat back down, and Katie spoke rapidly. "There were all these young people there. Girls I had never met before, and they came up to shake my hand and ask me how I was doing. We played volleyball, much like we do at our youth gatherings. The young people on both sides of me spoke with me while we played."

"There were boys, weren't there?" *Mamm* asked, still not looking at Katie.

"*Yah,* it was Roy's birthday party, so boys were invited. But the boys didn't do anything wrong, and neither did I."

Mamm was looking at her now, the lines even deeper on her face.

"Everyone was awfully nice," Katie insisted. "And we had cake and ice cream afterward. The boy whose birthday it was even thanked me for coming, when it should have been me thanking him for inviting me. Oh *Mamm,* you don't know how *wunderbah* it was to be accepted and talked to. I can't tell you even half of it."

"Come then," *Mamm* said, getting to her feet. "This is even worse than I'd imagined."

"But we did nothing wrong!" Katie repeated. "And I was so happy with these young people. I want to go back again. They invited me, and Esther said she would take me. Don't you want me to be happy? Please, *Mamm?*"

Mamm stopped in front of the stair door and opened it. "Just go to bed, Katie. You've had enough excitement for one night. Those young people have apparently made a big impression on you, but the feelings you experienced won't last. What we have here is real, not what's out there in the world. I hope you'll see that before it's too late."

"I want to be happy," Katie said quietly. "And I want you to be happy like I was happy tonight."

Mamm kissed Katie on the cheek. "You don't know what you're talking about. Those people have addled your brain. Go to sleep now, and we'll talk about it later."

Katie sighed and slipped up the stairs, stopping at the door to her room to look back at her *mamm,* who was still waiting at the bottom of the staircase and holding the kerosene lamp in her hand.

"Good night," Katie said to the silent form before entering her room. *Mamm* would never change her mind about the Mennonites. Never in a million years. And yet Katie knew she wanted to go back . . . needed to go back. And she had to keep praying that *Mamm* would open her heart to *Da Hah*'s grace. *I need a* daett, *and* Mamm *needs a husband.*

CHAPTER TWENTY

Emma sat on the edge of her bed listening to the silence of the house around her. Katie would be asleep upstairs by now, but Emma couldn't sleep. Not after hearing what Katie had to say about her evening with the Mennonites. Her daughter had not only entered a serious stage of rebellion, but she was enjoying it. What was a *mamm* supposed to do?

She looked at the empty side of the big bed where Ezra used to lay all those years ago. His voice echoing Katie's words still haunted her, causing waves of guilt to wash through her mind. How could she be so wrong? It seemed almost impossible to believe, and yet it must be true. Even while she kept on telling Katie the same things she always had. It was all so confusing, between Katie attending the Mennonite youth gatherings, and thinking that Ezra wouldn't approve of the way she was living.

Emma pushed the thoughts of Ezra away. She would have to find the strength to get through this problem. But how? She could be strong, but strong was no longer *gut* enough. She could give Katie lectures, but she'd already tried that. She could appeal to their love for each other, but Katie already knew that. Besides, it seemed to make no difference.

Emma stood and paced the floor of the bedroom. She soon moved out to the kitchen. Here she'd found peace an hour ago praying for Katie. She'd even dropped off for a few minutes of sleep. Perhaps she could find calm here again. She had to. Life couldn't be lived in the confusion that was tearing her heart apart. Dropping to her knees, Emma tried to pray, but she could only groan as Katie's face rose before her. How happy she had looked when she arrived home. Oh, how deceiving the world out there was! How could an innocent girl like Katie be expected to withstand its charms?

And Katie wasn't to blame really. She was only reacting to what her life had been so far. *The blame is mine,* Emma thought. She should have seen this coming and done something about it. She should have known Katie would be tempted. After all, Emma

194

had been tempted when she was young. Tempted to love someone who would never love her back. But not even in her wildest dreams of loving Daniel Kauffman had Emma stepped out of the Amish faith.

Emma searched her mind for answers. Perhaps she should have allowed Katie to attend more of the Amish youth gatherings. Katie might have become a bigger part of the community and felt less alone and neglected. She might never have been lured in by Mennonite young people.

Emma groaned and got to her feet. She grabbed her shawl from the living room closet and walked outside. The late moon hung over the horizon as Emma stood on the front porch. Its pale light reached halfway across the wooden floor. Emma moved over to the shadows where the swing was. She sat down. Holding still, she wrapped her shawl around her shoulders.

She looked across the front lawn and tried to pray again, but no words of praise or plea would come. Instead, words of complaint formed in her mind. She couldn't allow that. *Da Hah* did what He did, and it was always for the best. Yet how could that be? How could Ezra's death have been for the best? Had he lived, this would not be happening. She was sure of it. Yet Ezra was with

God and His angels even now walking on streets of gold. He knew only happiness and joy. He was wearing the crown *Da Hah* had no doubt given him when he arrived — a crown well deserved for his life of righteous faith lived on this earth. Ezra had even believed love would come to her frozen heart long before *Da Hah* had used Katie to accomplish the task. For that faith alone, Ezra must be wearing a crown several feet high.

Emma gazed at the moon for long moments. Apparently Ezra still thought love could grow in her heart again. Be how could that be true? She had frozen her heart solid for too many years.

And she was now left to walk on this earth with only Katie as a companion. That had seemed *gut* to her for all these years. She'd been strong, and there had been enough mercy from *Da Hah* to live on. But none of this was *gut* enough now. Not if she lost Katie. Life wouldn't be worth living, and losing her would forever lay on her conscience. How could she look forward to the day when she would see Ezra again? A look of disappointment would be on his face for sure now. She believed Ezra would have been told what had happened before she arrived — that Katie had been lost. And

Emma wouldn't receive a heavenly crown after such a failure.

Emma moved the swing with her feet as sobs racked her chest. The soft groanings of the wooden slats under her were like the rumblings in her soul. Emma drew comfort from the sound. At least something in this world understood her agony and shared the pain. Oh, she would do almost anything to win Katie back. Almost anything!

That thought hung in the night air for a moment. Anything? Would she really do *anything*? What was anything? Going to talk with Deacon Elmer? *Nee,* that wouldn't do any *gut.* Making a trip to Lancaster to speak with her brothers whom she hadn't seen in quite a few years years? Emma shook her head. They wouldn't know what to do. No doubt their own children were into *rumspringa,* and they would tell her to take a deep breath and calm down. They'd tell her things would get better after awhile. But things wouldn't get better. She was certain of that. She knew Katie, and Katie was very serious about what she was doing.

What *gut* was there in being willing to do anything when there was so little she could do? Emma pondered the question. No doubt many a parent had been where she was now. They had been willing to cross the ocean on a paddleboat, crawl a hundred miles on their knees, disgrace themselves in front of their entire communities if only their child could be brought back to them.

What she needed was someone to stand by her side, Emma decided. Someone who could feel what she was feeling. Someone who would be as desperate as she was about saving Katie. Someone who could share her groans. Perhaps even someone who could find the words to pray when she couldn't. Did she have someone like that? Yes! The thought raced through her mind. Emma leaped to her feet. Behind her the swing swung sideways against the house, hitting with a loud whack. Emma's hands flew to her mouth. "Not Jesse Mast!" she said out loud. But he wanted to marry her, didn't he? He had come over twice now. And he would care about Katie, wouldn't he? And he would pray for her. He would offer advice in words Katie would understand. Jesse did so for his own children. And wouldn't Ezra approve of this? He certainly wouldn't approve of how she was living now.

More thoughts flew through Emma's head like busy bees buzzing around their hive. She'd just said she would do anything to save Katie, hadn't she? But *this*? She couldn't again marry a man she didn't love.

Yah, the last time *Da Hah* had given mercy, and love for Ezra had come eventually. But she had been innocent then. Now she knew what it was to feel that deep stir in her heart, that longing for a man's attention. *Nee,* she could never open her heart to another man.

Yet . . . could she . . . would she . . . consider it for Katie's sake? And there had been Ezra's voice so clearly spoken that night on the basement steps. After all these years of protecting her heart? It was almost too much to imagine. There would have to be a miracle to change her heart. There was no question about that. Emma lifted pleading eyes toward the porch ceiling. What was she to do? She had to save Katie. She *had* to. But how could she do this great wrong against a godly man like Jesse? He wanted to marry a woman who would eventually love him. But even if she were willing to wed, that was something she couldn't promise. What if the miracle didn't happen the second time? What if it wasn't like it had been with Ezra?

Emma paced in and out of the moonlight. She saw the faces of Jesse's children pass in front of her. She remembered them one by one. Leroy, the oldest, who sat in the church services, his face stern just as the elder child's should be. That spoke of a father who knew how to raise godly children. Her hands trembled.

She kept going, running the list of Jesse's children through her mind. Willis was the tallest one even though he wasn't the eldest. Mabel was taking care of the whole household by herself since her *mamm* had passed. Many times Emma had driven by their place in the past year and noticed the wash had been done early and was on the line flapping in the wind. No girl who knew how to work so diligently could have a *daett* who didn't know how to raise children.

Jesse's second girl was named Carolyn. She never seemed to get noticed at church; she usually stood quietly with girls who were her age. And she'd grown even quieter in the year since her *mamm* had died. Was that not also a sign of a *gut daett*?

And the youngest boy — Joel. He'd grown a lot the last time she'd noticed him. He was a well-behaved child, Emma remembered. She sat on the porch swing again. They were all angels, she decided. Especially Joel. She remembered brief glimpses of his face during Sunday services. His head would be in his *daett*'s lap and he'd be sound asleep during long sermons. Joel didn't run around the house after the services or need calling down like some of the other boys did. The younger children were the first to be spoiled, she knew, but Joel didn't seem spoiled.

Indeed, Jesse must be a very *gut daett.* She could see nothing but positive signs of it. And this was the same Jesse who asked her hand in marriage! Emma leaped to her feet again, this time the swing whacking the back of her legs. "I can't believe I'm considering this," she said aloud. And yet Emma knew she was. Not just for Katie's sake, but for her own as well. Emma limped into the full moonlight and lifted her face to the heavens. "Oh *Gott im Himmel,* how could You forgive me for what I've done?"

Emma answered her question with a groan. "Forgive me for what I've done. Speak to Katie please, *Da Hah,* even as she is sleeping. Touch her heart with repentance. Let her see the wrong way she's traveling and how she's hurting people much more than she knows. Help me, please, as I try to change."

Emma waited, but the weight on her heart remained. "Please let Your will be done, even when I am so weak," Emma prayed. She took one last look around before she went back inside the house. She left her shawl lying on the living room couch, went into her bedroom, and slipped into bed. She must think no more of her troubles tonight. She pulled the covers tight against her chin and finally drifted off into an exhausted sleep.

CHAPTER TWENTY-ONE

The following morning Jesse sat at the breakfast table finishing the last of his eggs and bacon. He filled his bowl with steaming oatmeal and added some brown sugar and cream. Out of the corner of his eye, he saw that Mabel was watching him. She would be worrying about the food, no doubt, wondering if the eggs had been done like *Mamm* used to make them.

"Everything's great!" he said with a smile.

"Was the bacon okay? Not too crisp?"

"*Yah,* dear. It was done to perfection. I like it crisp. Both you and Carolyn are doing an excellent job keeping the house."

Mabel's face still looked concerned. "Smell the oatmeal before you taste it, *Daett.* It may be burned."

"It tastes fine to me," Leroy said from his place on the back bench. He was gulping down each bite.

"You wouldn't know if there were charcoals floating in your oatmeal," Mabel snapped. "So be quiet. I'm asking *Daett.*"

Jesse shook his head at him when Leroy opened his mouth to snap back.

"It's fine, Mabel," Jesse said. "I keep on saying that, but you don't believe me. Both of you girls do very *gut* with the housework."

Mabel didn't look satisfied. Her bowl was sitting empty while she watched him.

Jesse lifted his spoon to his mouth. *Yah,* it was burned a little. Millie would have known to take the oatmeal off the top and not scrape the bottom of the pan when serving it. Should he tell Mabel? It wasn't that bad, just a bit scorched.

"It's not bad," he offered.

"You have to tell me the truth, *Daett.*" Mabel had tears welling in her eyes. "I can take it."

"I've never seen such a crybaby in my life!" Leroy declared. "The girl is ruining what little breakfast we do have."

"Okay, that's enough out of you!" Jesse said. "This oatmeal does have a little burnt flavor to it, but it's not that serious. You're doing fine, Mabel. Next time don't scrape the bottom with your spoon if you think it's been on the stove too long."

Mabel smiled a little and then made a face at Leroy after she dried her eyes. "At least I don't come stomping into the house with my boots full of manure like you do. When you start seeing a girl, I'm going to tell her how you stink up the whole house and how you'll do the same once you're married."

Jesse laughed, hiding the sound with a loud clearing of his throat. The girl had a cutting tongue — though funny now, it might not feel so humorous to her future husband.

"I'd not do anything like that," Jesse said to Mabel. He turned to Leroy. "And stop teasing your sister. She's doing the best she can."

Leroy grunted and finished his oatmeal in silence.

Jesse continued with his oatmeal too. His face grew long again at this latest example of the problems he faced. Not only did he need a *frau,* but his children needed a *mamm.* He was trying to take care of that need with his visits to Emma, but so far neither his children nor Emma were obliging.

He'd dreamed of Emma last night. She'd been sitting somewhere in her house with tears in her eyes. There had been a rush of night air as he was running around the outside of the house trying to catch her attention. Around him the sound of buggies going somewhere echoed loudly. Over all that, he'd been sure he saw the light of a kerosene lamp playing on Emma's face as she wept over a great sorrow. It was very confusing, and dreams rarely meant anything anyway, he decided. He didn't need a dream to know Emma had a soft heart under those stern lines on her face. How he knew, he wasn't sure, but he did. She would look beautiful if she smiled more often . . .

Jesse finished the last spoonful of his oatmeal as the sounds of buggy wheels came from the driveway. Mabel was the first to jump to her feet and rush to the window.

"It's Ruth!" Mabel exclaimed.

Jesse groaned. Now what was *that* woman coming around for again? He'd almost begun to raise his hopes that he'd been wrong in his opinion of her. Perhaps Ruth had the sense after all to stay away. But obviously she didn't.

"She's getting out of the buggy," Mabel said, as if that were some great accomplishment.

Of course she's coming in, Jesse almost said. *She wants to be your mamm.* But he kept the words in his mouth. The woman was teacher to his two youngest children, and they needed to respect her.

"I'm going outside to meet her!" Carolyn

shouted as she raced toward the front door.

Leroy glared after Carolyn, but he didn't say anything.

Jesse saw the look and figured Leroy was as much in favor of Ruth's intentions as the rest were. He just didn't like the interruption this was sure to bring to the morning routine.

"She's taking something out of the buggy!" Mabel hollered.

A twinkle came into Leroy's eyes.

"She bringing in pies!" Mabel announced, heading for the front door.

Jesse stood up and pushed his chair back. Leroy was laughing now, his earlier irritation apparently forgotten. The boy had way too much figured out, Jesse thought. But then Ruth's intentions weren't much of a riddle. She was about as devious as a bale of hay coming down the hay chute. She smacked you upside the head, leaving no doubt as to what she was up to. The problem was Ruth thought she was running in the dark. All the while her buggy lights were on and shining brightly.

Leroy and Willis stayed at the table, but Jesse headed for the front door. Little Joel followed him, all smiles as he jumped up and down when Ruth came up the front porch steps.

"How is everybody?" Ruth asked with a laugh as she gathered Joel in her arms. Mabel and Carolyn stood smiling near the top step.

Ruth set a large plastic pie carrier with at least three pies on the porch floor. Jesse's mouth watered at the sight even with his best efforts to do otherwise. He bent down to peer through the plastic. One of the pies looked like it might be pecan. They all looked absolutely delicious. He opened his mouth to say so, but caught himself. There was no way Ruth Troyer's tricks were going to work on him. It would take more than pecan pies to get into his *gut* graces. At least the kind of graces needed to say marriage vows.

Ruth reached over to give Carolyn a long hug before letting go to fuss with a piece of hair sticking out the front of Carolyn's *kapp.*

"My, my!" Ruth exclaimed. "Someone didn't wash your hair very well on Saturday night."

Jesse almost laughed. Ruth had been seeing Carolyn all week and hadn't noticed her hair until she came up on his front porch.

Mabel looked horrified. "Oh, Ruth! I do the best I can. And so does Carolyn. But it's hard to know exactly what to do sometimes."

"Now, now," Ruth cooed. "I know it can't be helped. But you'll be learning how to do these things well before too long . . . I hope."

Ruth looked over Mabel's shoulder at Jesse, her eyes accusing, as if she blamed him for this situation.

"The girls need a *mamm*," he admitted. "We all miss Millie a lot."

"Of course. We all do," Ruth said mournfully. "But we can't question the ways of *Da Hah*. He takes away with one hand what He gives with the other. That's what I told myself when Homer up and died on me. I must say it comforted my soul something awful during those terrible hours and days."

"I see you've brought pies," Jesse said, changing the subject. "You know you didn't have to. The girls are doing a *gut* job keeping the household going."

"That's what you tell yourself." Ruth moved closer to him. "But I hear the other side of the story at school from Carolyn and Joel. Not that they complain, but running a household was never a burden *Da Hah* meant to be laid on the shoulders of two such young girls."

Jesse pulled back a step. "I know that. I've been praying about the matter, but *Da Hah* has not yet opened the door for another *mamm* for the children . . . or a *frau* for myself."

Ruth glared at him. "I say a man can do too much praying about that matter. As I told Homer many a time, sometimes a thing's so plain it makes a man almost blind."

"I guess," Jesse allowed. He saw things plain enough. It would only take about two months to get Ruth to say the marriage vows with him. Likely sooner if he allowed her to hurry the wedding preparations. The problem still remained though. He just wasn't interested. Ruth's face changed to a smile now, the effort quick and effective. The woman could change expressions faster than a cloud's shadow racing across summer-kissed ground.

"I'm glad to see you're taking the matter seriously, Jesse," Ruth said. "Remember, *Da Hah* always supplies manna from heaven wherever the need is." When Jesse remained silent, Ruth continued. "Well, I had better be getting on now. I like to get to the school early, before anyone else gets there. Up before dawn, the Good Book says. That's where the blessing of *Da Hah* lies."

Jesse watched Ruth go down the steps, not sure what to say or do other than stare at the offering of pies she'd left on the porch. They did look awfully *gut.*

Mabel must have thought he'd lost all his manners. She hollered across the lawn, "Thank you, Ruth, for these wonderful pies. What kind are they?"

"Peach, apple, and pecan!" Ruth rattled off without looking back over her shoulder. "I stayed up late last night baking so they would be fresh this morning."

"You didn't have to," Mabel hollered after Ruth. "But pecan is *Daett*'s favorite. That'll be the first pie I learn how to make for him."

Jesse caught himself before he groaned out loud. Mabel had no idea what she'd just said. Now there would be no getting rid of the woman. She'd be stopping in every week with her offering of pecan pies.

Ruth turned around, beaming. She hollered back, "I didn't know which one would be the best, so that's why you have several different kinds to choose from. But now I know. I hope someone will be willing to eat the others."

"Leroy and Willis eat anything!" Mabel called. She waved before picking up the pie canister. "I'll have this washed and send it back with Carolyn tomorrow."

"Take your time," Ruth yelled back, dismissing Mabel's comment with a wave of her own. "I'll see you later, Joel and Carolyn. And you too, Jesse."

Jesse left the two youngest standing on the front porch waving to Ruth as he went inside the house. Mabel followed him carrying the pie canister.

"Don't you think she'd make the perfect *mamm* for us?" Mabel said softly. "She brought you pecan pie — your favorite."

Jesse groaned aloud this time. The situation had just become intolerable.

CHAPTER TWENTY-TWO

The day after the Mennonite youth gathering, *Mamm*'s face was still drawn as if she hadn't slept all night. Katie noticed and did her best to make the morning go easy. She'd gotten up early and started on the barn chores. Then she came inside to prepare breakfast. Now she was helping *Mamm* clean up after the meal.

Katie considered that bearing up under *Mamm*'s continued disapproval was going to be more difficult than she'd imagined. Yet there had been such happiness in her heart when she returned from the youth gathering last night. There would be no turning back. If she could only explain to *Mamm* that nothing sinful had happened. That all she'd done was talk with some Mennonite girls and boys and spoken briefly with Roy Coblenz, the boy who had invited her. She hadn't done anything wrong. In fact, *Da Hah* was leading her, and she was going to trust Him.

How could feeling happy be wrong? How could it be evil to want the attention and acceptance of friends? Did *Mamm* really think it was? How could she? *Mamm* seemed to think acceptance couldn't be found anywhere but among her own people or here at home with her. That's what the real problem was. But even if she knew how to explain this, *Mamm* probably still wouldn't believe her daughter was right.

Should she try one more time? Katie glanced toward *Mamm,* who was wiping the top of the kitchen table. It was no use, Katie decided. Only an apology and a vow to never attend another Mennonite gathering would bring a smile back to *Mamm*'s face. And even then, *Mamm* probably wouldn't trust her right away. She would want proof that Katie meant to follow through.

And if the truth were told, Katie probably couldn't stay away from the Mennonite youth gatherings even if she did promise her *mamm.* Her heart was already longing to see Margaret and Sharon again. What a joy it would be to hear their happy chatter and see the happiness in their eyes as they spoke with her. They thought she was a perfectly normal human being. They didn't know she was known as Emma Raber's daughter and what that meant. Likely they had never even heard of the odd widow Raber of the community. They accepted Katie for who she was on her own.

Mamm cleared her throat, and Katie froze. "I don't suppose you've changed your mind about attending the Mennonite youth gatherings, have you?" she asked.

Oh, Mamm, *please,* Katie wanted to beg. *Didn't you see how much joy was on my face last night?* Instead, she took a deep breath and said, "I'm sorry for the trouble I'm causing you, *Mamm.* I really am."

"Then please come back to me, Katie." *Mamm* came over and wrapped her arms around Katie, pulling her close. "And I'll try to change the things I've been doing wrong."

Katie hugged her back even though her heart was pounding in her ears.

"It's that job at Byler's that's partly to blame," *Mamm* continued. "It's exposing you to these temptations. I wish you'd quit."

Why did she have to decide between breaking *Mamm*'s heart or her own? Katie wondered. "I'm not going to quit Byler's, *Mamm.* And I'm still with you," Katie said quietly. "Is it so wrong to feel happy when someone likes you?"

Mamm let go a bit to hold Katie at arm's

length. "*I* love you Katie. I've always loved you."

"It's important to me that others also love me." Katie struggled for more words. How could she explain this to *Mamm*?

Weariness crossed *Mamm*'s face. "But the Mennonites, Katie? *Da Hah* has given us each other."

Katie clung to *Mamm*'s hands. There was no use explaining or trying to justify herself. Her words would only tear at *Mamm*'s heart.

Mamm turned to sit down. She pulled a handkerchief out of her dress pocket and dried her eyes. "I know I haven't done everything right with you. I just wish you weren't going through this rebellious stage. I never had to, and I turned out okay. Look how *Da Hah* sent me your *daett* to love even after what I'd done. I was happy with my life. Why can't you be?"

"I'm sorry," Katie whispered. "I can't be happy with your life because it's not my life. That's not how *Da Hah* has willed it." It was no use saying more, even if she could find something more to say. And she was already late leaving for work. Katie squeezed *Mamm*'s hand and left the kitchen to go to her bedroom. Minutes later she came down dressed for work. *Mamm* was still sitting at the kitchen table, dabbing her eyes. Katie

216

almost rushed over to her, but she forced herself to walk out the front door.

If she stayed, they would only talk in circles again, and *Mamm* wouldn't understand anyway. And Katie really did need to be at Byler's on time. And she certainly wasn't going to quit working there. Byler's had been the doorway through which this new life had come to her, and closing it would be like turning her back on what she'd experienced. On that point *Mamm* was right. The job at Byler's was to blame — but it was to blame for *gut* things.

Katie hurried toward the barn and harnessed Sparky. Leading him outside, she swung him under the shafts and hitched him up. Katie pulled herself up into the buggy. Slapping the reins gently against Sparky's back, she drove down the lane. Looking back at the house, she saw the shadow of *Mamm* standing behind the drapes of the living room window to watch her leave.

Mamm does love me, Katie told herself, her breath coming in sobs now. They loved each other, and somehow they would make their way through this hard time without destroying each other. How was that to be done? *Mamm* was already being destroyed from the looks of things. And Katie was afraid she'd be if she listened to *Mamm.*

Not attending the Mennonite youth gatherings again would be like crawling into a deep, dark hole after seeing the light of the morning sun rising over the horizon. She hadn't known how dark her life had been until last night. Now there could only be a going forward. Surely *Da Hah* would look down and have mercy on a poor girl and her *mamm* who didn't know how to keep the love they had between them from slipping away.

Katie passed two buggies. Although her eyes were blinded with tears, she waved to whomever it was. She saw no hand waving back, but it didn't matter this morning. What mattered were the things happening inside her. She was being asked to leave what she loved to seize the feelings that drew her heart.

Katie wiped her eyes as she pulled into the parking lot at Byler's. Arlene's buggy was already there, so Katie unhitched Sparky and rushed inside. Hopefully Arlene wouldn't notice she'd been crying. Katie took a quick look around and saw no one. She rushed to the bathroom in the back, sneaking around one aisle when she saw Arlene ahead deep in conversation with Mrs. Cole.

Katie splashed cold water on her face once and dried with a paper towel. She looked in the mirror at the unsatisfactory results. There were still splotches of red under her eyes. Katie ran her finger over her cheek, remembering *Mamm* standing behind the living room window drapes and almost burst into tears again. She choked back the sobs and washed her face again. It looked worse now, so she gave up and marched out with her head up and a smile pasted on her face. Perhaps if she acted confident and cheerful, no one would notice.

Katie heard Arlene and Mrs. Cole's voices ahead of her, and she kept her head turned away as she came around the corner.

"Good morning!" Mrs. Cole called out.

Katie stopped and forced a smile as she turned to her boss. "*Gut* morning," Katie returned.

"We're almost ready to open," Mrs. Cole said, glancing at her watch.

"*Yah,* I'm ready," Katie said as she hesitated before heading on. Mrs. Cole was again deep in conversation with Arlene. Katie gathered herself together, and took her place behind the register. *Da Hah* had been with her, she told herself. No embarrassing scene had occurred, and soon her eyes wouldn't show any signs of redness.

Katie smiled to the customers coming in, giving little waves of her hand. No one seemed to notice her misery, and she began to breathe easier.

"How are you this morning?" Arlene asked from behind her.

Katie jumped.

Arlene laughed. "Scared you, huh? Or are you feeling guilty about that Mennonite birthday party I heard you went to last night?"

"I'm not feeling guilty," Katie said at once. "I had a *gut* time. And they are the nicest people I've ever met in my life."

"Whoa there!" Arlene laughed again. "Did Roy Coblenz ask you home or something?"

"Of course not," Katie shot back. "But he was quite nice to me, and he's very *gut* looking."

Arlene eyes got bigger. "Why, Katie Raber! You're changing right in front of my eyes. I do declare, you even have rosy cheeks this morning. Have you fallen in love? Just like that?"

Katie thought of laughing, but she didn't. "I'm not in love." Well, she might be in love — with Ben Stoll. But it probably wasn't love if the other person didn't love you back. Katie's ears perked up as Arlene went on.

"Talking about love, listen to this. Ruth

Troyer has been talking openly at the women's sewing about how widower Jesse Mast needs a new *mamm* for his children. She just talked on and on about it last week, my *mamm* said. John Yoder's wife finally asked her right out why she doesn't make herself available. *Mamm* said Ruth kind of held her head in the air, like she'd already thought of that idea and planned to do something about it. That's one bold woman, I say, setting her *kapp* for Jesse. But then who knows what a person would do if she were getting older like Ruth and didn't have many options available."

Katie caught herself before she gasped aloud. She must not reveal that *Mamm* was affected by this in any way. If Arlene found out that Jesse had been over to their house twice to speak with *Mamm* of marriage, this would really set the women's tongues to wagging. And neither her *mamm* nor she needed such a thing happening on top of everything else that was going on. Katie turned away from Arlene and opened her register in hopes a customer would come quickly to her station. As if in answer to her wish, a woman came out of the bread aisle and headed straight for Katie's register.

"Well, talk to you later," Arlene said as

another customer approached Arlene's register.

Katie took a deep breath. She smiled at the woman in front of her as she began scanning the grocery items.

At least for now *Da Hah* seemed to be looking out for her.

CHAPTER TWENTY-THREE

Jesse drove his buggy through the falling dusk, keeping Lucy on the right side of the road as an *Englisha* car approached. He let the lines go slack as Lucy moved away from the ditch once the vehicle passed. He stared off toward the horizon. The silence of the evening hung heavy in the air. There wasn't much of a sunset, Jesse noticed. Just a clear sky with the sun disappearing from sight. Clouds would add color — not that he liked clouds in the sky — but *Da Hah* did make them for a purpose.

A slight smile crept onto Jesse's face. If clouds added color to one's life, then he must have color running all the way through his right now. He'd left Mabel in tears back at the house after he told her where he was going. There'd been no reason to hide his destination. Mabel would find out anyway. He figured if he told Mabel ahead of time, the news would be easier to take. But he'd been wrong. And now he was deliberately seeing a woman his children objected to. And on top of that, a woman who didn't want to see him.

He was a fool, he supposed, to even make another try with Emma. But his hopes remained high. Perhaps Emma would listen to reason tonight. The problem was he had no new reasons to give her. Just the old ones — all of them already rejected by Emma. He'd already said, "I think *Da Hah* wants us together" and "I find a love stirring in my heart for you."

Jesse sighed, thinking about it. He couldn't get all mushy with words again tonight. But he could ask Emma straight out to marry him. If there was anything he'd learned from his relationship with Millie, it was to follow his heart. And *Da Hah* had stirred his heart in Emma's direction. He was certain of that.

His feelings must not cause him to act like a teenager in love. That much he knew. Jesse smiled at the thought of love-struck teenagers and how they pursued each other with constant glances and mushy words. *Nee,* that wasn't how he felt about Emma, but his affection for her was genuine and would make for a happy marriage — if only she could see it.

He could always ask for Ruth's hand in marriage. He'd thought long and hard about the matter again. She was obviously available, and the children loved her. She would make a decent wife, he supposed, although she didn't stir his heart the way Emma did. The woman did know how to cook. The pecan pie she'd brought over certainly had been lip-smacking *gut*. Perhaps it wouldn't be so bad to have pecan pie every week. He might fatten up with such *gut* eating, but he could use some fattening. Jesse looked down at his stomach and smiled. "It'll take more than pecan pie, I'm afraid," he said out loud. Lucy twirled one ear back as if she were listening.

The Rabers' house appeared ahead of him, and Jesse leaned out of the buggy to look up at the sky. He murmured, "You'd better give me a little help this time, *Hah,* or she's over the fence, I'm afraid."

Lucy quickened her pace as they approached the place. He might as well arrive looking like an eager teenager, he decided. Keeping up the speed, he steered into Emma's driveway, causing his buggy to tilt sideways. Perhaps he could get Emma's attention with reckless driving if nothing else. He pulled to a stop with a loud "Whoa!" He leaned out and then leaped to the ground. He reached for the tie rope under the front seat and secured Lucy to the hitching post. He turned around and, not seeing anyone, marched up the sidewalk and knocked on the front door. Footsteps came at once, and he took a step back.

The door opened and Katie stood there smiling.

"*Gut* evening, Katie," Jesse said. "Is your *mamm* home?"

"*Yah,*" Katie said and motioned with her head. "Would you like to come in?"

She was looking strangely at him, Jesse thought, but there was also hope and happiness in her eyes. He glanced down at his shirt and pants. Perhaps he still carried crumbs from Ruth's pecan pie? But nothing appeared out of order. *"Nee,"* he said, taking off his hat. "Please tell your *mamm* I'll wait for her on the porch swing." He might as well be a real youngster and go for the swing right away, he figured. This would be a proper courting tonight — if any courting was going to happen. Emma might have nothing more to say to him than she had before. Basically "a *gut* day to you" and "a *gut* farewell."

Katie nodded and closed the door.

Jesse walked over to the porch swing and sat down. It was *gut* to sit on the swing again tonight. Farm work didn't leave much time or inclination to sit on swings. A man needed a woman to remind him what swings were for — reflection and meditation on the better things in life. He jumped to his feet when the front door squeaked on its hinges. Emma appeared wearing a slight smile on her face. He stepped toward her, and she offered him her hand.

"*Gut* evening. I thought that was your buggy coming in the driveway," Emma said.

"*Gut* evening," he managed. "Is it okay if we sit out here awhile?"

"*Yah.*" She led the way to the swing and sat down.

He sat beside her and looked out across the fields. With that smile of hers his thoughts had forsaken him. The glow of her beauty had appeared for just a moment. Why was the woman so friendly tonight? he wondered.

"I hope you didn't mind my sending Katie to the door," Emma said, glancing sideways at him.

He cleared his throat. "Of course not. I expect you were busy. I guess I have to stop these sudden trips over here. I know I'm making a nuisance of myself."

Emma looked away and didn't say anything.

Jesse waited. Whatever Emma was preparing to say couldn't be easy. She was obviously struggling for words.

"I've been thinking . . ." Emma's voice came out a whisper. "I've been thinking about you . . . coming over here. And . . . and about what you asked me . . . and about what I told you."

"Yah?" Jesse waited. When she didn't continue, he added, "I know I spoke plainly about what I was interested in. If I have troubled you, I'm sorry. I came tonight again . . . in the hope I could ask again and perhaps better express my understanding of what I believe *Da Hah* is telling me."

"You keep coming," she said, not looking at him. "Even when I told you I wasn't interested."

"Yah," he allowed. "It is my way. I do not know any other."

"Do you plan to force my hand?"

Jesse glanced at her, his look sharp. "I wasn't meaning that at all. I would never try that, Emma."

She pondered the words, and Jesse settled back into the porch swing, waiting again. Whatever was troubling her, he wanted to hear the details. The discussion might not lead to the question of marriage, but if Ruth could bring pecan pies over to tempt his heart, he could listen to a woman's troubles in the hope of winning hers.

When Emma still said nothing, he offered, "I'm sorry if I'm not courting you properly. I know I'm not exactly a youngster anymore. At my age I find it hard to think of driving home from a Sunday evening hymn singing doing a proper courting."

A hint of a smile formed on Emma's face, but she shook her head. "It's like this . . ." Emma paused and her voice grew stronger. "I've been thinking about your offer to wed me." She gave him a quick glance out of the corner of her eyes.

"Yah?"

Her voice trembled. "Is this still what you wish?"

"Emma . . ." He reached over to touch her arm. "Of course it is. I wouldn't be here if that wasn't what I wanted."

She stared across the fields before meeting his gaze. "What if I told you I was willing to wed, but that I don't love you?"

He grasped her hand now. "Emma, this is often the way it is between older people who have been married before. We can't expect our hearts to pound like two wild, young folks's hearts."

A thin smile spread across her face and then vanished. "What if I never love you,

229

Jesse? I mean, I would be with you, yes, but what if my heart were never truly yours?"

He held her hand for a long moment before replying. "You had a great love for Ezra, didn't you?"

She nodded.

"I would not hold that against you, Emma." He took both of her hands in his. "My heart also hurt deeply when Millie passed. But *Da Hah* can bring about something new between us. I believe this with all my heart."

Emma hung her head. "That may be your faith, but it's not mine . . . yet. And there is something else . . ."

"Yah?" Jesse waited again.

She finally met his eyes. "A big part of the reason I'm considering this, Jesse. It's because of Katie. She needs a *gut daett.*"

"For Katie?" He wrinkled his brow. "Katie's a decent girl, I thought."

"Katie has taken up with the Mennonites," Emma whispered.

"Oh." His voice fell. "I did not know this."

Her fingers moved in his. "Does this change your mind, Jesse? If it does, I won't hold it against you."

He caught his breath. "Emma, *nee,* it does not. But I don't know if I can be of much help with her if her mind is set."

"You can," she said without hesitation. "You would be a *gut daett* for Katie, regardless of what happens. You might even win her back to our faith."

He was staring at her now, her words having sunk in. "You would wed me . . . because of Katie?"

Her gaze was steady. "I have told you the truth. That is part of the reason. I will not hide behind a lie. I think that *Da Hah* is no doubt very displeased with my life right now. There are changes I need to make, but I still will not hide the matter from you."

His thoughts raced. This was something he hadn't expected. The woman was willing to accept his offer partly because of what he might be able to do for her daughter. Well, she was being honest. What more could he ask of her? He glanced at her again. "And what if I fail in winning Katie back to the faith? Would you regret your decision to wed?"

She didn't wait long before answering. "I don't think so. Katie needs a *daett,* and I think you're a man with whom it would be easy to live with. And I know I need to change. Ezra would want that for me."

"Thank you." Jesse looked away. The woman spoke plainly; there was no question about that. But he must also make his

231

confession. His conscience wouldn't allow any other option. He squeezed her hand. "There are some things I must also confess."

"You?" She gave a little laugh.

"*Yah,* me. I was just thinking of Ruth Troyer and her pecan pies."

"Ruth Troyer!" Emma sat upright on the swing. "What does Ruth Troyer have to do with you and pecan pies?"

"I just finished eating one of her pies before I came over here."

"You've been asking her to bake pecan pies?" Her eyes narrowed a bit.

He laughed. "Believe me, it was the other way around."

She settled back into the swing and stole a glance at his face. "Has Ruth been getting anywhere with those pecan pies?"

"Would I be here if she were?" He gave her a warm smile.

She looked away. "Perhaps not. But does this mean you'll be wanting pecan pies every week?"

Jesse laughed. "That was a question I forgot to ask you. Can you bake pecan pies?" He grinned.

The man has a sense of humor, Emma thought with a slight smile. "Not like Ruth can," Emma admitted. "Nobody can bake pies like Ruth."

He gave her hand a squeeze and then reached up to touch her face. "Emma, I am teasing. For someone as sweet as you — and as beautiful — why would I need pecan pies?"

"You really are a tease, Jesse. How will I ever get used to you?"

He smiled. "I know I won't have any problems getting used to you."

He used both hands to turn her face toward him. She didn't resist and met his eyes. But her lips trembled as her hands reached up and rested on his shoulders.

"Emma," he whispered, "I already love you more than I should."

"You are too *gut* for me, Jesse. You shouldn't even be . . ."

He touched her hand. "There is something else I must tell you, Emma. It won't make any difference to my purpose or heart, but it should be said."

"Yah?" Her eyes searched his face.

"Most of my children don't wish me to marry you."

She pulled away from him. "But you still came. Why?"

He shrugged before admitting, "Because I love you, Emma. And I know we can make it work with *Da Hah*'s help."

She didn't answer but buried her head in his shoulder.

CHAPTER TWENTY-FOUR

The next morning Katie awakened to *Mamm* shaking her by the shoulder. "Get up! It's already late."

Sitting upright, Katie threw the bedcovers aside to climb out of bed.

Mamm didn't say anything more. She left, her footsteps fading down the stairs.

It can't be that late, Katie thought, looking out the bedroom window. She stood up, trying to recall what had happened the previous evening. Jesse Mast had visited again. The memory was clear now. She could hardly believe her eyes when *Mamm* sent her to the door. Had *Mamm* known anything about Jesse's coming? She hadn't mentioned anything, so it was unlikely. And what had the two talked about out there on the porch swing for so long? *Mamm* wouldn't be changing her mind about marrying Jesse, would she? *Nee,* that seemed next to impossible. Katie had tried to stay up late to talk to her *mamm,* but she became sleepy and finally went to bed with Jesse and *Mamm* still on the porch. There had been no sound of Jesse's buggy leaving before she'd fallen asleep.

Dawn was now breaking, red streaks of light running skyward. *Mamm* was up early, so she must be feeling *gut* about whatever happened last night. Katie pulled on her chore dress and went downstairs. *Mamm* had already left for the barn, so Katie went into the washroom and pulled on her boots. She headed for the barn. A few stars were still out on the western horizon, twinkling above the roofline of the barn. Katie pushed open the door to see *Mamm* bringing in Molly and Bossy through the back door. The two cows mooed at the sight of the piles of feed lying in front of the stanchions. Bossy made a dash for it, arriving first as usual. Behind Bossy, Molly lumbered along and put her head through her stanchion to eat. *Mamm* snapped the two neck sleeves into place.

Katie moved closer. "Okay, tell me what happened last night, *Mamm.* You're acting strangely this morning."

"I'm not acting strangely," *Mamm* protested, but she avoided Katie's gaze.

"*Yah,* you are," Katie insisted. "So you

might as well tell me what happened."

Mamm met Katie's eyes. "I have agreed to marry Jesse."

"You've agreed to marry Jesse!" Katie could scarcely believe her ears. "That's a miracle, *Mamm.*"

A slight smile crept across *Mamm*'s face. "Maybe and maybe not. I think it's for the best."

Katie was puzzled. "But *Mamm,* that's not like you at all. I was hoping for something like this, but . . ." Katie let the thought hang.

"Weren't you the one pushing me to marry him?"

"*Yah,* I guess. How did Jesse talk you into this?"

"I guess even an old woman can change her mind," *Mamm* said, handing Katie a milk bucket. "It was hard, but I'm glad I did it. Jesse is agreeable and, *yah,* I'm coming around slowly."

Katie stood there for a minute before she sat down beside Molly and began milking. It seemed so incredible! *Da Hah* was clearly moving right in front of her eyes. If *Mamm*'s heart could be changed, anything was possible. *But . . .* She paused to think. Something wasn't right here.

"Mamm?" Katie leaned out to look around Molly. "Why did you agree to marry Jesse?"

Mamm didn't say anything, and Katie was about ready to ask again when suddenly *Mamm* spoke up.

"I thought it would be best — for you and for me."

"Does this have anything to do with my going to the Mennonite youth gathering?"

Mamm took even longer to answer. "It might be best if Jesse and I keep our reasons between the two of us. There are some things that can only be shared between a man and his future *frau*."

Katie leaned her head against Molly's flank as she began milking again. *Mamm* never changed her mind without a *gut* reason. Could Jesse have brought some new reason to light last night that persuaded her? If he had, it must really have been something. But hadn't *Mamm* asked her that night she went to the birthday party if she would change her mind about attending Mennonite youth gatherings if . . .

"What are you thinking?" *Mamm* had come over to stand beside Katie with her milk bucket in one hand.

Katie stood up. "Are you marrying Jesse because of me? Tell me the truth, *Mamm*."

Mamm drew in a deep breath. "*Yah,* but only in part. I'm sorry, Katie, but I didn't know what else to do. I can't go on like this by myself. I need a husband. I see that now."

"You mean to help with me?"

Mamm's gaze didn't waver. "You're a wonderful daughter, Katie. I have no complaints in that area, but you are considering attending more Mennonite gatherings. And that's something I can't handle by myself. But it's more than that . . ."

"And you need Jesse's help?"

"*Yah,* Katie. I admit the fact."

Katie held her breath for a long moment. "*Mamm,* I won't stop going to the Mennonite gatherings because of what you and Jesse plan. I do want you to marry him. In fact, I'm very excited about it. But I don't believe you should agree to marry him because of me."

Mamm touched her arm. "Don't worry, Katie. I believe things will turn out okay. Jesse and I spoke for a long time last night. We both agree that our problems can best be handled together."

"What problems?" Katie asked and then winced as the thought hit her. "Am I now a problem?"

"*Nee,* Katie," *Mamm* said. "Jesse has problems with his children. They need a *mamm* just as you need a *daett.*"

Katie took a deep breath. "You're not telling me everything, *Mamm.* What is it?"

Mamm was silent, so Katie continued. "Well, then when is the wedding? Or is that also a big secret?"

A shadow crossed *Mamm*'s face. "We haven't decided yet. But soon. We won't be waiting too long."

Katie caught the look and said, "*Mamm*, why are you troubled? You had best tell me."

"It's not what you think." *Mamm*'s eyes sought Katie's face. "Please, just trust Jesse and me on this."

Katie waited, not moving.

Mamm stiffened. *Oh, please forgive me, dear* Hah, *but I can't keep this from my daughter.* She faced Katie. "The truth is that most of Jesse's children don't want me as their *mamm.*"

Katie froze and then half turned around. The two cows behind her were bathed in the morning sunlight streaming through the barn window. Hanging from the ceiling, the gas lantern hissed, its light a feeble effort against the power of the sun. Bossy switched her tail and snapped Katie on the arm. The pain stung just like *Mamm*'s words. They went deeper than the pain in her arm — even to her very soul, turning there into a flaming fire of shame.

Of course Jesse's children didn't want *Mamm*. She should have guessed it. *Mamm* was Emma Raber, which was even worse than being Emma Raber's daughter. That would also mean they didn't want Katie in their family either. This miracle had more thorns than any rose she'd ever seen. Why was *Da Hah* making them go through this?

"It's not as bad as it sounds," *Mamm* said. "Jesse and I talked this through. I won't tell you everything he told me, but I believe everything will be okay. I'm going over to spend time with his children soon. Jesse thinks we should start getting to know each other better as quickly as we can."

Katie knew shock was written all over her face, and she couldn't help the words that came out of her mouth. "You're going over to meet people who don't like you? How can you do that, *Mamm*? They're not going to change their minds."

"They're Jesse's children," *Mamm* said. "They will do what their *daett* tells them."

"Does Jesse think children are just little people who can be pulled around by strings?" Katie asked. "How can he put all of us in this situation? It's not right."

"It'll be okay." *Mamm* swung her bucket of milk. "That's all I can say about it now."

Katie had no response, so *Mamm* continued. "That's enough about it. We'll just have to trust *Da Hah*. And now we must finish the chores or you'll be late for work."

Katie remained silent as they worked. She threw down hay for the horses and turned the cows out into the barnyard. Her emotions were in turmoil. This couldn't end well. She thought of Mabel. She had such a fierce will. Mabel as a friend would be a *wunderbah* thing, but Mabel against her would be an awful problem. Katie had wanted a *daett* so badly, but now she could see the wedding . . . *Mamm* and Jesse saying the marriage vows. Afterward, they would all move into the same house, and Mabel would be scowling at her across the breakfast table each morning. Mabel might have to accept her *daett*'s decision on whom he married, but she wouldn't have to open her heart to either Emma or her daughter. Hearts were things that couldn't be pried open by man. She knew that from experience.

Yah, she'd wanted this, but now that it was here, her trust in *Da Hah* had fled far away. There was no way she could live in a house where she would always be disliked and known only as Emma Raber's daughter. Here at least she lived as Katie, and the Raber name only followed her outside these walls. Now *Mamm* was asking her to move where it would follow her into the most private sanctuary of her life. No Amish boy would ever want to bring her home to such a place.

"Come!" *Mamm* pulled on Katie's arm. "A *gut* breakfast will give us both courage."

Katie said nothing as she followed *Mamm* into the house. It would take much more than a *gut* breakfast to solve these problems.

CHAPTER TWENTY-FIVE

During breakfast Katie and *Mamm* continued their talk. *Mamm* told her more of the things Jesse had said last night. He'd spoken about *Da Hah*'s leading and of love growing again in their hearts. Jesse said that nothing was impossible with *Da Hah,* and that this could well be a miracle straight from heaven. The words sounded strange coming from *Mamm,* but Katie already believed them in her own heart, so there was really nothing to disagree with.

How fast things could change! It almost made one's head spin. And maybe that was the way *Mamm* had felt about her not that long ago. She imagined that could be possible. One thing she knew for sure — *Mamm* had finally opened her heart to Jesse's love, even if it was for the wrong reason. But Katie wasn't going to cut off her relationships with Margaret and Sharon just because of this. Especially not with the problem of Jesse's children ahead of her. Now more than ever she needed *gut* friends. Besides, that wasn't the way *Da Hah* worked. He didn't begin something of value only to throw it away the next day. Her new friendships with Sharon and Margaret were definitely something of great worth . . . and from *Da Hah* Himself.

"You have a good day now!" *Mamm* said after they'd hitched Sparky to the buggy and Katie had climbed in. "I'm thinking things will work out okay."

"I'll see you this evening," Katie said, trying to smile. She left the buggy door open and waved to *Mamm* as she went out the lane and turned toward the Royal Farms intersection. She allowed Sparky to take his time. Even with the extra moments spent talking with *Mamm,* she wasn't running late. Katie sat back in the buggy seat and allowed the morning air to flow over her face. It felt so *gut* to relax after the news *Mamm* had told her about Jesse's children. *Mamm* had tried to put a positive and hopeful spin on the subject by saying Jesse could handle things. But Katie knew that her *mamm* dreaded facing Jesse's children. All the signs were there when *Mamm* thought she wasn't looking. The silent stare and the worried look when any mention of Jesse's children came up. *This is not going to work,* Katie told herself. But just as quickly the thought raced through her mind, *Maybe I'm wrong.* Maybe Jesse's children would accept them in the end. *Mamm* seemed so sure they would. Maybe *Da Hah* would touch the lives of Jesse's children in the days ahead and bring about change. That would also be a miracle. So many had been happening already, could there be another one? Katie sighed. She would wait and see if *Mamm* was right. If Jesse persuaded his children to change their minds, it would be a *wunderbah* thing to attend church on Sundays and the hymn singing in the evenings and have people think of her as Jesse and Emma Mast's daughter.

Katie looked up to see a buggy approaching. She froze on her seat. It was Ben Stoll's buggy. Ben must be working out in this direction again. All of the feelings for Ben came rushing back. Would he wave this morning? Katie held her breath as the buggy went past. A faint flicker of an arm flashed in the window of the passing buggy after she waved. *Yah,* Ben had noticed her. He really had! And he had waved!

Katie tried to slow the pounding of her heart as the sound of Ben's buggy died away. Maybe this was another sign of what

Da Hah was doing. Where might this end? Katie let happy thoughts flow over her as she passed Bishop Jonas Miller's place. The bishop's *frau,* Laura, was coming out of the barn. She paused to wave at her. Katie pushed the buggy door open and wildly waved back. Let Laura think what she wanted. And let Mabel despise her if she wanted to. *Da Hah* was on her side.

Katie arrived moments later at Byler's. She unhitched Sparky and tied him at his usual spot along the back fence. An *Englisha* car roared in behind her, and Katie jumped. Esther always did like a grand entrance, and this morning Katie was glad for it. It matched her own happiness. She waited until Esther had parked and climbed out of her car.

"It's so good to see you this morning!" Esther gushed. "It seems like a year ago since I saw you even when I know it was only yesterday."

Katie smiled and nodded. With Esther, it wasn't necessary to speak a single word. She apparently had plenty to say all by herself as she chattered away.

"There's so much going on, it seems. There's another gathering later this week, and with all the busyness at work . . ." Esther led the way toward Byler's employee entrance.

"There is a lot going on," Katie agreed when Esther had stopped talking long enough to catch her breath.

Seconds later Esther's stream of words began again. "There's this big shindig this Saturday night at our place, and I'm inviting our youth group and some other special people."

Katie was walking fast, trying to keep up and listen at the same time.

"Anyway, we're roasting hot dogs and marshmallows over a bonfire after we cut wood at Widow Grace Harmen's place. We'll sit around and eat, and talk, and have a grand time. I'd like you to come. If you will, I'll pick you up at 6:30."

"I would love to come!" Katie said as they went in the store. "It's nice of you to invite me even though I'm not really part of your youth group."

"Oh, you are almost," Esther assured her. "I know Margaret and Sharon would be really disappointed if you didn't come. I was on the phone twice with Sharon since the birthday party, and she asked about you both times. And the gathering is for a worthy cause — helping an elderly widow get enough wood in for the winter. I wouldn't think of not having you there."

"I . . . um . . ." Katie swallowed hard. She planned to go, but she didn't wish to leave the wrong impression by being too eager. She still had roots in her old life.

"I won't hear any objections," Esther interrupted. "And if you don't come, I'll tell Roy. He'll come down and pick you up personally. Now what would your mother think if a Mennonite boy pulled into your front yard to pick you up?"

"You wouldn't!" Katie gave a nervous laugh.

"Oh, yes I would!" Esther said, smiling over her shoulder as she raced away.

Yah, she would indeed, Katie thought as she watched Esther disappear behind the deli counter. She would accept Esther's offer — even if it meant another *kafuffle* with *Mamm.* Katie was going to walk through the door *Da Hah* was opening for her.

"Good morning!" Arlene said from right behind her.

Katie jumped again.

Arlene laughed. "Thinking about some charming young fellow now that you're running around with the Mennonites?"

Katie tried to get a quick laugh out, but it sounded more like a snort.

"The time is coming closer, you know," Arlene went on, "when some charming fellow takes you home — whether he's Mennonite or not."

When Katie didn't say anything, Arlene continued her teasing. "Your heart is going to go pitter-patter all the way home."

"Stop it," Katie said with a smile. "Nothing like that is going to happen. My friends are all girls."

"Ah, so you're going to play hard to get then."

"Quit it!" Katie said. "It's not like that at all."

Arlene smiled but didn't say anything more.

Katie took her place at the register, and moments later Mrs. Cole appeared, greeting them cheerfully.

"Good morning, girls. I hope everyone is ready to go. It's going to be a big day again. Our anniversary sale begins today."

"*Gut* morning," Katie said. "I'm ready!" And she was, Katie thought, even if she faced some tough days ahead.

Katie received her first customer moments later. A younger woman with a baby sitting in her cart sucking on his thumb. "Hi there," Katie cooed. The baby broke into a big smile, his thumb falling into his lap. "What's his name?" Katie asked as she rang up the woman's items.

"Travis," the young mother said. "He'll be two tomorrow, and he's doing really well with our early morning shopping trips. I've found that's the best time for him. I guess he'll be a morning person like I am."

"Of course he's doing well." Katie put her face close to Travis and smiled at him. "What a sweet little darling."

Travis responded by sticking his thumb back in his mouth and staring at her for the rest of the time it took to complete the checkout. He was still staring at her as his mother rolled him out of the store. Katie waved to them until they vanished in the parking lot.

All morning the line of customers never stopped, just as Mrs. Cole had predicted. By 11:30, Katie's fingers were numb. Thankfully lunchtime wasn't far away. There was only one more customer in her line, and after that she planned to shut down.

"Hi!" Katie snapped out the greeting without looking up.

"Hello," a boy's voice said.

At the sound, Katie jerked up her head. "Roy!" she exclaimed.

Roy laughed. "I didn't mean to startle you. I was just picking up my lunch from Esther back at the deli. I'm trying out one of the glorious sandwiches she keeps talking about."

"Sorry I didn't notice you before," Katie admitted as she collected herself. "I guess I'm a little tired. It's been busy all morning."

"That's okay," Roy said. "Esther told me you might come to the gathering Saturday night. We're going to cut wood for widow Grace Harmen's winter stockpile and then go to Esther's to relax and eat. We'd all love to have you come."

"*Yah,* I'm planning to," Katie said as she rang up his purchase.

"I'll look forward to seeing you then." Roy paid Katie, picked up his sandwich, and left.

Everything was pointing in the right direction, Katie decided as she shut down her register. *Da Hah* was on her side, sending her encouragement along the way. How else did she explain Roy stopping by to give her a special invitation to Esther's gathering? And Ben Stoll had waved to her this morning. How *wunderbah* was that? "Thank you, dear *Hah,*" Katie whispered, a smile playing on her face. Someday *Mamm* would understand what she was doing by attending the Mennonite youth gatherings. She would have to.

CHAPTER TWENTY-SIX

The Friday afternoon sun beat down on Jesse as he moved bales of straw from the barn to spread in the horse pens. Leroy and Willis had already left for the house and were likely waiting impatiently even now for supper to begin. Well, they could wait a few moments longer. They were young and needed to learn that patience is a virtue, he decided. Jesse closed the stall door just as one of the workhorses snorted.

"Wanting some oats for your evening dessert?" Jesse asked out loud. "Well, I think you've earned a little, though if I give you some I'll have to give everyone oats. But then I guess you've all earned a little extra by working in the fields so hard today, haven't you?" He dished out a small amount of oats into all the feeder boxes. The workhorses plunged their noses in, chewing with vigor. Jesse watched them a moment before returning to his musings.

The children should have been told by now that Emma was coming over tonight. In fact, he should have mentioned it this morning right after breakfast. But he couldn't bring himself to speak the words. Not that he was having any doubts about marrying Emma, but waiting until the last moment to tell the children couldn't do any harm. It might lessen the time tempers had to gather into storms.

The truth was that the family had to move on. Millie was gone, and Emma was the right *frau* for him, even though the children would object and say she wasn't the right *mamm* for them. It would be his job to persuade them otherwise. He admired Emma's strength and courage. Plus her honesty on why she'd agreed to the marriage hadn't been necessary, but it was *gut.* She could just as easily have agreed to his proposal and left him in the dark as to the real reason. But Emma had told him everything.

The love in his heart was growing by leaps and bounds for this shy and mysterious widow. Ezra had obviously won her heart, and surely he also could. She would be as much of a treasure as Millie had been. That *Da Hah* was willing to allow him a second chance at love was almost too much to believe. How so much grace could be given to one man was beyond him. But *Da Hah* was known for His plenteous supply, was He not?

Jesse closed the barn door behind him and hurried across the front yard to the washroom door. He'd taken up enough time. He stepped inside and heard low voices rising and falling in the kitchen. He listened while he washed, but he couldn't make out the words. Jesse dried his hands and face before he pushed open the washroom door. Silence fell in the kitchen.

"Supper ready?" he asked.

"Yah." Mabel was now all smiles. "I have mashed potatoes tonight — and gravy. For meat we have some steaks I fried. I know they should probably be done differently, but I don't know how."

"I'm sure the food will be excellent," Jesse said, pulling out his chair.

Jesse sat down and was bowing his head when he paused. Why were they all looking at him when they should be getting ready for prayer?

"What is it, Mabel?" he asked since she seemed the focal point of this mysterious staring. Leroy and Willis had slight smiles on their faces, but Mabel and Carolyn were beaming from ear to ear.

"Teacher Ruth is coming over after supper tonight," Carolyn announced, taking up the role as spokesperson. "Friday nights work best for her, she told me. She's coming to teach Mabel how to bake her *wunderbah* pecan pies."

Jesse swallowed hard. "Ruth Troyer is coming here . . . tonight? Who invited her?"

Jesse had visions of Ruth working in his kitchen as Emma drove her buggy down the lane. There would be words spoken between the two women he didn't wish to hear. There might even be feelings stirred up that *Da Hah* Himself would have difficulty making right again.

"Daett," Mabel was saying, the word dangling in the air, "no one invited her. Today at school she said something to Carolyn about coming, and Carolyn knew how badly I want to learn how to bake pecan pies, so she mentioned that. Then Ruth said she'd come over after supper. She would have come this afternoon, but she had piles of papers to grade and couldn't get away."

Jesse groaned. The schoolteacher was going to be the ruin of him yet. If he didn't get her stopped there would be disaster ahead — and that was putting it mildly.

"Surely you don't mind," Mabel continued. "You can sit in the living room and read *The Budget* like usual. If things go late, you can go to bed. We won't bother you at all. Ruth said she doesn't mind what time we get done, and I don't either. I'm more than willing to lose some sleep to learn how to make those pies for you."

"Won't that just be great?" Carolyn piped up.

"Can we pray now?" Leroy asked. "Pecan pies are all fine and dandy for the future, but I'm starving right now."

"Yah!" Willis added his agreement. "There won't be any pecan pies to eat tonight anyway. Not if I know women. They'll have to cool before they let us close, and I'm not staying up that late."

"You certainly won't!" Mabel snapped. "You'll wait for supper tomorrow night, and you'll also wait until *Daett* has sampled one. I want him to have the first bite."

Jesse cleared his throat. "Ah, children, I don't think this is going to work out. I don't want Ruth coming over tonight. I had something else planned."

"Daett!" Mabel protested. "You know I want to learn how to bake pecan pies."

"There will be other times to learn how to bake pies," Jesse told her. "Tonight is not the night."

Mabel didn't say anything more.

Jesse took a deep breath and said, "Can

we pray now?" He bowed his head again, but Carolyn spoke up before he could begin.

"Teacher Ruth will be here any minute."

Jesse sighed. "I suppose so." He got to his feet and checked out the kitchen window, but he couldn't see a buggy coming. He turned back to face them. "Someone will have to drive up to the schoolhouse right now and tell Ruth that it doesn't suit us tonight to have company. She can come some afternoon, but not tonight."

There was silence in the kitchen as they all looked at him.

"And it needs doing right now," Jesse said. "Carolyn is right that Ruth may already be on her way."

Jesse glanced at Leroy first and then at Willis. There was no way he could go himself. What a sight that would make — him riding to the schoolhouse after hours when anyone who saw him would know Ruth was there alone.

"You're surely not going to send one of us?" Leroy said. "I'll die if I don't get some of Mabel's steaks pretty soon. I've been starving since four o'clock."

"I guess neither of you will be going then." Jesse sat down again. His doom was sealed. And Emma hadn't even arrived yet.

Willis shuffled to his feet. "I'll go, *Daett*.

It's not that far."

"What a saint," Leroy muttered, also rising. "Let me at least help you get the horse ready."

They were young and would survive. Jesse watched their broad backs disappear through the washroom door.

As Jesse readied for the third time to pray, the washroom door opened and Leroy walked in, followed by Willis.

"We're too late. Ruth is already here," Leroy announced. "Her buggy is rolling in now."

"Are you sure?" Jesse leaped to his feet. "It could be . . . someone else."

"It's her buggy, I'm certain," Leroy said.

Jesse didn't move, his hands grasping the edge of the kitchen table. Now what was he supposed to do?

"Can we eat?" Leroy asked. "My stomach has about given up and is now eating its own flesh."

"*Yah, Daett.* I agree with Leroy," Mabel said. "Supper is getting cold. Perhaps Ruth can even join us."

"She will not join us," Jesse said before bowing his head. He began his prayer. "Our great and merciful Father, creator of the world and all that lies in it. Look tonight upon our poor, weak hearts and give us Your grace for another evening. Give us Your blessing on this food, and bless the hearts and hands that have prepared it. I thank You for Mabel and Carolyn and the boys and all the work they do around the place. Forgive us where we have failed You. Watch over us this evening and during the hours we sleep, that we may awaken to another morning to serve You again. Amen."

Leroy dove for the potato bowl almost before Jesse was through speaking. The boy heaped a great pile on his plate. He passed the bowl to Willis and reached for the gravy Mabel had waiting for him.

"*Daett,* please eat your supper," Mabel said. "I'm sure Ruth will sit in the living room quietly until we're finished. That is, if you still won't invite her to join us."

"All right then," Jesse said. "I'll invite her to supper, but then I'm leaving. I have things I have to do."

He left the table and the astonished looks on the faces of his children. There wasn't a minute to spare, he figured. Emma might already be on her way to his place, and there was obviously no way Ruth was going to be talked into leaving. Her tongue would wrap around any objection he came up with.

Jesse left through the washroom and headed across the lawn. He met Ruth crossing over to the house.

"Well, *gut* evening," she cooed.

"*Gut* evening," Jesse replied, his eyes looking cold, he was sure. "I just learned from the children you were coming."

"I hope I'm not causing any inconvenience." Ruth's hands fluttered about. "Mabel does so want to learn how to bake pecan pies. You know, the ones *you* love."

"I know," Jesse said. "The children are still eating supper. Why don't you go in and join them? Mabel will be available afterward for her lesson."

"And you?" Ruth's eyes were bright. "Have you eaten?"

"*Nee,*" Jesse said. "I have someplace I have to be. If I'd known you were coming . . ."

"Oh . . ." Her hands fluttered again. "Maybe next time. Perhaps we could arrange things better."

"Perhaps, but why don't you go on inside now? Mabel is expecting you."

Jesse turned and walked into the barn. He closed the door behind him. He took Lucy out of her stall and strapped the harness on her, all the while muttering, "That woman will be the death of me."

CHAPTER TWENTY-SEVEN

Emma drove her buggy slowly toward the Mast place, allowing her horse to take his time. Tears formed in her eyes, and she brushed them away. Jesse and the children didn't need to see her all tear-stained when she arrived. Jesse would think she was troubled over her agreement to marry him, and the children would wonder what was wrong. In reality, Emma was upset at Katie's announcement when she arrived home from work earlier this week.

"I'm going with Esther to a shindig at her house on Saturday night — after the youth group does some charity work," Katie had said as soon as she walked through the door.

"I wish you wouldn't," Emma had said. "Jesse is going to be your *daett*. He'll be what you told me you wanted."

"That's all fine and *gut*," Katie had said. "But I'm still attending the Mennonite youth gatherings."

Emma had pressed her lips together and held in the words that wanted to leap out of her mouth. *You can't do this, Katie! No one ever comes back who gives in to the Mennonites.* But words like those would only drive Katie away. Why couldn't Katie be less impulsive? Why was she throwing so much of her life right out the door? But Emma was trying to change her ways — and speaking less of her mind to Katie might be part of that.

A movement ahead of Emma interrupted her thoughts. It was a buggy, and whoever was driving toward her was pushing hard. The horse was almost breaking into a gallop. Any young man wouldn't do that to his horse, and older men usually weren't in such a hurry. So who could this be? Emma's hands tightened on the reins as the buggy came closer. She pulled toward the ditch. Whoever this was, he needed plenty of room to pass.

Instead of keeping up the rapid pace, the buggy slowed. When it neared, the door flew open. Jesse leaned out, waving his hand.

Emma gasped and pulled to a stop. She leaned out of her buggy, waiting while Jesse climbed down and came running toward her. He looked troubled. Had there been an accident? She breathed slower and held her horse steady.

Jesse approached her open buggy door.

"What is it?" Emma asked, leaning further out the buggy.

"There has been a change in plans," Jesse said. "It's not going to suit for us to meet with the children tonight."

"Okay." Emma managed a smile. "I can come some other night. What is it? Relatives stopping by? Did they chase you out of the house? You sure were in a hurry."

"Not exactly . . ." The troubled look grew worse on his face. "Let's say one of the children's friends showed up. They claimed it was the only night that would work."

Something didn't seem quite right about his explanation, and Emma wondered if Jesse was telling her the whole story.

"I'm very sorry about this," Jesse continued, obviously sensing the question racing through her mind. "It's just best if you don't come to the house right now. We'll try to speak with the children some other night. Perhaps first thing next week."

"What if this friend shows up again?" she asked, watching as he winced at the question. He was definitely hiding something.

"I don't think she will," Jesse managed. "I'll tell the children she's not to come back again."

"Oh, so this visitor is a *she*. And *she's* the children's friend. Is she also your friend?"

"Like I said, I'm sorry." Jesse wasn't looking at her now. "I had no idea this would happen . . . really."

"Perhaps you'd better tell me who this woman is?" Emma tried to smile.

Jesse blinked before looking away. "It's kind of hard to explain. But there's really nothing going on, believe me, Emma. She's just the children's friend."

"You said that before, but you haven't said who she is."

"Please, Emma." His eyes begged for mercy. "It makes no sense to me either. Why my children are the way they are or how they've gotten me into this fix tonight, I'm not sure. I will straighten it out. I really will."

"Please tell me who is at your house," Emma said softly. "I need to know."

He didn't answer right away. "Look, Emma. I haven't had any supper yet. We were already running late before this person came. This is a little too much for me to deal with tonight. Tomorrow I'll come over and explain to you. She's leaving as soon as she's done teaching Mabel how to bake pecan pies."

"She's teaching your daughter how to

bake *pecan* pies?"

He was obviously searching for the right words. "*Yah,* but it wasn't my doing. It just happened — between Mabel, and Carolyn, and her. It's Carolyn's teacher."

"Ruth Troyer? She's baking pecan pies at your house tonight?"

"It's not what you think, Emma. Please . . ."

"Then why is she still at your house?"

Jesse tried to laugh. "That's exactly what I mean. She's still there because of the children. But she won't be for long, and she won't be back."

Emma stared into the distance, tears not far away. "So this is what has been going on all the time? You haven't told me the whole truth, have you, Jesse?"

He lifted his hand in protest. "Just wait a minute, Emma. That's not true at all. If it were true, I wouldn't object to you coming down to my house."

"I think I'd better go, Jesse." Emma pulled on the reins and turned her horse around in the middle of the road. Emma managed to control her emotions enough to swivel around on the buggy seat to look back. Jesse ought to be in his buggy by now and heading for home.

Emma gasped at the sight behind her.

266

Jesse wasn't returning home. He was coming after her, and his horse was almost galloping again. She slapped the reins and picked up speed. Minutes later she looked back again. Jesse was even closer now.

"Get up!" Emma hollered. Her horse laid his ears back and increased his speed. She had to get away from Jesse and the pain that was throbbing in her heart. But her horse couldn't keep this speed up for long. He wasn't that young, and neither was she, Emma decided. And what if someone saw her and Jesse Mast tearing through the community like two young people racing on a Sunday night after a hymn singing?

Emma pulled back on the lines before checking on the buggy behind her again. Surely Jesse wouldn't be crazy enough to come alongside her and try to speak with her. Well, if he did, she wasn't stopping. What had she been thinking? Emma slowed down even more as her lane came up ahead of her. Perhaps Jesse would drive on by. If he did, no one would know what had happened between them. He would appear to be on an evening errand. But if he followed her in . . . Emma held her breath as she turned down the driveway. She glanced back. *Yah,* Jesse's buggy was following. He was actually coming to her place. He had to know he was embarrassing himself, but he was still coming. Was he telling the truth? Was Ruth at his place for a reason other than what she'd assumed? Why else would a man make such a fool out of himself by following her home?

CHAPTER TWENTY-EIGHT

Ruth glanced around the kitchen table, taking in Mabel and Carolyn's smiling faces. Mabel had jumped up moments ago to refill her water glass, even though she'd tried to wave the girl away. If Jesse would only be this easy to win, her task would be an easy matter, Ruth thought. But the man was not cooperating.

Ever since Joel had let slip in school that his *daett* thought they all needed a new *mamm,* she'd jumped into action. But a lot of *gut* that was doing. She was apparently making no headway at all. And now Jesse had gone rushing off to somewhere unknown the minute she arrived for the evening, even murmuring about not having eaten his supper. If she'd been wise, she would have started work on winning him months ago. By now they might even be married, if she'd acted sooner.

Now not only had Jesse left so abruptly,

but there was something else amiss here. Mabel was smiling, but she had a distant look in her eyes. The same went for Carolyn. Did they know where Jesse had gone in such a rush? Was his departure due to her presence? If so, she needed to know. But would it be proper to ask? And how would she ask?

Ruth studied Leroy's face. He was busy chewing on the last of his steak. He had avoided looking at her since the moment she arrived, so the boy must know something and was trying to hide it.

Taking a deep breath she looked toward Jesse's empty plate at the head of the table. She turned to Leroy. "Is your *daett* coming back anytime soon? I see he hasn't eaten yet."

"I don't know," Leroy said without looking up. "*Daett* didn't tell us how long he would be gone."

Did she dare ask more? *Yah,* she did. "Does he do this often?"

"No," Mabel said at once. The other children nodded their agreement. "He just had to take care of something."

"And you don't know what it is?"

No one said anything, and Mabel looked close to tears.

"Where could he have gone without eating his supper?" Ruth asked. "Surely one of you has some idea where your *daett* went?"

"He sometimes goes over to see Emma Raber," little Joel piped up. "Maybe he went to see her."

"Joel!" Mabel gasped.

"Well," Joel defended, "*Daett* does. And I know because I heard you and Carolyn talking about it."

"Is this so?" Ruth asked Mabel. "Your *daett* is seeing Emma?"

Mabel broke into tears. "Honestly, I don't know where *Daett* is. He's been acting so strangely lately. And, *yah,* he has been going over to see Emma Raber. He's even been talking to us about asking her if she would be his *frau.* All the while I can't even stand the thought of that woman taking *Mamm*'s place."

"Of course you can't," Ruth said, rising to put her arm around Mabel's shoulders. Mabel buried her face in Ruth's apron as sobs racked her body.

What a mess! Ruth thought. But thankfully the children were apparently not in agreement with their *daett*'s plan. In fact, they must be hurting worse than even she could imagine. Here their beloved *mamm* had died not that long ago, and now their *daett* was threatening to bring Emma Raber, of all people, into the house as their *mamm*.

"I can understand perfectly how you feel," Ruth said, giving Mabel a squeeze.

"I'm sure *Daett* has his reasons," Mabel said between sobs.

"And Mabel has been working really hard," Carolyn spoke up. "She's been running the whole household. Of course I help her, but *Daett* says it's too much for us."

"Come!" Ruth pulled both girls tightly against her in a hug. "You're both overworked, that's the problem. You'll feel better if you finish your supper and go into the living room. Tonight I'll take care of the dishes. You won't have to do anything."

"But I want to learn how to bake pecan pies!" Mabel wailed.

"Now, now," Ruth soothed. "Let me clean up the kitchen, and then we can see how you feel. You've already had a hard day, and pecan pies take a long time to make. I can see you're troubled tonight. I will come back some other Friday evening. Then we can work on them."

"I knew it!" Leroy exclaimed. "With all this fuss there won't be any pecan pies tomorrow."

"You're just spoiled!" Mabel jerked her head up from Ruth's apron. "I work my fingers to the bone for you, and that's all

272

you worry about — when we can have pecan pies for you."

"I didn't mean anything by it," Leroy said, backing off. "I'm sorry. And you do work hard for us."

Mabel sniffed and wiped her eyes. Ruth released her embrace of Mabel and Carolyn and retook her seat. So Jesse was clearly making serious advances to Emma Raber. Joel's remark wasn't as innocent as she had at first thought. The children were crying out for her help. For all Ruth knew, Jesse might have already asked Emma to marry him. He probably couldn't bring himself to tell his children the awful fact. Or was Emma putting Jesse off for some reason? But Emma wouldn't turn down an offer of marriage from Jesse Mast in a thousand years. She had nothing to lose by snatching up one of the most eligible widowers in the community. None of this made any sense to Ruth. But neither did Jesse rushing off and leaving his children alone the minute she arrived at his house.

"We have to keep the food warm for *Daett.*" Mabel interrupted her thoughts. "I'm sure he's coming back soon."

"Of course he is," Ruth agreed. There was no sense in making this look worse to the children than it might be. They'd already suffered enough. "We can keep the food warm in the oven, and keep his plate on the table."

Mabel nodded, smiling again.

"Now you two go into the living room to rest while I clean up," Ruth told both girls.

"I'm going to help," Mabel insisted.

"And so am I," Carolyn added.

"Can we please be excused?" Leroy asked from the back bench. "I don't have all night to sit here."

"Of course you can leave," Ruth told Leroy.

He didn't move. He just stared at her.

"We have to pray," Willis spoke up. *"Daett* never lets us leave the table without giving thanks to *Da Hah."*

"Oh, of course!" Ruth bowed her head at once. She knew they'd needed to pray, but her mind was all mixed up right now. Likely the children wouldn't hold this mistake against her since they looked confused themselves. The poor things. They really did need a *mamm* to take care of them, and she would be more than willing if Jesse would get his thinking cap set on straight. Some men were like that. They couldn't see anything even if it sat in plain sight right in front of their eyes. Jesse was wasting his time running after the widow Raber. The nerve of the man. He really was mixed up in his mind, and here she was worrying about a little thing like forgetting prayer at the table.

Da Hah would help her figure out what she needed to do. She couldn't afford to lose Jesse. She and Homer had never been able to have children — even though she'd often desired to gather a young one born in her own home into her arms. She'd wanted to see him grow up and sit at their table. How she'd longed with all her heart for that day while Homer was still alive. But the answer from *Da Hah* had always been *nee.*

Now the desire was stirring in her heart again. She wanted her own children, born as gifts from *Da Hah*'s hand. She should never have allowed her work at the schoolhouse to take her eyes off what she really wanted. Ruth took a deep breath and pronounced, "Amen."

Leroy and Willis's heads came up at once. They leaped to their feet and disappeared upstairs. Joel smiled at Ruth for a brief moment before following his brothers. Ruth rose and tried to shoo the two girls out of the kitchen again, but they stood their ground.

"We want to learn how to make pecan pies," Mabel said again.

Ruth gathered both girls into a big hug,

squeezing so hard Carolyn giggled. Ruth turned her face away as tears sprang up in her eyes. She'd always wanted girls to call her own. Now here they were, no longer babies but still young enough for her to mother. Perhaps this would be just as *gut* as having her own children.

She could begin to win Jesse by wrapping her arms of love around his children. They still needed things from her — even if it was only instructions on how to make pies. Later there would be many other things she could teach them. And before long they would be young ladies, and the boys in the community would be making eyes at them. She could guide them through the maze of the feelings growing up created in a young girl's heart. Each day she would see that they got what daughters deserved. And only the best boys would be *gut* enough for her girls. Thank *Da Hah* she'd arrived in time. Whatever Jesse was up to tonight — including visiting Emma Raber — it would have to be stopped. It shouldn't be that hard to accomplish. Didn't she already have her foot in the door, so to speak?

Carolyn wiggled loose from Ruth's arms and began to take the dishes to the counter. Mabel went to the sink, filled the pan with water, and put it on the stove to heat. Well, she would join them, Ruth decided. Sometime soon Jesse would come home, and she would tackle the subject with him alone — whatever time of night that was. There was no way she was going to leave these girls alone tonight.

"I wish you could come more often," Mabel said, looking up at Ruth. "It feels so like home again with you here."

"Oh . . ." Ruth said, tears forming in her eyes, "I would so love that, Mabel. You have no idea how much I would. Both of you are such lovely girls."

"I don't know about that," Mabel said.

"Mabel smiled to Mose Yutzy the other Sunday," Carolyn announced.

"She did?" Ruth cooed as Mabel turned red. "Well, that's *wunderbah*. But aren't you a little young yet, Mabel?"

"It's not like he's asking me home," Mabel protested.

"But someday he might," Ruth said. "And that would be such a *gut* catch."

Mabel turned a deeper shade of red, and Carolyn laughed.

"Stop it!" Mabel snapped at Carolyn. "Or I'll rub it in once you smile to a boy."

"I'll hide my feelings better than you do," Carolyn said.

"Now, now, girls," Ruth said. "We're all

different and show our affections in different ways. There's no right and wrong in how we love those who are close to our hearts."

Both girls smiled at her and soon at each other. *It feels so* gut, Ruth thought, *to mother these children.* Already it was happening. They would flourish under her care, she was certain, as would the three boys. And perhaps *Da Hah* would still see fit, in His great mercy, to give her and Jesse a little *bobli* of their own. But she had to stop thinking about such things right now. Her face was getting a little red, and this would be hard to explain if Carolyn or Mabel noticed. First things first. Right now she had to take care of these girls, and then she'd wait until Jesse came home. Surely he would be home long before the pecan pie lesson was over. Jesse couldn't be gone for hours — not without supper in his stomach. No man was capable of such a thing.

CHAPTER TWENTY-NINE

Emma climbed down from her buggy. She tossed the reins out the storm front with a quick flick of her hand. She glanced back to see Jesse climbing down from his buggy and walking toward her, leaving Lucy standing in the middle of the lane.

Jesse approached Emma as she was unhitching. He kept his voice low. "Would you please let me explain?"

Emma took a moment before she looked up. "Could you explain better in the house, perhaps?"

Surprise must have shown on his face, Jesse thought, because Emma smiled. She tilted her head before saying, "Or on the swing, if you wish."

Jesse cleared his throat. This was quite confusing. Somewhere along the ride, the woman had changed. He recovered with effort. "I would love that."

"Are you going to tie up then?" Emma

glanced toward Lucy, who was standing in the middle the lane bobbing her head up and down.

Jesse nodded. He returned to the buggy to retrieve the tie rope from under the seat. While Emma continued unhitching, Jesse led Lucy to the hitching post and tied her up. He returned to Emma just in time to hold the shafts as she led her horse forward. He followed her to the barn and waited at the door. He almost offered his help with pulling off the harness, but decided not to. Emma was capable and might think he was taking liberties where they had not yet been given. He had been taking plenty of liberties, he acknowledged, but tonight was not the night to push things. He watched while she put her horse into a stall. Emma glanced at him as she walked to the barn door. What she was thinking was hard to tell. But what could he expect from a woman who had just discovered she had a rival camped out in her intended husband's home?

They walked to the house, and Emma motioned for Jesse to sit on the swing. She sat down beside him. Jesse heard his stomach growl and looked away. That was something he'd forgotten, but the awareness of his hunger was coming back now that he was no longer racing after Emma.

"That's right, you mentioned you didn't have any supper," Emma acknowledged.

Jesse grimaced. "True, but supper can wait."

"So . . ." Emma said, "you said you have an explanation for why Ruth Troyer is at your house tonight . . ."

Jesse coughed into his hand. "*Yah,* of course I have an explanation." He paused.

She waited quietly while he gathered his thoughts.

"I began to think about asking you to marry me many months ago, Emma. At that time I wasn't thinking about Ruth in the least. In fact, I didn't think of her at all other than as my children's schoolteacher." Jesse glanced in Emma's direction.

"I'm listening."

Jesse nodded. "What I'm trying to say is that I never had — nor do I have — a romantic thought about Ruth. All I know is that recently she's been stopping by after school, making friends with Mabel and my two youngest children, and in general making a pest of herself. Now tonight when I have the evening planned with you, it was announced at the supper table by one of the children that 'teacher Ruth is coming over' to teach Mabel how to make pecan pies."

"No woman comes into a man's house without encouragement, Jesse. Not even Ruth Troyer."

He sighed. "I did eat her pecan pie the other day. But it's the children, really, who may have encouraged her. They really like her. I'm planning to deal with the problem — if that confounded woman gives me a chance."

Emma laughed a little. "Ruth doesn't give chances. You should know that by now."

"I know." He reached for her hand. "Really, I'm sorry about all this. I suppose it's my fault. I'm not used to dealing with these . . . um . . . tactics, shall we say?"

She met his gaze. "I believe you, Jesse. I know Ruth Troyer well enough."

His hand tightened on hers. "Thank you."

"I realized on the way back home that you wouldn't be making such a fool out of yourself by chasing after me if you didn't care a lot. I overreacted earlier. A woman thing, I guess."

He stared at her. "Emma, I'm coming to think you do care for me . . . at least a little."

She smiled. "*Yah,* a little. But even so, I'm still tender around my heart. I guess that's why I flew off the handle like I did. And you'll have to deal with Ruth. She can't go on acting like she is."

"I know." He glanced about.

"And what about the children?" Her fingers held on to his arm. "Their feelings worry me. I can't force your children to love me. Especially if they've taken a shine to their teacher."

Jesse hung his head. "Perhaps I wasn't seeing things clearly, but you can win them over, Emma. Don't underestimate yourself."

Emma sighed. "This is new to me too, Jesse. You'll have to give me time. So will they."

He touched her face. "*Yah,* time is on our side. You'll see."

She dropped her eyes.

"*Da Hah* is with us, Emma. Don't forget that." He drew her close. "Now, I suppose I'd better go home and take care of my problem with Ruth. And you and I will schedule another night with the children."

She smiled. "*Yah,* you might be right. First, come inside. The least I can do is give you supper."

"There's supper waiting at home," he protested. "I know you weren't expecting company."

"You think I can't cook?"

He laughed. "Now you're sounding like Mabel — always worried you don't measure up. Of course I'm sure you can cook. But you don't have to tonight. It doesn't take me that long to drive home. Not any longer than it does for you to fix supper, I'm sure."

"Come in," she repeated. "I don't want Ruth Troyer feeding you supper."

He smiled. "Ruth will be long gone by the time I get there."

Emma gave a snort. "That's what you think. But let's not speak of her anymore." She rose and Jesse followed her example.

As they entered the house, Katie came out of the kitchen and made a dash for the upstairs.

"Please, Katie!" Jesse held up his hand. "Please join us while your *mamm* prepares some supper for me. I'd like to speak with you."

Katie stared at him before joining him on the couch. "So, is this your first lecture on me not running with the Mennonite youth group?"

"Katie!" Emma exclaimed after she gasped from the kitchen doorway.

"Well," Katie said, before Jesse could speak, "I'm not going to change my mind about going to Esther's gathering tomorrow night. I might as well get it out in the open."

"Katie, mind your manners now," Emma warned.

Katie lowered her gaze. "I'm sorry, but

the two of you did come racing in here like two teenagers."

Jesse chuckled. "That's okay. I suppose we do look a little old to be acting so young. But even adults have things to work out."

Katie looked at him. "So why is *Mamm* back so early? And why were you tearing after her in your buggy? Did the meeting with your children not go very well?"

"I don't think you should be asking any of these questions," Emma interrupted. "Please go upstairs, Katie, while I fix Jesse supper."

Katie leaped to her feet, but Jesse stopped her. "I don't want to go against your *mamm*'s word here, Katie, but I do want to speak for myself."

There was a moment's silence . . . until Emma nodded for Jesse to continue.

"It's like this. I have some things at my house that need taking care of. Things have gotten a little out of control, shall we say, and tonight your *mamm* didn't get to meet my children. Your *mamm* was very decent about understanding my problem, and I think we can work it out."

He waited as Katie seemed to think on what he'd told her.

"Okay, I see. But about Saturday night. I'm not going to change my mind. And I feel uneasy about how the two of you were acting tonight. It must have something to do with your children not liking *Mamm.*"

"I think I would feel very uneasy myself if I were in your shoes," Jesse said. "And I hope you enjoy your Saturday night out with your friends. What did you say their names were?"

"I didn't," Katie said, a look of surprise crossing her face. "But it's Esther, Margaret, and Sharon."

Jesse smiled. "I'm sure they're very nice girls."

"*Yah,* they are. I think you'd like them." Katie rose. "*Gut* night then — to the both of you."

"*Gut* night." Jesse turned toward the kitchen as the stair door closed. Emma was staring at him.

"Is that all you have to tell Katie? You hope she has a *gut* night at the Mennonite youth gathering?"

He shrugged. "*Yah.* I thought that was the best thing to tell her. I don't want to argue with her tonight."

Emma winced. "I was hoping you'd persuade her not to attend the Mennonite gatherings." Emma didn't wait for an answer before she disappeared into the kitchen. Jesse stood up and followed her, finding

Emma standing by the kitchen window and gazing out across the darkened lawn.

He slipped his hand around her waist and pulled her close. "I love you, Emma, and you love me . . . at least a little bit. Isn't that true?"

She didn't answer. She just laid her head against his shoulder for a moment before pulling away. Emma pointed to the kitchen chair. "Sit. I'll have something for you to eat in a minute."

Jesse obeyed while Emma rushed about the kitchen, setting the table, getting food out, getting pots and pans out, but never looking at him. His stomach growled again at the sight of the steaming meat casserole she pulled out of the oven fifteen minutes later.

"Eat!" she commanded, setting the casserole amongst the jam and butter bowls. He reached for her hand and Emma sat down beside him, bowing her head along with his.

"You do love me, don't you?" Jesse asked when they were done with the silent prayer.

Emma said nothing, but she met his gaze with tear-brimmed eyes. He reached over and gathered her in his arms for a long moment before letting go. She dished out his food and sat beside him while he ate.

Chapter Thirty

As Jesse drove home later that evening, he watched through the open buggy door as the stars twinkled on the horizon. Wild and giddy thoughts rushed through his mind. Emma had certainly shown him tonight at the kitchen table that she loved him, even if she continued to refuse to say so. He hadn't quite dared kiss her when he left, but it wouldn't be long before he would. He smiled at the added bonus that Emma was a decent cook.

Yah, he would have to deal with Ruth tonight. He must remain understanding with Ruth, he supposed. What else other than pies did Ruth have to work with in her effort to win his heart? He had to do something. Emma had understood his explanation tonight, but she was a woman and could take only so much. If Ruth kept hanging around, he couldn't expect Emma to keep her mind open about the matter.

He'd come close enough to losing Emma tonight. Thankfully, Emma had been impressed with his wild chase after her, though at the time he'd felt a bit foolish racing after her.

Jesse pulled back on the reins and stopped Lucy before turning into his driveway. In the semidarkness ahead, Ruth's buggy took shape. It was parked in the same spot it had been when he left. Well, what did he expect? Emma had warned him. Of course the woman was still here. And she was likely keeping Mabel and Carolyn up late baking pies when both children should be in bed. Carolyn had school tomorrow, and Mabel needed her sleep for the work she did at home.

Jesse pulled up close to the barn, jumped down, and unhitched. He took his flashlight out from under the buggy seat and led Lucy into the barn. He slipped off the harness, turned Lucy into her stall, and with the flashlight beam bouncing in front of him, walked out of the barn and made his way across the yard.

He paused to listen before opening the washroom door. There were no voices coming from the kitchen, and only the faint light of a kerosene lamp was shining under the door sash. Ruth had to still be here if her buggy was in the yard, but where were the two girls? Had she sent them to bed? Jesse pushed open the kitchen door. The smiling face of Ruth appeared at once. She was seated at the kitchen table with two pecan pies in front of her.

"Welcome back," Ruth whispered. "I already put the children to bed. I hope you don't mind."

Jesse stayed frozen by the door. Finally he spoke. "Why are you still here?" If she thought he was going to sit down and eat pecan pies with her at this hour of the night, she was sorely mistaken.

Ruth ignored the look of irritation on Jesse's face. She waved her hand toward the chair. "We need to have a talk, Jesse. Where have you been all evening?"

He remained standing, staring at her.

"Sit down," Ruth said, still smiling. "It's not decent for a man to dash all over the countryside in the evening when he doesn't have a *frau* home to take care of his five children."

It was as if she were quizzing a first-grader on his flashcards, Jesse thought. He didn't move.

She gave a little shake of her head. "It's the truth, Jesse. Even if I have to be the one saying it. Thank *Da Hah* I came by tonight when I did before someone else dropped in and saw the way you're using these children. It's a crying shame, Jesse. And an outright disgrace. The children told me you've even been doing this during the day-time — dashing over to Emma Raber's place for talks with her. Is that where you went to-night?"

Jesse gave up glaring at her and sat down. The woman would have to be dealt with, but this would be harder than he'd thought. She made him feel like he was still taking the bottle on his mother's knee.

"I'm glad you're listening to me, Jesse," Ruth continued, no longer smiling. "This is the first *gut* sign I've seen all night. I must say, I feel hope rising in my heart for your situation. Maybe this can be taken care of before your children are damaged worse than they already have been."

"What are you talking about?" Jesse finally managed to get out.

"You don't have to look at me like that. I'm the one who has been home with your children all evening while you've been out doing who knows what. Are you behaving yourself, Jesse?"

"Of course I am!"

"And have you had supper? Mabel insisted that we keep food out for you. For myself, I would have let you go hungry because, I do declare, sometimes even grown men never get out of their childhood."

"Emma fed me supper," Jesse said, watching Ruth's face.

"So you *were* there?" Ruth glared at him now. "What a disgrace, Jesse. Acting like that in front of your children. You're worse than a love-struck teenager."

Jesse was quiet for a moment. He got to his feet and said, "I'm going to take you outside to your buggy, and you can wait there while I get your horse. After that, I will hitch up for you, and you will drive on home where you belong."

"I'm not going anywhere, Jesse," she said. "Not until I've told you what's on my mind."

He leaned forward and said in voice loud enough to echo throughout the house, "I want you out of my house, Ruth Troyer. Right now!"

A look of horror crossed her face as feet upstairs landed on the floor with a loud thump and came running down the stairs.

"Look what you've done now!" Ruth hissed as the stair door burst open and Mabel's frightened face and tense body appeared in the opening.

"Is something wrong, *Daett*?" Mabel asked.

"Nee," he said. "Everything's fine, Mabel. I'm sorry I hollered. Now please go back to bed."

Mabel was taking in the situation, her eyes moving between the two of them.

"Please, Mabel," Jesse repeated. "Go back upstairs. Ruth and I need to finish talking."

Mabel didn't move, but her face brightened. "Did you see our pecan pies?"

"Yah," Jesse said. "They look *wunderbah*."

Mabel still wasn't leaving. "We haven't tasted them yet, *Daett*. We wanted you to be the first."

"That's very nice, Mabel. I'll try them tomorrow. Now go to bed."

"Ruth said they might be cooled enough to eat by the time you got home."

Ruth stood up. "Yes, dear, they are. But your *daett* has other things on his mind at the moment. I'm sure he'll enjoy the pies tomorrow night for supper."

Mabel disappeared a second later, and Jesse waited until her footsteps died away before he turned back to Ruth. "I meant what I said, Ruth. I want you to leave now."

She responded by sitting down.

"I'm not going anywhere until I've had my say."

What was he to do? Carry the woman out to her buggy? Of course not, but neither was he going to stay here and listen to more of her lectures.

"I've already told Mabel," Ruth said. "So there's no use hiding yourself from the truth."

He turned toward her. "You told my daughter what?"

"About Emma Raber's history — all the important points, at least. The ones that were fit for Mabel's ears. And believe me, it was enough to make for an awful lot of explaining on your part if you continue to insist on seeing Emma."

Jesse gripped the back of his chair. What was the woman referring to? Emma didn't have a rough past that he knew of — other than living alone and keeping to herself. Of course, there was that thing with Daniel Kauffman, but that was years ago.

"I know men are blind half the time when it comes to women," Ruth was saying. "And they can't see out of the other eye the rest of the time. But still you don't have to act surprised, Jesse Mast."

"Has anybody ever told you to mind your own business?" Jesse said between clenched teeth.

She smiled and folded her hands in her

lap. "Not when it comes to five motherless children — all of whom I love with my whole heart. And not when they have a *daett* who can't see what's plainly in their best interest."

He met her gaze. "If you think I'm going to marry you, Ruth, you are sorely mistaken."

Her face fell for a moment, but Ruth gathered herself together. "That is up to *Da Hah.* I have not said anything about marrying you, Jesse. It's the children I'm thinking about, and what's best for them. If you can find a decent woman in the community or from some other community, perhaps, who loves the children and whom they can love back as their *mamm,* I'll be satisfied. I know I'm not the only *gut* woman around."

He glared at her. "Whom I marry is none of your business."

"It *is.*" Ruth didn't blink an eye. "I'm their teacher. Well, Carolyn and Joel's, and the rest of them love me too. Until you can do better than that, I will be here for them."

Jesse's thoughts raced, but at the moment he didn't dare speak them. He finally turned toward her. "Tell me what you told Mabel about Emma."

Ruth's face beamed. "I'm glad to see you're coming to your senses, Jesse. I was wondering there for a moment."

He held up his hand. "Just answer the question."

"I'm not your pupil," she sputtered. "But for your children's sake I'll tell you about Emma. She has a history going all the way back to her young-folk days when she fell deeply in love with Daniel Kauffman. And storming out after his wedding right in front of the happy couple themselves. What a disgrace that was!"

"*Yah,*" Jesse said and paused. "And half the young-folk girls were in love with Daniel Kauffman. Thankfully Millie wasn't included amongst them."

"But not like Emma," Ruth insisted smugly. "Emma thought she could hide her love from everyone, but she lived and breathed for the slightest smile and word from Daniel. Even after Daniel began dating someone else, Emma hung around, refusing to let any other boy take her home. Only when Daniel married did she give up and marry Ezra. Of course, she was older by then. But her connection with Daniel at his wedding was plain for all to see."

"And what has that got to do with me and my own?"

"Why, Jesse, because she's taking you for the same reason. Because she can't find anyone else. If Emma did it once with Ezra, she'll do it again with you. Do you really want a woman like that as the *mamm* of your children? All the rest of us married for love, Jesse. I was so in love with Homer I couldn't see straight when he came around. Even when *Da Hah* didn't give us children, I loved him with all my heart."

Jesse stood up. "Come now, Ruth. It's time for you to go home."

"Does this mean nothing to you? Think about what — or whom — you are bringing into your house, Jesse. Think about your children."

"I will do that." He motioned toward the door. "Now it's high time for you to go home so I can get my sleep. I have a big day in the fields tomorrow, and I'm sure Mabel is probably lying awake upstairs worrying about us until we stop talking down here."

She didn't budge.

As Jesse moved toward her, Ruth jumped up. "You don't have to treat me like this. I'm only trying to help."

"And I thank you for the pecan pies." He led the way out the front door. "From now on, I don't want you stopping by. In fact, I forbid it."

"We will see about that, Jesse," she sputtered as she followed him across the yard.

"I will do what's right."

He left her standing by her buggy and went to retrieve her horse from the barn. He held the bridle once he had the horse hitched up as Ruth climbed into the buggy. He stepped aside and gave the horse a slap on its haunches. The horse lunged forward, and Jesse heard Ruth gasp as she drove past him.

She would be back, he knew, as he watched her buggy lights going down the road. Ruth Troyer still had a few tricks up her sleeve, if he didn't miss his guess.

CHAPTER THIRTY-ONE

Jesse rose well before dawn the following morning and climbed out of bed in slow motion. His head was still fuzzy, which was understandable considering all he'd been through last night. Women were enough to give any man gray hair, and Ruth was the worst. She had more nerve than a dozen foxes in one henhouse.

Jesse rubbed his head and dressed in the dark. He'd hoped things would look different after a *gut* night's sleep. Didn't they usually? But it was apparently not to be. Ruth's meddling still looked like the nightmare it was, even when he tried to convince himself she really did care for his children and couldn't be entirely blamed. But there remained just as much trouble this morning as there had been last night after her buggy lights had disappeared in the darkness. She'd be back, he was still sure of it. And no doubt she'd left in her wake terrible tales to poison Mabel's mind against Emma. What a mess this was indeed.

Well, some things would have to change around here, beginning with straightening Mabel out. Perhaps he could have a long talk with her, explaining that Ruth's opinion of Emma was a little misguided, especially considering her own interest in getting married. The situation was complicated by the fact that part of Ruth's tale was true. Emma had been, or thought she'd been, in love with Daniel Kauffman. That much made sense. And she had made that mad dash out of the wedding. But so what? In the end, Emma loved the man she married. Nothing he'd ever seen in Ezra and Emma's relationship had given any other indication. So Emma couldn't be faulted in the matter.

Jesse left his bedroom, opened the stair door, and hollered, "Time to get up! Everybody out!"

He didn't wait for a reply but walked over to light the gas lantern at the kitchen counter before he headed into the washroom. He paused as he heard light steps coming down the stairs. That would likely be Mabel, wanting to speak with him before the chores. And he needed to take the time for a few words with her. But the real conversation would have to wait until later.

There wasn't time now to counter Ruth's nasty news and opinion about Emma.

"The nerve of that woman!" Jesse muttered, stepping back into the kitchen. He greeted Mabel. "*Gut* morning."

"*Gut* morning, *Daett,*" Mabel said, wringing her hands. "Did Ruth tell you everything last night?"

Jesse sighed. The subject already made him weary. Maybe he ought to snap out orders like some *daetts* did instead of using persuasion on the hearts of his children. He could simply tell Mabel to accept what was going to happen. But that wasn't his way.

Mabel's eyes were pleading. "I wanted to speak about this when I came down last night. But I thought it was better if I waited until this morning when Ruth was gone."

"*Yah,* that was for the best," Jesse agreed, leaning against the doorframe. "Ruth didn't share anything I wasn't already aware of or that I care about. I think it best if we wait until after breakfast to speak at length about this. I don't want to rush through this with you because this is a very serious situation. It's important to me that we talk and get things straightened out."

Mabel hesitated, her face questioning. Then she relented and walked over to the counter where she began to take down the breakfast dishes.

"Be sure Carolyn gets up to help you," Jesse said before he left.

Mabel nodded.

Jesse walked across the lawn, swinging the lantern. When he pushed open the barn door, the first thing to meet his eyes was a smashed gate on a horse stall. The second shock was the listless form of one of his workhorses lying on the floor. An empty oat bag lay on the concrete floor with a few kernels still scattered around.

"What's going on here?" He hollered the question even though no one was around but the farm animals. He ran to the workhorse, grabbed its halter, and pulled up hard. The horse lifted its head, but it fell again when Jesse let go. Jesse ran over to the smashed gate, where he saw that most of the boards were broken inward. That could mean only one thing. Something from the outside had broken in. But what and who?

In a flash he remembered dragging Ruth's horse out of here last night. It had been dark, and his only light had been the flashlight. He hadn't looked around. His mind had been on getting the woman on the road, not on what her horse might have done inside his barn.

"Confound it all!" Jesse said out loud. "The nasty thing kicked down my gate."

Jesse looked around again. There could be no other answer. Ruth's horse had kicked the stall door, and from there the workhorse had pushed his way out and stuffed himself with grain. Jesse returned to the listless horse and pulled on the halter again. He succeeded in getting the animal up and walking a few steps. Behind him the barn door opened, admitting Leroy and Willis.

Jesse hollered, "Come over here boys, quick!"

The boys rushed over, and Jesse gave the halter to Willis. "Take this horse outside and see if you can walk this off. I don't believe the bag was more than half full. Leroy, grab a lead rope for your brother."

Willis took the halter while Leroy ran to get the lead rope. After giving it to Willis, he stared at the smashed gate. "What happened here?"

"Ruth's horse must have kicked the door in last night," Jesse said. "I didn't notice it when I took her horse out to hitch up."

"You didn't see something like this?" Leroy looked incredulous. "That's as plain as day."

Jesse wanted to tell Leroy he'd been distracted, that the woman had messed with his mind, but maybe it was best that Leroy didn't know about his troubles last night.

"I only had my flashlight," Jesse said instead.

Leroy didn't look convinced.

"Go, Willis!" Jesse motioned with his hand toward the back barn door. "We have to get that horse walking around. If necessary, run him around the barnyard. Anything to get that feed moving through the digestion cycle."

"Come on, boy!" Willis shouted as he snapped on the rope and pulled hard. With much straining he got the horse out the back door and started on the first go-round in the barnyard.

"What a woman," Leroy said, still staring at the smashed gate.

Jesse almost laughed, but he coughed instead. Leroy was already putting way too many things together. Soon he would be laughing at his *daett*. Jesse decided he'd better make a trip back to Emma's today and set the wedding plans in motion before anything worse happened. Would Emma be willing to rush the wedding date? Probably not. He'd have to let things run their course. And there was still much work ahead. For one thing, his children's hearts and minds needed to be persuaded.

"Come on," Jesse told Leroy. "We'd better begin the chores."

"I thought I heard shouting last night after I went to sleep," Leroy said. "Did you and Ruth have a fight or something? Was it somehow connected to this?"

Jesse laughed out loud this time. "We did have a frank discussion," he admitted. "But it had nothing to do with horses kicking in gates."

"I take it you're not getting along too well with the woman," Leroy observed. "Was that why you didn't see the smashed gate last night?"

Leroy was right, but Jesse didn't feel like admitting it.

His son didn't seem bothered by his *daett*'s silence and continued with his thoughts. "I think she's using Mabel's heart to wrap you around her apron strings. Maybe you ought to get rid of the woman before something worse happens than her horse kicking down the gate. She might take to burning down the barn."

Jesse laughed again. It felt *gut* to finally have one child on his side — and so suddenly. But then maybe it hadn't been so suddenly. Leroy was smart. They all were smart, even Mabel. It was just that her heart strings were being plucked by Ruth. Mabel

305

shouldn't be blamed for that woman's manipulation.

"I'm still going to enjoy her pecan pies tonight though," Leroy commented. "So maybe on second thought you ought to marry the woman so we can have pecan pies every day."

"Come on now," Jesse said through a smile. "Enough talk. We have to get these chores done without Willis's help. I expect we'll do good to save that horse without a large vet bill."

Leroy nodded and disappeared into the hayloft. Jesse took a quick look into the barnyard to check on Willis's progress. Willis was doing a great job. He was already moving the horse along at a brisk trot. "That's the way to do it!" Jesse hollered to Willis before going to open the gate for the cows. The cows pushed past him to get to the feed.

"I'm going back and forth, except I just walk him when I get tired," Willis hollered back. "Is that okay?"

"That's the best we can do." Jesse slapped the last cow as she stopped half in and half out of the doorway. The cow lunged forward, and Jesse followed her inside. With the cows eating, he closed the stanchions and then began the milking. Leroy soon came to help, and they finished only fifteen minutes later than normal.

Willis was still working the horse in the barnyard when Jesse let the cows out.

"How's it going?" Jesse asked.

"Okay." Willis slowed to a walk. "He's passed gas several times."

"That's what I was hoping for. Come on. We can go for breakfast now. I think the horse will be okay now. If things still look iffy after breakfast, you can walk him some more."

The three men walked back to the house and entered through the washroom door after cleaning up.

Mabel had the table laid out with eggs, bacon, oatmeal, and toast.

Jesse seated himself at the head of the table and bowed his head. They prayed silently and, after a few moments, Jesse said, "Amen." Mabel passed the plates of food around like usual, though Jesse noticed her face seemed drawn.

Behind them the first light of day came through the window, overwhelming the weak kerosene-fueled lamplight.

"When is teacher Ruth coming again?" Carolyn asked, breaking the silence.

Jesse cleared his throat. "I don't know, honey. But not very soon."

"I like having her here," Carolyn said. "She can make pies in just a jiffy. I don't think Mabel or I will ever learn how to make them that fast."

"It doesn't matter how fast you can make pies," Jesse said. "And you will see teacher Ruth at school."

"You don't like her pies?" Carolyn asked.

"Of course *Daett* does," Leroy answered the question. "Everyone likes pecan pies."

Carolyn didn't look satisfied. "I think Ruth wants to come and live here all the time. That is, if *Daett* will ask her to be our *mamm.* She could teach us how to make pecan pies fast someday."

"She'd probably burn down the house first," Leroy muttered.

Mabel gasped and flew to her feet. "Don't you be running down Ruth, Leroy. She is already as close to a *mamm* to me and Carolyn as we've had since *Mamm* passed."

"*Yah,* Leroy. Let's not tear someone down." Jesse kept his voice low. He had to soothe this situation or they would all be fighting each other before long. But Leroy wasn't paying attention to any soothing words.

"Well, I'm telling you that Ruth's horse kicked down our gate last evening. And for no *gut* purpose. And that nearly got one of

308

our workhorses killed by this morning."

"That's not possible!" Mabel shouted. "Neither Ruth nor her horse would do anything like that. At least not on purpose."

Jesse opened his mouth to say that Leroy was indeed telling the truth, but he changed his mind.

Leroy wasn't backing down either. "I think this woman is completely out of her place. I finally figured it out last night. Not that I was totally blind to her schemes before, but I see clearly now. That woman is using you and Carolyn to weasel her way into this home and get *Daett* to marry her."

Jesse raised his hand to silence Leroy.

Mabel's face was fiery red. "I want to tell you something, Leroy Mast. It's that Emma Raber who is causing all this trouble. Ruth told me all about her last night — how she was in love with somebody while they were all growing up. Emma followed the poor boy right up to his wedding day, trying to lure him away from his girlfriend. And then she shamed herself by making a scene at the wedding and driving out right in front of the bride and groom when they left the service."

Leroy blinked and looked away. "I'd not heard that," he said.

Mabel continued. "Then Emma lured a

new boyfriend into her clutches only weeks after the boy she loved married. She's like a spider, Leroy. A sneaky spider who is trying to catch *Daett* in her web. How else can you explain why *Daett* is so taken with Emma when Ruth loves all of us and would be our *mamm* tomorrow if *Daett* would only ask her?"

"Wow!" Leroy shook his head. "Thank *Da Hah* neither of them are after me."

Jesse stood up. There would be no talking with Mabel after breakfast as he had planned. She wouldn't be persuaded very easily, he could see that clearly now. Ruth had done her work thoroughly. It was high time he brought this conversation to an end. He motioned for silence. "I want to make something clear to all of you. I've asked Emma Raber to marry me and be my *frau*. And once she says the wedding vows with me, she will be your new *mamm*. And that's the end of the conversation and the end of the story. And I don't care what Ruth has to say about it or about Emma."

"What a story!" Willis added. "Can we at least eat the pecan pies this morning? A little sliver, perhaps?"

"I don't care." Jesse kept the smile off his face as he looked around at all of them. "Let me say this once again. I want to hear nothing more about Ruth Troyer or anything negative about Emma Raber. Got it?"

They fell silent as Jesse sat down and finished his breakfast. He was being a little rough, he figured, but he was tired of this. Ruth was getting under his skin, and a man could only take so much. The sooner the wedding vows were said with Emma, the better.

Mabel, he noticed, was making an attempt at hiding the pecan pies. He stopped her with a lift of his hand. "Cut those pies up, Mabel. And into big pieces."

"But it's breakfast time," she protested. "Pies should wait for supper."

"I want all that pie eaten now." He allowed his irritation to show.

Mabel glanced at his face and then rushed over to the counter for a knife.

Leroy was grinning from ear to ear.

CHAPTER THIRTY-TWO

"Here we are!" Esther's cheerful voice announced as they bounced to a stop beside a dilapidated barn. "Widow Grace Harmen's place, and it looks like everyone is here already."

Katie craned her neck to look at a long line of cars parked beside them. There were quite a few.

Katie clasped her hands in front of her, surprisingly feeling a bit overcome with a sudden case of shyness now that the planned Saturday youth gathering had actually arrived.

"Come on!" Esther's voice cut through her thoughts.

Katie climbed out of the car as Esther smiled her encouragement and asked, "Are you okay? You seem a bit . . . absent."

"I'll be okay," Katie said, straightening a wrinkle in her dress with a brush of her hand.

Esther's smile widened. "You look just fine, Katie. Better than any of the rest of us do."

Katie didn't say anything as she followed Esther across the yard.

A car door slammed beside them, and Katie jumped. It was Emery Yoder, the Amish boy from the community who had been at the last gathering. Tonight he had on a quite *Englisha*-looking pair of jeans adorned with a new belt and a nice T-shirt. Obviously Emery was on *rumspringa*. If *Mamm* could see him it would do nothing to alleviate her fear about Katie being here. Emery greeted her with the briefest of nods and was quickly chatting with Esther like they were old friends, which Katie was sure they weren't. Esther, though, could speak with any boy for hours, even one she barely knew.

Emery snapped open his car's trunk and hauled out a shiny new chainsaw. Esther gave an appreciative gasp. Emery shrugged as if this were nothing. "Borrowed Dad's chainsaw. He purchased a new one last week."

"Then maybe you'll let me take a turn?" Esther asked as she eyed the chainsaw.

Emery laughed. "Why? Do you think because it's new it'll be easier to handle?"

Esther made a face. "Of course not. I grew up handling chainsaws."

"I hear you're treating us to a feast over at your place after the woodcutting," Emery said. "Byler's premium sausage links and cheese-filled hot dogs. To say nothing of marshmallows by the pound."

Esther's laugh filled the evening air. "That's only for men who cut at least a cord of wood tonight and who personally haul loads of wood up to widow Harmen's woodshed without breaking a sweat."

Emery laughed. "And how do you propose to grade these heroic efforts?"

"I'll be keeping tabs on everyone!" Esther shot back.

Katie's thoughts drifted away from their banter. How like Emery to ignore her, making no attempt to include her in the conversation. But then she shouldn't be surprised. Emery was Amish, and this was only the second time he'd seen her in these new surroundings. And she was acting like she always did at the Amish youth gatherings — withdrawn and quiet. Emery couldn't be faulted.

They were approaching the edge of the woods now. A wave of sound assaulted their ears muffled only by the dense, surrounding trees. A few of the young people were standing along the edge of a fencerow. The boys mostly were carrying chainsaws and listening to an older woman speak.

The woman turned to greet Esther and Katie with a cheerful, "Good evening! I'm so glad you could all come out tonight. You don't know how much this means to me, having my firewood cut each year. It would cost me a fortune to hire someone. And I wouldn't be able to save a penny over the expense oil or gas would cost me. Thank you. Thank you so much!"

"That's perfectly okay," Esther said. "We're glad to help again this year, Grace. And don't you worry yourself for a minute." Esther studied the older woman for a moment. "Are you sure you should be out here tonight? The air could get chilly by the time we're finished . . . and with your arthritis and all . . ."

Grace dismissed Esther's objections with a quick wave of her hand. "It's good for me to get out of the house."

Esther nodded. "Grace, I don't think you've met Emery and Katie."

The older woman nodded to Katie and Emery. "Thanks so much for coming."

Esther asked, "Are you coming over to our place for the hotdog roast afterward, Grace?"

Before the woman could answer, Emery excused himself and headed deeper into the woods toward the roar of chainsaws.

"I'm afraid I'd better not tackle that much tonight," Grace said, her gaze lingering on Emery's retreating back. "What a nice young man — just like all of these young people. Is he your beau, Esther?"

Esther's laughter filled the woods. "I hardly know him, Grace. But from what I know, Emery's a nice man. He's Amish, like Katie here."

"Oh, Amish!" Grace turned her gaze on Katie. "Such nice people. Thanks for coming, Katie."

"You're welcome," Katie said with a bright smile.

"Well, I need to get to work helping," Esther said, patting Grace on the arm. "Now, if you get cold, you'd better go on back to the house. Do you want one of us to stay with you?"

Grace hesitated. "I'm sure all of you are needed to help carry out the wood."

From her voice, Katie could tell she wanted someone to stay with her. "You go on," Katie said to Esther. "I'll walk back to the house with Grace."

"Would you?" Esther's face lit up.

"Well, it would be nice to have someone

help me back to the porch, at least," Grace admitted. "Once I'm settled in . . ."

"I'll stay with you as long as you need me," Katie assured her, taking Grace's arm.

Esther gave Katie another grateful smile and disappeared into the woods.

Katie turned to lead the way back to the house, still holding Grace's arm. When Katie noticed the elderly woman was breathing hard, she slowed the pace.

"Thank you," Grace said. "I'm not young anymore. I guess that's difficult to admit once one gets old."

"You're doing fine," Katie said, giving her a warm smile.

As they neared the house, another car arrived. Katie waited while Grace greeted the two arriving boys with their chainsaws. It was Bryan and John, the ones who had played beside her at the volleyball game. They gave Katie a quick smile before moving on toward the woods. They had remembered her! Warm circles ran around Katie's heart. Their looks had carried the type of expression friends gave each other. They considered her, Katie Raber, a friend!

"Thanks for coming up with me," Grace told Katie when they reached the porch. "I think I'll sit right here and watch the proceedings for awhile."

"Can I get you something?" Katie asked. "A warm blanket?"

"No, you go on back now." Grace waved her hand in the direction of the woods. "I take care of myself all day long, and now that I'm here on my porch, I'll be fine. Young people need to be around young people, not around old fogies like me."

Katie smiled. "I'll stay if you wish."

"I won't hear of it." Grace dismissed Katie with another wave of her hand.

Katie retraced her steps and, with a final glance over her shoulder toward Grace, entered the woods, following the sound to where the chainsaws were roaring their loudest.

She finally found Esther.

"Is Grace okay?" Esther asked.

Shouting over the noise, Katie said, "She wants to sit on her front porch. She said she was fine and sent me back to work."

"Good. You can help over here," Esther said, leading Katie to where several of the girls were helping to fill low-slung trailers pulled by tractors. One was already filled and ready to head back to widow Harmen's woodshed. Several of the girls climbed on, but Katie stayed behind, moving over to work on the half-empty trailer. She caught sight of Margaret and waved. Margaret waved back and mouthed, "Good to see you."

Katie felt warm feelings flood over her again. And it wasn't just Margaret's greeting. It was also the warm acceptance she felt from everyone here.

For the next hour, the trailers kept making trips back and forth. As darkness began to fall, Roy Coblenz shouted, "That's enough for tonight. Let's get everything loaded that we've cut and head out."

There were a few grunts of agreement as the last of the wood was hauled out. Katie rode on the last trailer, hanging on for dear life as it bounced across the field. Grace was waiting for them beside her front porch, offering her thanks as they went past. At the woodshed, Katie helped unload until the job was done and everyone headed for their cars. Katie and Esther made their way to Esther's Corvette and climbed in. With a roar, they took off, falling into line with the stream of vehicles moving out the driveway. Grace was at the end of the short driveway now, waving and smiling.

Katie rolled down her window. "Good night! Take care of yourself, Grace!"

Grace called back, "And thank you, Katie."

"She's very appreciative of the help," Esther said. "It's nice to do things for people when they're so thankful."

Katie wondered if maybe she should thank Esther again for all she was doing for her . . . like bringing her to these gatherings and being her friend. But before she could put words to her thoughts, they were pulling into Esther's yard. The sight before her took Katie's breath away. A huge pile of coals glowed in the darkness, with occasional bursts of flame shooting skyward.

"Mom and dad got it just right!" Esther said as she parked her car. "And timed it just right too."

"It's beautiful!" Katie gushed, stepping out of the car. Margaret came bursting out of the darkness before she could say any more, giving Katie a hug and taking her by the arm.

"You're mine now and for the rest of the evening," Margaret said, leading her off in the direction of the coals. "I've been wanting to speak with you all evening."

"Why?" Katie knew she sounded startled.

Margaret laughed. "Nothing special. Come, let's get in line. This supper won't last long. It's pretty late already. The wood hauling went longer than we expected."

"Do you do this every year?" Katie asked. "Cutting wood for Grace?"

"We have for as long as I can remember. Don't your young folks do things like this?"

"Oh, *yah,*" Katie answered at once. She didn't add the rest of her thoughts though — about her lack of friends among her community. There was no sense in spoiling this *wunderbah* evening.

"I could eat a dozen hot dogs," Margaret said as they approached the table where the food was laid out. Margaret took up one of the roasting forks and slipped two hot dogs on it. Katie did the same, holding up her hand to shield her face after they walked over and held the hot dogs over the open coals. The warmth of the fire spread over Katie's skin, matching the warmth that had been warming her heart all evening.

CHAPTER THIRTY-THREE

On Monday morning, Emma filled the old Maytag washing machine with water before tugging on the starter rope. On the first try, the pulley jerked back so hard Emma gasped. She straightened her back before grasping the rope again. With one hand steadied on the rim of the washer, she pulled hard with the other. The motor roared to life. She dumped the load of dirty clothes in and added soap. The roar of the motor rang in her ears. She closed the lid and wiped her hands before going up the basement stairs into the kitchen. There she collapsed into a chair and buried her head in her hands as a groan escaped her lips.

Jesse had at least tried to speak with Katie the other evening when he was here, and hope had stirred in Emma's heart that perhaps her daughter would see the mistake of her ways. Surely Katie's eyes would open now that *Da Hah* was having mercy on all of them again. But things looked so different this morning after her talk with Katie. Katie was having none of putting a halt to her social life. She'd gone to the Saturday-night Mennonite youth gathering and was looking forward to the next gathering. What a mess! People didn't become attached to the Mennonites and then return to the Amish faith. Emma's heart sank thinking about what this might mean.

For one thing, she had to trust *Da Hah* more and not grow desperate like she was apt to do. And she was doing the right thing. There was this stirring in her that any decent man would cause in a woman's heart when he pursued her. It wasn't love yet . . . and might never be. But she'd felt this same lack of emotion when Ezra first took her home. There had been no promise then that love would follow, nor were there any now. But she'd been honest with Jesse about the matter, and it would just have to be *gut* since he didn't seem to think it was a big issue. *Da Hah* would surely not hold her to account for something she couldn't help.

Emma sighed. Life without Katie felt empty. What had she done wrong, anyway? Emma pondered the question and soon came up with plenty of answers. None of them made her look like a very decent mother. She'd given Katie plenty of reason to doubt her in the past. All those lectures she'd given about love and marriage had been a mistake. She could see that now.

What had been wrong with her back then? Those old fears felt like wild imaginations now. Thankfully *Da Hah* was moving her away from all that, even if Katie wasn't fully with her any longer.

Emma stood and walked over to the kitchen window. The barn sat flooded in bright sunlight. Their two cows stood in the barnyard chewing their cud. Emma groaned and wrung her hands. If only Jesse were here this morning to speak with Katie. Emma caught herself up short. Jesse hadn't done that well convincing Katie the other evening. But she couldn't be blamed for wishing he had, she supposed. Besides, they weren't yet wed, and he had his own children to care for. Perhaps things would go better when they had Jesse's full attention. Emma's thoughts lingered on Jesse's conversation with Katie. He'd wished her well with her plans to attend the Mennonite youth gathering. Didn't Jesse know the girl needed to be handled with a firm hand and not encouragement to continue in her wrong ways? *That's enough thinking about this,* Emma told herself. She hadn't done that well with Katie either. But the negative thoughts continued to rush in.

Emma gave up with a sigh. What if Jesse didn't know how to help Katie straighten out her life? Emma felt herself turn cold at the thought. Look at all the trouble they were running into already. For one, Jesse's children didn't want anything to do with her, and Katie didn't want anything to do with Jesse's children, and Ruth was surely wagging her tongue all over the community by now, telling everyone what a great mistake Jesse was making in courting her.

Emma tried to calm her sagging emotions. She knew once what love was. What if *Da Hah* was allowing it again? Was there not hope rising in her heart? Impossible as both love and helping Katie seemed, she must not turn back. Even in the face of great difficulty . . . even with Ruth Troyer around. Anger stirred. What nerve that woman had, coming right into Jesse's home and baking pecan pies for him. Why, if that was all it took to win a man's heart, she should've been baking pecan pies years ago instead of sitting here raising Katie on her own.

A smile played on Emma's face. The truth be told, even Ruth Troyer knew that baking pies wasn't the whole story. That was why she weaseled herself into the hearts of

Jesse's children first. So why didn't she, Emma Raber, go over and charm Jesse's children too? Emma laughed out loud at that thought. She had no more hope of winning the hearts of Jesse's children than Ruth had of capturing Jesse using pecan pies. Emma was a strange woman to Jesse's children. She was a heartbroken woman, a woman who had lived alone for years, a woman who had her own daughter to raise. What chance did she have with Jesse's children?

Questions raced through Emma's mind. Why did life have to be so hard? Why did Ezra have to die? Why couldn't he have lived these years on earth with her? They would have had more children by now, and Ezra would have known how to deal with Katie.

Emma paced the floor. She had to stop thinking like this. It couldn't be pleasing to *Da Hah.* He had taken Ezra, and she needed to be strong. An answer would come for their problems. Katie couldn't be lost completely. How could she? She was her daughter. She'd raised Katie with great love in her heart. That had to mean something.

Emma glanced at the clock on the kitchen wall and gasped. The load of wash was still in the basement. What in the world was wrong with her? She'd come up to work in the kitchen and had spent all the time thinking about her troubles instead. And now she was leaving the load of wash in for much too long. Emma raced downstairs and swung the wringer around to turn the rollers on. She set the empty hamper on a wooden bench behind her and began to feed the wet wash through. The roar of the motor filled her ears, but even then the questions didn't stop.

She had fallen into her old ways this morning. She'd spoken for twenty minutes or more with Katie this morning after breakfast, like she always had during Katie's growing up years, but the words no longer seemed to take root. Emma knew better, but hadn't been able to stop herself. Katie still listened, but it was different now. Katie heard with her ears, but she no longer heard with her heart.

Emma kept running the wash through the ringer with her mind miles away, thinking back over the years. If Ruth Troyer wished to damage her relationship with Jesse, she could bring up her crush on Daniel Kauffman and her mad dash out of his wedding. Likely Ruth knew the story. Her feelings for Daniel had been pretty obvious to anyone who was watching. Not that Jesse would have noticed. He saw nothing but Millie in those days, and boys didn't usually notice such things anyway. But Ruth had reason now to spread her knowledge abroad. And Ruth would remind Jesse of this common knowledge. The question was whether Jesse would care.

Emma ran another piece of wash through the wringer with her brow wrinkled in concentration. There had to be something she could do about this problem. Perhaps she could join Ruth in her bold venture into Jesse's home? She could answer Ruth with her own method. But how was she to do that? Did one drive up to Jesse's house and knock on the door? Jesse wouldn't be in during the day. He'd be out in the fields working. Only Mabel would be at the house, and her eyes would blaze with fury at Emma Raber showing up on her doorstep. Especially if Ruth had spread her vicious gossip.

Emma ran the last piece of wash through the ringer and refilled the washing machine. A widow everyone thought was strange would probably look worse to Mabel than a meddler like Ruth. And a daughter's heart would be close to her *daett,* especially after her *mamm* had passed away. This couldn't help but have an effect on Jesse.

Emma wiped away a quick tear thinking about it. She mustn't blame Jesse for what he wasn't doing, Emma told herself. He showed no signs of being influenced by Mabel's opinion. He loved Mabel and brought *gut* correction at the same time, like a *gut daett* should. This was something Katie had never experienced. If Ezra had lived, he would have loved Katie with all of his heart, and Katie would have loved him in return. But all of that had been lost, and she'd done a poor job of filling the gap.

Emma's eyes filled with tears as she walked outside into the blazing sunlight with her hamper of wet wash. She was Emma Raber, she told herself. She'd lived many years withdrawn from her people, and now she was reaping the consequences of that behavior. Katie was forsaking her, and Jesse's children were rejecting her. And she couldn't blame either — not one bit. She would act exactly like they were acting if she were in their shoes. If there was any trip she ought to make, it was a fast one over to Jesse's place to inform him that he should never visit her again. But she refused to give in even to that despair. No doubt this was *Da Hah*'s way of showing her that she wouldn't be getting off easy for the wrongs done in the past. No one ever did. Who was she to think that love could spring up in her heart again — if it really was love — without trouble coming with it? *Da Hah* was giving again, the *gut* and the bad, and she must accept both from His hand.

Emma set the hamper of wash on the ground and began clipping the laundry to the line, letting the tears run freely down her face. In all her lectures with Katie, Emma had always been certain they had a precious love between them. Yet she must try to see things as Katie was seeing them. What she had called love was to Katie nothing more than a muddy puddle of water lying in the barnyard — something fit for Molly and Bossy to stomp around in. Had she failed to supply the fresh rivers of love that all human beings needed each and every day?

Emma walked back to the basement in silence and began running the next load of wash through the ringer. Yet *Da Hah* had not allowed her to die in this house alone. She must not be in despair. He'd sent Jesse to her. She must keep hoping and believing, even if Katie didn't see things her way and even if Katie never stopped going to the Mennonites. That was the only answer.

CHAPTER THIRTY-FOUR

Later that day Emma stood at the kitchen window watching her wash flapping in the wind. The plate she'd used for her lunch lay on the table behind her. The pan of warmed-over casserole was also there, still steaming. The bread bag was tied shut, with the butter and jam jars closed. The meal, meager though it had been, had lifted her spirits. Emma turned and transferred the plate to the sink. She ran water and soap over it and left it on the counter. Her wash should be dry by now, she figured. She needed to keep working to keep any dark clouds at bay. They would be back soon enough, with so much of her life still filled with unresolved trouble. But she would pray harder and trust *Da Hah* for His mercy. That was something that had never failed her.

Emma went down the basement stairs and picked up the empty hamper to go outside. She arrived at the clothesline. The first piece was dry, and so was the second one. Her hamper was half full when she heard buggy wheels on the road coming in from the east. Emma straightened her back and stared in that direction. It was from there, she thought, that she and Jesse had come racing home on Friday night.

Emma smiled at the memory. She'd been stealing brief glances behind her all the way home. Jesse had looked so earnest while seated on the buggy seat, his eyes blazing and his beard flying over his shoulder. Still she had kept her horse moving at a fast clip for most of the journey, not ready to give in yet. She must learn to give in sooner, she told herself, especially when *Da Hah* was at work. And she must even do so when anger was rising inside of her over a perceived injustice. How much had she already missed in life through her stubbornness and fear? But life was surely changing now, and she must also be thankful for that.

Out on the road, a woman leaned from the buggy to wave. Emma waved back. The woman looked like Bishop Miller's wife, Laura, but it was hard to tell with the *kapp* in the way. Emma watched the buggy disappear into the distance before continuing to fill her hamper with wash. Someday she would be old like the bishop and his wife, and hopefully she'd have the same grace on her life then that the bishop and his wife had now. It could easily have turned out differently. She could be bitter at heart and even weirder than she was now. All of that would have happened if *Da Hah* hadn't worked a fresh grace in her life.

Da Hah was helping her, and she should do what she could to keep the dark thoughts at bay. And there was something she could do and should do. She must make that visit to Jesse's place. Even if self-invited visits were one of the low tricks Ruth Troyer practiced. Emma had reasons Ruth didn't. She was Jesse's promised one. It would do her *gut* to act like it, and Jesse would be pleased, she was sure. He had come over to her place often enough without asking her first.

On impulse, Emma hurried to take in her wash and dumped the pile on the living room couch before rushing out to the barn. If she hurried, she could be back before Katie came home from work. Jesse's place wasn't that far. And she wouldn't stay that long anyway.

Emma threw the harness on her horse and led him out of the barn. She hitched him to the buggy. Moments later she was urging the horse down the road, trying to keep

thoughts of Ruth's Friday night visit out of
her mind. It would do no *gut* even remembering such things. No doubt Jesse had
taken care of Ruth and sent her packing.
But what if he hadn't? Emma pushed the
dark thought away, but it wouldn't leave.

Was she making a mistake? Should she
have stayed home and let Jesse come to her?
That's what she had always done before.
There was still time to turn back, Emma
told herself. But she couldn't do it. That
would be giving in to fear, would it not?
She couldn't give in again. Not now when
she was so close. Emma clutched the reins
as the negative thoughts descended on her
like rain clouds opening up during a wild,
summer thunderstorm.

How had she ever imagined that marriage
to Jesse was possible? How could she be a
gut mamm to Jesse's wonderful children?
How did she dare think that Mabel and
Carolyn would ever speak well of her? They
had lost their real *mamm* not that long ago,
and they had opened their hearts to Ruth.
She was dreaming impossible dreams when
it concerned Jesse's children. No smiles
would ever play on their faces at the sight
of her. There would never be little feet running to meet her and hugs given when they
arrived. Kind words would never be spoken

in her presence. Jesse would never sit beside her on his living room couch looking on approvingly as she mothered his children. She would never feel at home in Jesse's kitchen — not after Ruth had been there with her pecan pies to steal their hearts.

And for Katie it would be even worse. Katie might join the Mennonites for *gut* the week after the wedding, her heart broken over how she was being used. Emma knew she clearly wasn't *gut* enough to be the best *mamm* to Jesse's children. She was not even *gut* enough to love Katie. All of this was so plain to see now. Emma squeezed her eyes shut, slapping the reins and moments later pulling into Jesse's driveway. Her head was now pounding with pain. Maybe it was just as well she'd come. Now she could tell Jesse the truth and be done with it. This marriage idea was not going to work.

Emma glanced around. No one was in sight, so she stopped the horse by the hitching post and climbed down. She pulled the tie rope out from under the front seat and tied the horse before she glanced toward the house. She couldn't see anyone, but Mabel would no doubt be waiting inside. There was no way she could go in there. Not with her heart in despair like it was.

"Dear *Hah,* help me," Emma prayed. "I

don't know what I should do now."

Emma looked across Jesse's fields and spotted a team of horses in the distance. Jesse and his two boys must be working way back there. It would look mighty strange for her to go tramping all that way on foot. Yet she would do so because she had to find Jesse. To get there the shortest way was through the barn, she figured. Let people think what they wished. Jesse would know what words needed to be spoken to soothe the turmoil in her head and heart.

Emma pushed open the barn door and entered. She paused a moment to adjust her eyes. A slight noise came from behind one of the stalls, but she paid it no attention. The door to the barnyard was ahead of her, and that was where she needed to go.

She was halfway there when Jesse's voice stopped her. "Emma? What are you doing here?"

She didn't move as the blood pounded in her face.

"I thought I heard noises outside a moment ago," Jesse said. "But I was too busy with my harness repair to check."

She turned, taking in the leather harness draped over the wooden bench. Jesse's hands were oil streaked, but his face wore a big smile. Tears wanted to spring to her eyes, but Emma held them back. "Jesse," she whispered, and he smiled again. "I had to come over . . . I was thinking I could help out perhaps . . . but on the way these horrible thoughts kept coming. I don't know what to do. Maybe we shouldn't go on . . . you and I?"

"What are you talking about?" Jesse's hand swept the dust from the bench he'd been sitting on. "Come and sit down, Emma. You look pale."

She shouldn't sit down, Emma told herself, shaking her head. She should go home.

Jesse stood and stepped closer. "Come, you're going to pass out if you don't sit."

"I'm not going to pass out!" she wanted to shout. The truth was she didn't know if she could speak at all. Jesse's eyes were doing strange things to her heart. She was nothing but a weak woman, Emma thought. She was unable to handle life, and her heart was going where it had no business going. What right had she to even think she could love this man enough to make him happy?

"Emma." Jesse took both of her hands and led her over to the bench. Emma sat down before breaking out into sobs.

Jesse waited until her cries had died down before asking, "What's wrong, dear?"

"I'll be okay," Emma choked out. "My

thoughts just got dark on the way over here. It's . . . it's the past, I think. It's too many years of living by myself with just Katie . . . of thinking only of the two of us. Of dwelling on my own pain."

"Emma, don't," Jesse murmured. "Who has been saying these awful thoughts to you? Has Ruth visited you?"

"Ruth?" Emma shook her head. "Of course not. She wouldn't do something like that."

Jesse didn't look convinced.

Emma ignored the topic of Ruth. She had more important things to think of right now. "It's just that your children don't want me. And Katie isn't going to stop running around with the Mennonites. And you don't know everything about me either. If you knew the truth, you wouldn't want to marry me."

"I see." Jesse still held her hands. "Do you want to tell me what that truth might be?"

"Nee." Emma looked away. "I suppose Ruth has already told you."

His voice was quiet but clear. "I'd like to hear your side."

Emma's head spun. So her fears weren't without reason. Ruth had spoken with Jesse, and he was doubting her. Perhaps she was already lost. But she must tell her side.

There was no other way but the truth, no matter what Jesse would decide. Thankfully her tears weren't running now. And it was best this way — that Jesse know the truth from her lips.

"I acted very foolishly in my youth," Emma began, not looking at him. "I had a serious crush on a boy — a man you know — Daniel Kauffman. Anyway, I hung on his every word and smile for years, even after he started dating another girl. I kept on hoping he would stop seeing his girlfriend and turn back to me. I kept hoping right up to their wedding day. Only when I heard them saying their vows did I give up. And then my heart turned to stone. I created quite a scene by storming out and driving out right in front of everyone — right past the bride and groom as they were coming out of the house."

She paused and listened to Jesse's breathing beside her. He seemed calm. Had she said too much? Was he going to send her away now? Did she need to get up and walk out the door?

"Go on," Jesse encouraged.

Emma jumped. "But I've told you everything."

"No, you haven't. Tell me about Ezra."

Emma drew in her breath, her fingernails

digging into the palms of his hands. What did Jesse want to know? But deep down she knew what he wanted, but she didn't want to tell him. It would be like tearing her heart apart for his eyes to look in and judge her. And she would be doing it in front of someone who might turn around and walk away, someone whose opinion she cared about a lot.

A cry sprang to her lips, but she choked it back.

Jesse was still waiting, saying nothing.

Emma took a deep breath and began. "I married Ezra because he was the first man who asked me after Daniel's wedding. I'd made such a mess of my life. I thought, 'Why shouldn't I?' Ezra loved me, *yah.* That's what he said anyway. And I knew it was the truth. Perhaps that's why I allowed him to go through with the wedding. I knew I would never love him. My heart had become frozen because of Daniel."

"But you learned to love Ezra?" Jesse's voice was soft beside her.

"*Yah,* I did. It was because of Katie." She took a deep breath. "My heart opened to him when Katie was in my womb. It was as if a great gift had been given to us from *Da Hah.*"

"How did you learn to love me?" His

fingers moved on her hand.

A sob caught in her throat. "I'm not sure that I do, Jesse. But I do know that Katie pulled my heart toward you. At first because I thought you could help her. And then I heard Ezra's voice in Katie's words, telling me how wrong I had been. You are a decent man, Jesse. Any woman could see that. It would be hard to not like you."

"Emma." He pulled her close to him, carefully keeping his oily hands away from her dress. "You shouldn't argue with what *Da Hah* is doing in our hearts. There is more going on than you know. And *Da Hah* doesn't make mistakes."

"But what about what I already told you? About Daniel Kauffman. About how I acted?"

"You speak like a truthful woman, Emma. And I'm okay with that. It's Mabel who is our problem."

"Mabel knows everything about me?"

Jesse frowned. "*Yah,* Ruth told her some things. But you are going to be *my frau,* Emma. We'll deal with Mabel together."

Emma wept, sobbing into his shoulder. He held her tight, even while being careful to avoid getting her dirty.

CHAPTER THIRTY-FIVE

Sometime later Emma still had her head on Jesse's shoulder. But she was laughing now at his continued efforts to keep his oily hands away from her dress.

"Let me get this stuff wiped off," Jesse finally said, unhooking his arm from around Emma's shoulders.

Emma took both of his hands in hers, looking up into his face. "I was once used to dirt on a man's hands, and I guess I can get used to it again." She held her breath as it looked like Jesse was going to lean forward and kiss her. It had been a long time since she had kissed a man. Things were moving so fast, but if *Da Hah* was in it as Jesse claimed — well, her heart was strangely filled with joy. She lifted her face toward his, working one hand loose to run her fingers through his beard.

Just then the barn door burst open behind them.

"*Daett,* I want to . . ." Mabel called as she rushed in.

Jesse let go of Emma's hand.

"Oh!" Mabel stopped mid-stride. "I see someone's with you."

Mabel knew *gut* and well there was someone with her *daett,* Emma thought, and she had known who that person was. *She surely saw my buggy outside.* Mabel was here not just to see what was going on, but to break up whatever was happening. Apparently Jesse had arrived at the same conclusion from the look on his face.

Still Jesse managed a smile. "Emma stopped by, and we've been talking."

"Oh . . ." Mabel shifted from one foot to the other.

"Come, shake Emma's hand," Jesse said.

"Nee." Emma heard her own voice counter Jesse's. "Mabel doesn't have to if she doesn't want to." She knew it wouldn't help Mabel's opinion of her if she were forced to do something uncomfortable.

"I don't mind." Mabel smiled and came closer. "*Daett,* I need you to look at the washing machine motor. It hasn't been running well this morning."

Jesse appeared perplexed. "You should have said something before this if it wasn't working. I'll check it this evening, Mabel.

Emma's here right now, and you're done with your wash for the day, aren't you?"

Mabel nodded while offering Emma her hand.

Emma shook it, trying to smile. "I'm afraid my hands are a little dirty." She turned both up for Mabel to see. Faint oil streaks ran across her fingers and into her palms. Mabel's eyes darted from Emma hands to her *daett*'s and then up at his beard, where small specks of oil glittered on several hair strands.

It wasn't that hard for Mabel to make the connection, Emma figured. Her hands had been in Jesse's beard, and Mabel would think they'd been kissing, which they had — or almost had.

Thankfully Jesse didn't seem all that concerned. He nodded as if to acknowledge the obvious. "*Yah,* Emma and I have been talking. I'm glad you came out when you did. I was wondering when we should tell you."

"Tell me what?" Mabel stepped backward.

"That Emma and I are to wed before too long."

"But *Daett*!" Mabel gasped. "Ruth was just here, and you know what she told you. How can you still do this?"

Jesse nodded. "I know this may seem a

little sudden to you, and I understand that. But like I said at the breakfast table, what Ruth Troyer said means nothing to me. She didn't say anything I didn't already know. And Emma is the one I've chosen for my *frau.*"

"But . . . but . . ." Mabel sputtered, stepping back and almost falling over a bale of hay as she burst into sobs.

Jesse moved forward and caught Mabel's arm. He helped her sit on a nearby straw bale, and then he sat beside her.

He would have put his arms around her shoulders, Emma figured, if his hands hadn't been so oily. She waited as Mabel's wails pierced the air and sent chills up and down her spine. *I will not run away,* she told herself. She slowed her breathing, willing herself to calm down. None of this was Jesse's fault. And neither was it her fault. She had not chosen Jesse. He claimed this was *Da Hah*'s doings. So how could she run away even if Jesse's children didn't yet understand? She couldn't, she decided, even if Mabel never learned to like her and even if Katie never came back to the faith. She needed to be strong now and stand with Jesse . . . with her intended husband. Only if he changed his mind and asked her to leave would she do so. She stood up and trembled as she walked to the bench where Jesse had been working. She looked around and found a clean rag. One was stuck in a corner where Jesse had no doubt placed it. It would do for now. She took the rag to him.

A slight smile spread across his face as he wiped his hands. Then he slipped his arm around Mabel's trembling shoulders.

"I don't understand any of this," Mabel whispered, sniffling hard.

Emma pulled her handkerchief from her dress pocket and handed it to Jesse, who passed it on to Mabel.

"This may be hard to understand," Jesse was telling her, "but like I told you this morning, I don't want any more discussion of what Ruth has to say about anything. Ruth is not your *mamm* and she never will be."

Mabel rubbed her eyes with Emma's handkerchief but didn't look up.

Emma moved over beside Jesse. "Should I leave?" she asked softly when he looked up at her. She could make a quick dash for the door, she thought. She wouldn't be running away — not if Jesse agreed it was best for her to go. She could come back another day.

Jesse shook his head and reached for Emma's hand.

Tears were close to coming again, Emma thought. How truly great this man was. He understood her anguish, but he wanted her to stay. Somehow he knew how to reach out to her. Somehow he knew what she needed. He even chose the right moment to give her courage to stay because he must have known that her running away would take more work later to fix. The way ahead might be long and hard already.

"Mabel," Jesse said, his voice now low, "I'm very sorry that you find this disappointing, but this is very important. You are my daughter, Mabel. And I love you and will always love you. I want you to like the woman I choose as my *frau*. But in the end, that choice is mine alone to make. My heart has to reach out and find the woman *Da Hah* has prepared for me. You can't be expected to see that, Mabel. No child of a parent who is making that kind of choice can always see what is right. I hope you can understand that a little. Can you?"

Emma looked away. Why did she have to be in on this conversation? She ought to be a thousand miles away while Jesse discussed this with his daughter. But she must learn to trust Jesse, just as she was learning to open her heart to him. If Jesse was to be her husband, she must be his *frau* in every

347

sense of the word. And the sooner the better.

Mabel was still sniffling and saying nothing.

"I want you to understand that Ruth is not seeing things like she ought to," Jesse continued. "Ruth is biased because she has her own interests to deal with. *Yah,* some of the facts she shared were true, but how she interpreted them was not. And she has no business interfering with what I know is best for all of us as a family."

This produced a fresh wail from Mabel.

Emma shifted from one foot to the other. Obviously Jesse was getting nowhere in this attempt to convince Mabel. Should she try to reach the girl since she was going to be her *mamm*? But how would she do that?

"I think you'll find that I'm right in time, Mabel," Jesse tried again. "Once you know Emma and Katie better. But this has been enough talk for one day. I don't think you're making the best impression on Emma either. I'm sure she wasn't expecting this kind of reception. Perhaps you should go back into the house now. I'll get Emma back on the road again, and tonight I'll look after the washer motor. Okay?"

Mabel nodded. Without another word, she jumped up from the straw bale and dashed out the barn door.

"I'm so sorry I couldn't help you out," Emma said. "I couldn't think of a single thing to say or do."

"That's okay." Jesse took Emma into his arms. "You came over here to talk with me, not deal with emotional teenagers."

"Mabel has a point," she said into his chest even as she felt his strong arms were close to squeezing the breath out of her.

When he didn't answer, Emma pushed away and looked up into his face.

"No, she doesn't," he said. "Mabel doesn't understand everything, and I'm not going to explain it to her. There are some things that are best left unsaid. And some things between a husband and *frau* shouldn't be shared. Mabel will get over this. Leroy already has, for which I'm thankful. The others will follow."

Emma hung her head. "I'm thankful you stick up for me, but I did do what Ruth Troyer said I did. Even if it was all those years ago."

He shrugged. "And Ruth imposed herself on my household, showing up without my permission, turning the hearts of my children in her direction with sweet talk and pecan pies."

"That's not half as bad as what I did."

349

Jesse smiled. "I think that's up to me to decide. And I have already done so. I want you as my *frau.* That is — if you'll still have me after this commotion."

"You know I will," Emma whispered.

Jesse wrapped his arms around her again. "Come now," Jesse said a few minutes later as he led her outside. "I'm sure you have things to do at home. And I have plenty to do around here myself."

Emma followed him on wobbly legs. She climbed into her buggy with Jesse's help. He untied her horse and threw the tie rope in the back. She waited until Jesse had come back around and stuck his head in the buggy door.

"Thank you again," she said. "For everything. You know just what to say to encourage me. You don't know how much *gut* you are doing me."

He laughed. "I'm sure it's not that much." He motioned with his head toward the house. "I'm the one who is asking great things of you. Don't worry, Emma. Mabel's a sweet girl. You haven't seen her at her best. Give her a chance to come around."

"I hope she'll speak to me," Emma said wistfully. She could imagine moving into the house after the wedding with a mute Mabel glaring at her.

"It'll be okay," he said. "Look, why don't you come over sometime next week? Bring Katie along, and we will try this introduction thing again."

Emma nodded.

"I'll see you then," Jesse said, stepping back from the buggy.

Emma took off, leaning out of the buggy to wave at him. Jesse was standing in the middle of the driveway, waving back. There was no sign of Mabel. The house windows were empty.

CHAPTER THIRTY-SIX

The next afternoon Ruth made her decision. She closed the schoolhouse door behind her, leaving a pile of ungraded papers lying on her desk. Today there was something more important that needed tending to. She would visit Jesse's place again and find out more about the matter that had troubled her all day. From what she'd gathered watching his children in school today, Jesse must have come to his senses and was ending this silly chasing after that strange Emma Raber. Although that hardly seemed possible considering how Jesse had ushered her so rudely out of his house last week.

But now, looking back, Jesse's actions were understandable in a way. And she would forgive him. After all, he had been exhausted that evening. Her words must have been quite a shock to him. But now it was obvious something had happened, if the looks on Carolyn and Joel's faces could be trusted. The fault might be hers in that she'd waited this long to visit Jesse again. Today Carolyn had sat at her desk for hours without smiling. Joel had refused to speak when she asked him what his sour mood was about. Likely Jesse was in meltdown mode at home, having been thoroughly embarrassed by the awful flaws in Emma he'd missed until she'd pointed them out to him. Men were like that. They had thin egos, and it didn't take much to send them over the edge. Well, it was time to offer her sympathy since Jesse was no doubt ready to open his mind, if not his heart, to her considerable appeal. She'd learned from life that the opening of a man's eyes to the world around him was not always a pleasant experience, regardless of how highly the preachers spoke in favor of it.

A man must be honest, the preachers said. Which was true, of course, but they never seemed to understand how important a woman's role was in helping a man see right. But she understood, and she would give an understanding ear to Jesse now that he was willing to see the truth. She'd expected this moment to arrive once Jesse had time to think things through. She had to admit the moment had come more quickly than even she'd expected. This did speak well for Jesse — even though she would have taken him as her husband if it had taken him weeks to back down from his obsession with that Raber woman. That's what it had been. Nothing but an obsession. Those sometimes overtook a man, and they needed correction. Apparently even Jesse Mast — the catch that he was — had his faults in that area. And she was exactly the woman he needed now that he was down.

Ruth slapped the reins against her horse's back as she drove up the road. Carolyn and Joel would have been home for over an hour now. She would have followed them right away, but she'd had to wait until everyone left the school. And, as usual when she was in a hurry, there had been an accident. One of the first-graders, little Elsie Yoder, had fallen on the steps right after school was dismissed and cut her knee. By the time the blood had been washed off, her tears wiped away, and her leg bandaged, time had slipped by.

If Ruth hurried now, she could still be back by five or so to finish grading papers. If any of the parents who lived in the area noticed her early departure, they would be pleased to see a light burning later at the school. They would know their teacher was busy at her duties.

And if Jesse asked her to stay for supper, she would have to refuse him. There would be plenty of opportunity to see him later now that he'd come to his senses. His children were her first concern, but she could only spend a few moments with them this afternoon. Her other duties came first at present.

Poor Jesse must feel awful for the words he'd spoken to her the other night. He might hesitate to see her because of embarrassment. But the sooner one faced one's mistakes, the better.

Jesse's house came into view ahead, and Ruth slowed to turn down the driveway. No one was around the barn that she could see, but it looked like Carolyn had just run into the house from the front porch. The girls must be in the house with Joel, Ruth decided. This was *gut*. It would give her a chance to speak with Mabel and Carolyn before she walked back to the field where Jesse was probably working. Of course, he might see her buggy and come up to meet her, but she wasn't going to count on that. Men didn't usually face their mistakes that easily.

Ruth tied her horse to the hitching post

and walked across the front yard and up the front steps. She was reaching for the doorknob when it opened to reveal Mabel's tear-stained face.

"Oh my darling Mabel," Ruth cooed, wrapping the girl in her arms. She squeezed so hard Mabel could barely breathe. Ruth didn't notice as she gushed on. "I came as quickly as I could when I saw at school today that Carolyn was so terribly upset. But she wouldn't speak a word to me about it, and Joel wouldn't tell me much either. I'm so sorry you have to go through this. Your *daett*'s breakdown must have been an awful experience, and so soon after your *mamm* passed away."

Mabel nodded and sobbed harder.

"Come!" Ruth led the way to the couch. "Sit down and cry all you want. And where is Carolyn? I wanted all day at school to give her a big hug, but the children would have started asking questions. And your family does have a right to some privacy while you go through this hard time."

"She's upstairs," Mabel managed to say. "I think she was tired of seeing me cry."

"Of course," Ruth cooed, giving Mabel another hug. "But we'll get through this. I really do think the worst will soon be over. That's the way men are, but I don't wish to speak ill of your *daett.*"

"You can say whatever you want about *Daett.*" Mabel paused to blow her nose.

"He's really a *gut* man at heart," Ruth assured her. "You will see that after he's calmed down. This is how things go when men can't see the truth and have to be shown by someone else. You must not hold this against him."

"But it's so hard," Mabel said. "You should have heard him talking to us this morning. It was awful."

"*Yah,* I'm sure." Ruth gave Mabel another hug. "But the worst is over now. Your *daett* means only the best for you."

"That's what he says," Mabel wailed, fresh tears pouring down her face.

Ruth patted Mabel on the arm. "At least he's talking some sense. It's a *gut* sign. Soon he'll be completely back to his senses and won't say such hard things to you again. But at least we can be thankful your *daett* has changed his mind about . . . well, about Emma Raber."

Mabel stared at her. "Changed his mind? What are you talking about? Nothing will change *Daett*'s mind about that woman."

"I knew her past would catch up with her. I just . . ." Ruth suddenly stopped speaking. "What did you just say, Mabel?"

Mabel dried her eyes. "Nothing is going to change *Daett*'s mind about Emma. I caught the two of them in the barn on Monday night after Emma made a special visit over here. *Daett* was holding her hand and looked ready to kiss her. I threw a big fit, and *Daett* told me he's going to marry the woman. This morning he told the whole family. *Daett*'s totally smitten, and I can't do anything about it. No one can."

Ruth's mouth was agape, and she said nothing for a long moment. Finally she said, "So *that's* why Joel and Carolyn were so upset. Are you sure about this, Mabel?"

Mabel nodded even as new tears formed. "We're going to live with this woman now that she has snuck her way into *Daett*'s heart. Will you still give me a lesson in baking even if Emma Raber becomes our new *mamm*?"

"I just can't believe this!" Ruth said, getting to her feet. How could she have been so wrong? Well, it didn't matter. At least she was here now to help these poor children. "I must speak to your *daett* at once!" she declared.

Mabel snorted through her nose. "It won't do any *gut*. I've tried everything."

"You're a young girl, Mabel." Ruth pulled herself together. "A grown woman needs to take care of this problem. I will speak with your *daett* myself. Where is he?"

Mabel shrugged. "In the barn fixing horse harnesses, I think."

"This can still be straightened out," Ruth declared as she headed for the door. Mabel followed close behind her.

Ruth held her head high as she marched across the front yard. She arrived at the barn and pushed open the door. Mabel chose to stay outside, giving Ruth a little nervous smile just before she went inside.

The nerve of Emma Raber, Ruth thought. *Coming right here to Jesse's place as bold as day, hunting down the man like he was a love-struck youngster who didn't have any other options.*

"Hello!" Ruth hollered, peering about in the low light.

"I thought I heard your voice earlier." Jesse appeared from behind the horse stall wiping his hands on a cloth. "I heard someone drive in. I'm very busy. What is it you want?"

Ruth walked up to him, stopping an arm's length away. "Is it true what Mabel is telling me?"

Jesse glared at her. "That depends on what she's telling you."

Ruth huffed before beginning to speak.

"You know *gut* and well what I'm talking about, Jesse Mast."

Jesse squinted at her. "I suppose you're referring to Emma and our plans to wed. This is none of your business, but you seem determined that it should be. I thought I told you to stay out of my family's business."

Ruth glared right back at him. "Someone has to look out for the welfare of your children, Jesse. And if you aren't interested, then their teacher is about as qualified as anyone."

Jesse moved a step closer. "It's the responsibility of the children's *daett* to see to their needs. And this *daett* is doing just that. And he's tired of you meddling in things that don't concern you. I made that clear to you the other night. Can't you understand our language, Ruth Troyer? Teacher or no teacher, you are meddling where you don't belong and where you aren't wanted."

She backed up a step. "You're telling me you will still see this woman? After you know she isn't interested in your children's welfare? Why, that woman can't even take care of her own child, Jesse. Katie's running with the Mennonites. Do you know that?"

"*Yah,* I know that." He pointed toward the barn door. "Now get out, Ruth! What's wrong with you anyway? Haven't I made it clear that you are not welcome here?"

"Wrong with *me*?" she shrieked.

He leaned toward her. "Let's see if I can bring this down to a level you can understand, Ruth. I know that teaching a schoolhouse full of children may have gone to your head. But unless you have a real complaint to make against Emma, something like breaking the *ordnung* or dating outside the faith, you don't have a leg to stand on. The past is the past. You won't keep me from marrying her. You can go to Bishop Miller himself with your story about Emma's past, and he's not going to do a thing about it. And do you know why, Ruth? Because no one cares. No one cared back then how some love-struck young girl felt, and no one cares now. No one did anything wrong back then, and no one has done anything wrong now. Do you understand?"

"I see you have a stubborn mind," Ruth countered. "After you have wed that woman, don't go complaining that no one warned you, Jesse Mast. And I hope *Da Hah* sends someone to take care of your children because I won't be available."

He leaned over and put his face close to hers. "Do you want to go to your buggy on your own two legs or do you want me to carry you out there, Ruth? I will do whichever is required."

She paled. "You've not heard the last of me. Something must be done for your poor children's sake." With that she turned and fled, slamming the barn door behind her. Out of the corner of her eye she caught sight of Mabel's white face, but she didn't slow down. Never in her life, Ruth thought as she climbed in the buggy, had she run across such a thickheaded man. This must be *Da Hah*'s *gut* mercy — showing her what kind of person Jesse was before she'd married him. But his children — the poor things — who was going to take care of them? Ruth drove out the lane, wiping away her tears. There was one thing she could do yet, and it was her responsibility to do it. She owed that much to Jesse's children. Emma must be paid a visit.

CHAPTER THIRTY-SEVEN

On Friday evening, Katie stood waiting in the yard, pacing back and forth. The time for another Mennonite youth gathering had arrived, and Esther ought to be here soon. Katie could have waited in the house, but she was too tense for that. *Mamm* was reading on the porch, swinging back and forth with one foot on the floor and the other tucked underneath her.

Why was *Mamm* so quiet tonight? In fact, she'd been pretty quiet ever since that afternoon she'd spent at Jesse's place. They were up to something, the two of them. But whatever it was, at least *Mamm* wasn't giving any more lectures. Still, she had begun their conversation this morning with a plea. "I wish you'd reconsider your plans for tonight, Katie. Everything is going to be all right between Jesse and . . ." But then *Mamm* had stopped as if she remembered something. Whatever it was, Katie wasn't about to change her plans to attend the Mennonite volleyball game tonight.

A roar sounded from up the road, and Esther Kuntz's fancy car came into view. *Mamm* looked up for a second before she dropped her eyes back to the page. Katie ran across the yard as Esther's car turned in. It was somehow different seeing Esther's car here rather than at Byler's. There it didn't seem out of place at all, but here was another matter. Perhaps she was making a mistake by allowing such a fancy thing of the world this close to their home. *"Calm down,"* Katie told herself. She wasn't driving a car like that, and she wasn't getting her own vehicle. She was only attending a Mennonite youth gathering, not joining the Mennonite faith. She only wanted to be with her friends.

Mamm was looking up again now that Esther had come to a screeching halt by the hitching post.

Katie gave a little wave of her hand, but *Mamm* didn't wave back. She was probably imagining Katie driving in her own car and out of her life forever.

"Hello," Esther greeted as Katie climbed in.

Before Katie could answer the engine roared under the hood, and she jerked back.

"Sorry!" Esther said with a laugh. "My foot slipped off the brakes."

Katie hung on as Esther quickly turned her car around. *Mamm* was watching them with a look of sadness on her face as they raced out of the driveway. Esther didn't have to tear around like she did, Katie thought. At least not in *Mamm*'s driveway. She almost said so, but then she changed her mind. She had no right to say anything to Esther about her driving if she willingly rode with her.

"Your *Mamm* looks so dreamy sitting on the front porch reading her book. What was she reading?" Esther asked as she accelerated onto the main road. The rush of the car pushed Katie back into her seat.

"*Pathway* stuff," Katie said, adding, "Those are Amish magazines."

"I've never heard of them. I wish my parents had time to sit on the front porch reading. Seems like we're rushing about all the time."

Esther could begin by driving slower, Katie thought as they raced around another curve. She smiled instead of saying anything. Esther was being nice to her, and she was now going to put the critical thoughts away and enjoy herself tonight with people who liked her.

Esther made it safely around another bend and stopped at a stop sign. Katie took a deep breath and asked, "Who's coming tonight?"

"Oh, just the usual gang," Esther said. "Some of the young people are gone, so we asked others from the neighboring churches to come. I think we'll have plenty of young folks to play volleyball."

"Are Sharon and Margaret going to be there?"

"As far as I know. They're around but not everyone always comes. You know . . . being busy and all."

"Yah," Katie agreed. "I hope Margaret and Sharon come tonight."

"Well, if they don't, you can hang around with me," Esther said.

"I can't thank you enough for bringing me again tonight," Katie said as they approached Esther's lane. Already lines of cars were parked by the barn and the volleyball net was set up in the front yard.

"It's nothing." Esther gave a quick shake of her head. "And besides, it was Roy Coblenz who invited you first. You can thank him more than me."

"But you invited me again," Katie replied, trying not to think of Roy. *He means nothing to me,* she told herself. And Roy had paid her little attention since his birthday party, which was perfectly fine. Friends were what she wanted among the Mennonites — not boyfriends.

Esther roared past all the cars parked along the driveway, pulling to a stop by their barn. Katie got out and glanced around. A cluster of girls stood near the house, and a few boys were batting the ball across the net.

"We'll have a great surprise for everyone later." Esther glowed as she hopped out of the car. "It's homemade ice cream being secretly made in the basement. Mom's probably getting things ready right now."

A bright smile filled Katie's face. "Homemade ice cream! That will be *wunderbah.*"

"I thought you'd like that." Esther motioned toward the house. "Maybe you can dash down to the basement later. Secretly, of course, when no one is looking, and give mother some pointers. We don't make homemade ice cream that often. Not like the Amish do anyway."

"I doubt if I'm that good at it," Katie protested. "*Mamm* always makes the ice cream at home."

Esther dismissed her words with a wave of her hand. "Come! Let's see why they haven't started the game yet." Esther led the way across the yard.

Katie saw Margaret break away from the group of girls and scurry toward them.

"Hi, Katie! I'm so glad you could come again," Margaret gushed, giving Katie a big hug. "It's so good to see you."

"And you," Katie returned. "I so enjoy my time with you and your friends."

"That's the way it should be," Margaret told her. "We want our visitors to feel welcome."

Katie winced at Margaret's words. Was she just a visitor? Someone who would disappear after a short amount of time had passed? No, she must keep up her trust in *Da Hah.*

"I expect you're hoping to see Sharon tonight," Margaret said. "But I don't think she's coming. They have some older relatives in for a visit. Not the kind you can bring to a volleyball game."

Before Katie could answer, a familiar voice spoke up behind her. "Well, look who's here."

Katie whirled around. Roy was standing there, smiling, holding out his hand. "Welcome back. Looks like they're about ready to start playing."

Katie smiled back. "*Yah.* It's good to see you."

Roy smiled and turned to move on. Katie stared after him. He too considered her a friend. It felt so good to be considered normal . . . one of the group. The newness of that feeling still hadn't worn off. Katie took a deep breath and walked over to where a group of girls was standing. She smiled a greeting. They all smiled back, a few saying, "Good evening."

"Good evening," Katie replied, stepping closer.

A few of them moved aside, giving her room within the circle like she belonged among them. No one was saying anything in particular right then. Their attention was focused on Esther, who was waving her arms around and shouting, "It's time to begin now! And if you boys can't figure out who will pick the teams, I will do so myself."

"You don't have to get yourself all worked up, Esther," one of the boys said, leaping into the air to grab the ball they'd been batting back and forth across the net. "We're just trying to get in some practice before the game begins."

Everyone laughed, and Esther joined in before saying, "Well, get to it then. And we have a little surprise waiting in the basement when everyone is done playing."

"Now what could that be?" another boy teased.

"You'll just have to wait," Esther told him. "Now, are you going to pick teams or not?"

"Of course," the boy said. "I'll volunteer, and so will John."

John groaned but he apparently found the plan agreeable because he began picking his team at once, calling out names.

In the ruckus that followed, Esther slipped up beside Katie and tugged on her arm. "Come. They'll get things straightened out, but now would be a good time to slip into the house. And don't worry about the game. When we come out, we'll both go on opposite sides, and everyone will be happy. They won't even notice us coming in."

Katie nodded and followed Esther. An older woman met them at the basement stairs with a bright smile.

"This is my mother, Mary," Esther told Katie. "Mom, this is Katie. She's going to help us with the ice cream."

"Oh!" Mary's smile was wide now. "I'm so glad you found someone who knows how to make homemade ice cream. But I hate to take one of the young people away from the game."

"Don't worry about that," Katie told her. "I don't know that much about ice cream making though."

"You certainly know more than we do," Esther asserted as she led the way downstairs.

"We're glad for any advice you can give," Mary told Katie when they arrived at the bottom of the stairs. A man who must be Esther's father had two huge ice cream freezers set up and attached to an electric motor. He greeted her with a hearty, "Ah, here we go. We finally have someone arriving who knows about ice cream making. I just borrowed these freezers, but I haven't made homemade ice cream in years."

"I don't know that much," Katie protested.

"She knows, so don't listen to her," Esther said.

"Name's Vern," Esther's father said as he extended his hand.

Katie shook it and smiled.

"Let's get busy then." Vern laughed. "How about you watch us, Katie, and tell us if we do anything wrong."

Katie nodded.

Mary began by emptying the bowls of ice cream mix she'd prepared into the round metal containers inside the freezers. Vern put the lids on, attached the cranks to the lids, and poured ice between the metal containers and the surrounding wooden tubs. He stopped when the ice came within a few inches of the top of the metal containers.

"Right so far?" Vern asked as he glanced toward Katie.

Katie nodded. "You don't want anything to get close to the lid."

"That's what I thought because I still need room for the rock salt, I think." Vern turned his words into action, pouring a stream of rock salt around the top of the ice. He threw a switch when he finished. Both freezers groaned into action, as the motors turned the metal containers round and round.

"At least you don't have to turn the crank by hand like we do," Katie said.

Vern smiled and hollered above the increasing racket, "How do I know when the ice cream is done?"

"When you can't turn them by hand anymore. That's the only rule I know." Katie told him.

"Obviously that rule wouldn't apply here," Vern said with a grin. "We'll figure out something, I suppose."

"Come." Esther tugged on Katie's arm. "Let's go. Dad can handle it now."

Katie turned to follow Esther upstairs, and

Vern hollered after her, "Thanks for the help."

"You're welcome," Katie hollered back. "But I really didn't do anything." She really hadn't, Katie thought on the way up the stairs. So maybe Esther's parents were just trying to make her feel welcome. Still, they had seemed truly thankful, so perhaps they really had wanted her opinion on ice cream making. It was a thought that sent positive feelings running around her heart.

CHAPTER THIRTY-EIGHT

Katie held her breath as Esther roared into *Mamm*'s driveway, her headlights cutting through the darkness and bouncing off the sides of the house. The hour was late, and if *Mamm* wasn't awake and waiting for her, Esther's noise and lights would wake her up for sure. *Mamm* being awake was the last thing Katie wanted at the moment. There was too much joy running through her from the wonderful evening she'd spent with the youth group. To see *Mamm*'s sad face would ruin everything. Perhaps tomorrow she could deal with her disapproval, but not tonight.

It had been such a great evening. First there had been the volleyball, and then everyone had sat on the lawn eating home-made ice cream and little cupcakes Esther's *mamm,* Mary, had prepared. And if that hadn't been enough, Mary had made everyone hot chocolate with marshmallows. Even better were the friendly chats Katie had with Margaret and several other girls.

Bryan and John, whom she'd met at Roy's birthday party, hadn't played beside her during the game tonight, but a different set of boys had. Bill and Charles, they said their names were. They both had spoken with her as the game progressed — nothing in particular, just friendly. And friendly was what Katie craved right now. Even Roy had made a point of saying goodbye to her. There was nothing special about his words either, which was *gut.* "Special" was something she couldn't handle right now. With a whirl, Esther swung her car around before coming to a stop.

"Goodnight, Katie," Esther said, still cheerful.

"Goodnight! And thanks for taking me," Katie said. Hopefully the dread of encountering *Mamm* wasn't evident in her voice. She'd caught a glimpse of light in the kitchen window, so *Mamm* was still up.

"Hope to do this again really soon," Esther chirped.

"*Yah.* Thanks again." Katie got out and closed the car door behind her. She did hope to do this again — and many times more. Katie walked across the front yard as Esther's car headed down the driveway, the headlight beams bouncing from the uneven road.

Katie went up the front steps and stepped inside. Standing still in the silence, she listened. There was no sound coming from the kitchen, so perhaps *Mamm* had just left the light burning for her. But then a chair scraped on the kitchen floor, and Katie's stomach sank.

"Katie, is that you?" *Mamm* called from the kitchen.

"Yah." Katie walked closer. She glanced into the kitchen and forced a smile. *Mamm* was sitting there reading her magazine. Her face had even more sorrow written on it than when she'd left, Katie decided. She looked away as the feeling of *Mamm*'s pain pierced her heart, especially as she now knew that next week she was going to do the same thing and the week after that. The Mennonite youth group was simply too *wunderbah* for her to stop attending. This was obviously going to take another miracle from *Da Hah* to figure out how to handle it.

"Sit down," *Mamm* said. "We need to talk."

Katie drew in a long breath and sat down.

"I assume you had a *gut* night." *Mamm* smiled but the effort looked forced.

Katie nodded, saying nothing. *Mamm* was

sure using different methods on her lately. Some of them hurt more than the old ones had. Apparently there was no lecture coming, so Jesse must already be teaching *Mamm* the best way her daughter could be "won back to the faith." "*Mamm,* if you're worried about me leaving the Amish, I'm not planning on that."

"That's *gut,*" Mamm said. "But that's not what I want to talk to you about."

Katie looked up with a startled expression on her face. "Has something happened?"

Mamm's smile was pained. "Not unless you count my planned wedding to Jesse Mast."

Katie looked confused. "You already have my approval."

"That's not it either," Mamm said. "I'd like you to come with me Tuesday night when I visit with Jesse's family."

Katie groaned. "I was hoping you'd go alone, *Mamm.* They hate me."

Mamm sighed. "They don't hate you, Katie. They don't really even know you . . . or me for that matter. I've already met the oldest girl, Mabel, and I think she's more heartbroken over losing her *mamm* than anything else."

"I can't do this." Katie stood. "Once you've said your marriage vows with Jesse

— if you get it done and we move in — that's one thing. Before that, they'll eat me alive."

Mamm tried to smile. "I know this is hard, Katie, but it's the least you can do for me."

"*Mamm,* please," Katie begged. "I'm too scared. And it's even worse now that I know how nice some folks can be."

Mamm looked pale. "How can my daughter say such things about her own people?"

"*Mamm,* please." Katie moved closer, touching *Mamm*'s arm. "I'm sorry. I didn't think how that would sound. And I have been treated nicely by many of our people in the community — just not by the young people."

Mamm sighed. "You've let awful things enter your heart, Katie. Our young people love you. Don't doubt the love of our people. And look how *Da Hah* sent me your *daett* to love me and now Jesse. How then can you run away from us, Katie?"

"I'm not running away," Katie protested.

"I wish you would come back to us, Katie," *Mamm* whispered. "It's still not too late."

So this was, after all, about persuading her to give up the Mennonites. Katie shook her head. "I'm still going back. I'm not like you, *Mamm.* I know you were a better

378

person than I am, but I can't do anything about the way I am."

"Katie . . ." *Mamm* stood to take Katie in her arms. "I don't mean that at all. And I didn't mean to bring up the Mennonites tonight. I guess I just keep slipping back there."

Katie didn't say anything, allowing her head to rest on *Mamm*'s shoulder. It felt *gut,* but she wasn't a little girl any longer. She was growing up. Pushing away, Katie sat down again.

Mamm held on to her arm. "Please, Katie. Come with me when I visit Jesse and his children. It would be so much easier for me if I weren't alone, and also easier for you in the long run. You don't want the wedding to arrive without knowing Jesse's children better."

Put that way, it made perfect sense, Katie thought. Only it didn't make perfect sense. When someone didn't like you, nothing made sense. But *Mamm* wanted her to go, and she really couldn't turn her down. And where was her faith that *Da Hah* could and would work things out?

Katie nodded. "Okay, I'll go with you."

"Oh thank you, Katie!" *Mamm* give her another big hug.

Katie squeezed her back this time.

Mamm finally let go, saying, "*Gut* night then. Remember, I love you."

"*Gut* night," Katie replied, finding her way upstairs in the dark. She lit a match and transferred the flame to her kerosene lamp. She sat down on the bed in the flickering light and stared out the window at the stars. They twinkled brightly back at her, seeming to smile out of the heavens. *What a sorry ending to a beautiful evening,* Katie thought. Not that *Mamm* was to blame. The trip to Jesse's house would weigh heavy on anyone's shoulders. But it would have been nice to come home tonight and spend the rest of her waking moments thinking about her fun evening before drifting off to sleep.

Now she was going to lie here and worry about how horrible things would be when they arrived at Jesse's place. They would sit in Jesse's living room with all of his children gathered around. They would be staring at Emma Raber's daughter from a close range. No doubt *Mamm* would have the worst of it, since she was Emma Raber. How in the world did *Mamm* plan to become these children's *mamm*?

But Katie had problems of her own to figure out. When *Mamm* married Jesse, she would have to move with *Mamm* to Jesse's house. Such a move would change so much, and in ways that couldn't be anticipated. For one, what was to become of her new life among the Mennonites? Could she still attend the gatherings? Would she still get to see Margaret and Sharon once in awhile? Yet she couldn't spend all her life around Margaret and Sharon. Life moved on, and so would Margaret and Sharon.

So what were her plans beyond enjoying her time with the Mennonite youth? Would she marry one of their boys someday? The thought sent shivers of fear up and down her spine. She'd often wondered what it would be like to make a boy happy, to see love shining out of his eyes for her. But never in her wildest imaginations had he been a Mennonite. If she joined the Mennonites she would have to change her dress, throw away her *kapp,* and buy a car. Katie stared at the flickering light. And she would have electric lights in the house, the kind Esther's *mamm* and *daett* had, which were turned on by a switch somewhere. She hadn't touched any of them, but she'd walked past them. Could she live in a house that had power from the outside world flowing through the wiring in the walls?

Katie shivered. *Nee,* that was a little too much to even imagine. Perhaps it was *gut* that *Mamm* had spoken with her tonight, and that she'd agreed to go along to Jesse's place. That way her options were still open either way. Perhaps by some miracle Jesse's children would like her, and she could have brothers and sisters of her own. Was that not what she'd wanted for years? It was, Katie told herself before she blew out the light. She would try hard next week to be nice to Jesse's children. She would tell them "hi" just like the Mennonite youth told everyone "hi." Jesse was a *gut* man. She'd always thought so. And perhaps *Da Hah* was bringing this thought to comfort her so she would help *Mamm* with Jesse's children. *Mamm* would need all the help she could get.

Katie slid under the covers and tossed and turned for a long time. She should get out of bed and pray, Katie thought. But she was too tired from the long evening. She would just trust that *Da Hah* was still guiding her life, and He had a plan for her that was more *wunderbah* than she could envision. With a slight smile on her face, Katie dropped off to sleep.

CHAPTER THIRTY-NINE

The following Sunday morning Katie sat beside *Mamm* in the buggy as they drove toward Bishop Miller's place for the morning services. Ahead of them other buggies had appeared on the road, all going the same direction. *Mamm* slapped the reins as hoof beats and the rattle of a fast-approaching buggy came from behind them.

"He won't try to pass you," Katie told *Mamm* after a quick glance back. "It's Joe Helmuth and his sisters."

Mamm smiled and relaxed. True to Katie's prediction, the sound of Joe's buggy wheels decreased as he kept his distance. If this had been Ben Stoll, Katie thought, he would have shown no such restraint. Ben would have raced around them even though they were within a hundred yards of where church was being held. Ben was a wild one, but her heart still beat faster on Sunday mornings at the thought of him. Had Ben really waved to her the other day? Or had that been an imagining of hers? The memory seemed foggy and distant now.

Katie glanced sideways at *Mamm* and pushed thoughts of Joe and Ben out of her mind. *Mamm* couldn't possibly know what she was thinking, and there was no need for thoughts of boys to flutter around in her brain right now. She would see both of them before an hour had passed, seated across Bishop Miller's living room from her.

What she should be thinking about was the upcoming Tuesday evening when they were scheduled to visit Jesse's family. It would not be an easy time, that was for sure. Likely the upcoming visit was the reason for *Mamm*'s tense look all morning. That and the *kafuffle* on Friday night about her running around with the Mennonites.

Nothing had been settled because nothing could be settled, Katie told herself. She would simply have to wait and see what happened. *Mamm,* on the other hand, was not waiting on anything. She was pushing full-steam ahead with her plans to say marriage vows with Jesse.

At least the decision to marry Jesse was no longer about her, which was *gut. Mamm* was falling in love — if Katie didn't miss her guess, though even *Mamm* seemed unaware of the fact. Regardless, that would make the sting of pain all the worse if Jesse's children didn't accept her. Katie would have to help *Mamm* by praying about this.

Mamm pulled back on the reins and turned into the driveway. The buggy stopped before they arrived at the end of the sidewalk leading into Bishop Miller's washroom, where they waited for the other buggies to unload the womenfolk. *Mamm* guided their horse to the row of buggies by the barn.

Mamm's continued relationship with Jesse was raising hope in her own heart, Katie decided as she climbed down from the buggy. Katie pressed her lips together as she unhooked the tug on her side of the buggy. There was no sense in crying here in public, even if no one noticed. It wouldn't help the situation. But she couldn't keep the thoughts from going on. What if Jesse really succeeded in his plan, and they could all be one happy family? She would have a *daett* and brothers and sisters. Wasn't that what she'd wanted for so long? Her friendship with Margaret and Sharon might be the foreshadow of what was coming. Katie held the buggy shafts as *Mamm* led the horse forward. Katie decided again she had to stop thinking about this right now. She forced herself to smile as Bishop Miller's oldest boy, Eben, came running up to take their horse. He looked tired this morning.

"*Gut* morning," Eben said to *Mamm* as he grabbed the reins to lead the horse away.

"Thank you," *Mamm* told him.

"You're welcome," Eben hollered over his shoulder as Katie followed *Mamm* toward the washroom. Always someone came for their horse — every Sunday morning. Usually it was one of the boys at whose home the church service was being held. But if the *daett* of the home had no older boys, someone still came. Emma Raber and her daughter, Katie, were a fixture that belonged in the bracket of those who needed help on Sunday mornings. Everyone knew it. That was something that belonging to Jesse's family would also change.

Katie held her head up, her *kapp* straight out as they crossed the open lawn in front of the men. They joined the line of women at the sidewalk. Katie kept smiling, thinking happy thoughts. She might be Emma Raber's daughter right now, but last night she'd been Katie, laughing and talking with people who saw her for who she really was — a human being in whose heart beat the same hopes and fears as everyone else's.

"*Gut* morning," Wilma Troyer whispered to *Mamm.* Her eldest daughter, Lizzie, nodded to Katie. Katie returned her smile. Lizzie had to be around fourteen years of age, and she wasn't with the Amish youth group yet. Hopefully, Lizze would never learn that she was Emma Raber's daughter and wasn't worth paying attention to.

Katie moved forward with the line of women, following *Mamm* toward the washroom door and keeping her head down. Dark thoughts were tormenting her. If *Mamm* had remarried five years ago, or even two years ago, perhaps there would have been a chance for things to improve. But it was too late now, Katie thought. She was too old. And Jesse's children would never accept her as one of their own. Even if they did, she would be an old maid before anyone else noticed. That was simply the way it went with people's reputations in the community. Such things moved at the speed of the icy glaciers the eighth-grade students had studied.

Katie's faith was struggling this morning, and she had to stop doubting. "Please help me, dear *Hah*," Katie whispered silently. "I don't want to give in to despair." Wilma was holding the screen door for *Mamm*. When she arrived, Katie shook her head as Wilma motioned for her to follow *Mamm*.

"I'll hold the door," Katie whispered.

Wilma smiled and followed *Mamm* instead. Katie held the door for them, undoing her shawl once she was inside the washroom and adding it to the pile on the table. *Mamm* had already gone into the kitchen, and Katie followed when she was ready. Peace was coming over her heart again, and she offered to shake hands with a few of the girls near the kitchen sink before slipping in with the line of unmarried girls. Moments later the older women began moving toward the living room. Katie stayed with the girls her own age, keeping her head down as they walked in front of the already-seated younger boys.

Moments later one of the men shouted out a song number, and the singing began. The bishop waited for the first line of the song to finish, before leading the way upstairs for the minister's Sunday-morning meeting. Katie stole a glance at the line of seated older boys in front of her. Most of them had their eyes on their songbooks. A few were leaning forward in concentration. She spotted Ben Stoll's distinct profile, and for long moments she watched him. What if Ben noticed her this morning? she wondered. What if he actually looked at her? What would she do? Pass out? Her heart was pounding already. It couldn't happen, could it? That wave from the buggy had been nothing but a fluke, Katie told herself. She looked back down and kept her eyes fixed on the songbook page.

A few minutes later, Katie wondered what Ben was doing. Glancing her way, perhaps? She just had to check. What if Ben chose this very moment to look up and notice her and she missed it? A few of the other girls were stealing quick glances across the room, and some of the boys she could see had their heads up. Still, she didn't look all the way to Ben's place on the bench. By the time the ministers returned from their meeting upstairs and the first sermon began, Katie took a deep breath and gathered her courage. She peeked across the room just as the minister rose to begin his sermon. His voice thundered through the whole house. Katie's gaze found Ben at once. He was smiling to someone on the bench of girls, but his gaze came her way almost at once. It was as if he'd been waiting for her to look his way, Katie thought. She gave him the sweetest smile she could muster. She could hardly breathe as a little smile played on Ben's face. He'd noticed her, Katie told herself as she quickly looked at the floor again. Ben Stoll knew she existed! *Da Hah* had given her a sign! She knew He had. He was going to make everything turn out okay.

So what did the other problems in her life matter? Questions like how long her friendship with Margaret and Sharon would last or was *Mamm* really going to marry Jesse would be answered. What if Jesse's children never liked her? Why should she wonder if she'd someday have to join the Mennonites and turn on electric lights and take out a driver's license? She wasn't going to worry about any of those things.

But she mustn't let her obsession with Ben get out of hand, Katie told herself. She had surely matured lately, and she had other friends who loved her now. And there were also *Mamm*'s warnings over the dangers of giving a man attention who might never truly return them. Still, today was almost too much to believe. Taking a deep breath, Katie forced herself to listen to the minister's sermon.

"*Da Hah* is a great and terrible *Gott*," the minister was saying. "He remembers the sins of the fathers to the third and fourth generation, but He also has mercy unto a thousand generations."

Katie stole another quick peek at Ben Stoll, but he was looking at the minister now. One smile was enough for today, she told herself. *Da Hah* was having mercy upon them all. Not just on *Mamm,* but on her also. She would get down on her knees when she arrived home this afternoon and not stop thanking Him for a very long time.

CHAPTER FORTY

On Tuesday night, Katie sat nervously in her side of the seat as *Mamm* drove the buggy toward Jesse's place. They had both buggy doors pushed open to allow the air to flow over their faces. The evening sun had almost set, and the shadows were stealing fast across the land. They'd eaten supper at the house before leaving, even though Katie had managed to get down only a few bites. She was more nervous than she ought to be. Her joy from Ben's smile on Sunday was still with her, but reality was also present. Whatever happened tonight, *Da Hah* would surely supply His grace. She was sure of that, but that didn't mean the journey or what was going to take place would be easy. *Mamm* was quiet as she drove. In fact, she hadn't really said much for some time now. It was as if the two women had said all there was to say between them and were now waiting for the storm to descend upon their heads. And there would be a storm tonight. Katie was also sure of that. *Mamm* knew it too, and yet she was driving straight into the troubled winds with her face firmly set. It took a certain kind of courage to do that, and *Mamm* was to be admired for it. She was doing this because it was right. She would do it even if there was pain involved, and even if that pain tore at her heart. And this might tear deep. *Mamm* was going not just to speak with a man she loved, but with his children who didn't love her.

Katie noticed a buggy approaching them. She gasped after she looked closer and saw that it was Ruth Troyer driving toward them. As she passed by, Ruth craned her neck around to glare out her buggy door at them.

Mamm tried to act like she hadn't noticed, but her lips were now set in an even straighter line than they had been before.

"Mamm," Katie said, reaching over to touch her arm, "I'm with you. And *Da Hah* will help us even if it hurts a bit."

"I know," *Mamm* said.

"You must love Jesse a lot," Katie said.

Mamm smiled. "I'm not sure about that, but I can no longer tell myself that I can just walk away from such a decent man. I've been without a husband for too long, Katie.

And you have been without a *daett*. I'm sorry for the way I've been these years since your *daett* died."

Katie acknowledged *Mamm*'s words with a nod, moving on quickly. "I think we should prepare ourselves for a rough evening. If Ruth's looks are any indication of what lies ahead of us, we will be glad if we come out alive."

Mamm managed to laugh but the sound was choked.

"Ruth is just going home from school," *Mamm* said. "She has nothing to do with our visit tonight."

There wasn't much conviction in *Mamm*'s voice, but Katie let the point pass. Ruth was likely up to some trick and had probably even stopped in at Jesse's place to give him one final chewing out.

They drove on, the sun dropping even further over the horizon. *Mamm* turned on the blinker lights as dusk fell. Jesse's driveway soon appeared, and *Mamm* slowed down to turn in. Katie searched the falling darkness ahead for any unusual signs. It would have been nice if Jesse were outside waiting for them, but that would be expecting a lot of him. He couldn't read their minds and know when they planned to arrive. *Mamm* had said that a certain time hadn't been set, just that they should arrive sometime after supper.

Mamm pulled to a stop, and Katie hopped out, grabbing the tie line. She ran in front of the horse and tied him to the post. Her courage was returning now that they'd arrived. After all, she was really just an observer tonight since she probably wouldn't do much more than pray anyway.

With a sigh, Katie followed *Mamm* up the sidewalk to the porch. *Mamm* knocked and before anyone answered, there was a noise behind them. Katie turned around to see Jesse hurrying across the yard to greet them. The barn door was swinging wildly on its hinges.

Katie had to laugh even though she hid her face with her hand. If Mabel was watching through the living room window, it wouldn't help if she noticed her soon-to-be sister laughing at her *daett* — even if Jesse was acting love-struck.

"You're here!" Jesse proclaimed, racing up the porch steps to grasp *Mamm*'s arm.

"I hope we're not late," *Mamm* offered, her smile a bit forced. "You said sometime after supper."

"*Yah.*" Jesse pointed toward the front door. "The time's perfectly okay. I was out in the barn waiting for you, but for some reason I didn't hear your buggy arrive. I must be getting hard of hearing in my old age."

Mamm's smile became more natural now. Katie relaxed when she noticed that.

"Come in, come in!" Jesse was holding the door open for them.

Mamm went inside, and Katie followed.

"Have a seat." Jesse motioned with his hand toward the couch. "I'll call the children."

A noise rattled out in the kitchen, and *Mamm* looked in that direction. She remained standing beside the couch though.

"Is Mabel out there?" *Mamm* asked Jesse.

He nodded.

Mamm didn't say anything more. She sank onto the couch, her face white again. Katie mentally shook herself and marched toward the kitchen doorway. She had no reason to be afraid of the girl, she told herself. Margaret and Sharon accepted her, and that was enough for now. And Ben Stoll had smiled at her. With that, she could face Mabel with some confidence.

"Let me go in," Katie said gently to Jesse. He stood aside as Katie entered the kitchen.

Mabel stood at the sink, her arms soapy from washing the dishes. When she turned around, there were tears streaming down her face.

"Mabel," Katie called out as she walked closer.

Mabel continued washing without uttering a word. Katie stopped, frozen in place until *Mamm*'s hand touched her shoulder. Together they stood there, saying nothing.

"Now, now!" Jesse's voice boomed behind them. "We can't begin the evening like this. There's no reason for this at all. Come, Mabel. The dishes can wait until later."

Katie unfroze and found her voice at the same time. "I'll help Mabel with the dishes," she said. "The two of you can talk with the other children until we're finished."

Jesse cleared his throat and sounded like he was going to say something. When he didn't, Katie looked behind her to see *Mamm* now wrapped in Jesse's arms.

Katie whirled back around, her face turning a flaming red as she tripped toward Mabel, catching herself by the edge of the kitchen table before she fell. Mabel had also seen the sight, and she was now staring out of the window. Katie steadied herself with both hands, the image of *Mamm* in Jesse's arms rushing through her mind. This was the part of *Mamm* being with Jesse she hadn't expected. Hopefully the two of them had moved away from the doorway by now or had quit acting like that. It wasn't a decent sight for unmarried young people to see. What would Mabel say about seeing her *daett* acting like that with *Mamm*?

Katie stole a quick sideways glance at Mabel. She had stopped crying and didn't look embarrassed.

Mabel spoke through clenched teeth. "Why are you two here?"

"You know why we're here," Katie countered.

"I wish you would just go away," Mabel said out of the corner of her mouth. "You've been trouble enough. We have a perfect woman who wants to be our *mamm*. And *Daett* would ask her if your *mamm* hadn't charmed his heart with her sneaky ways."

Angry words pushed against Katie's lips, but she held them back. Instead she said, "I'm sorry you feel that way. I think *Mamm* has fallen in love with your *daett*. And he with her."

Mabel snorted her disapproval.

"Well, it's true," Katie insisted, ignoring the insult. "Don't you believe that two people can grow to love each other?" Katie tried to smile through the fierce glare Mabel turned on her.

Mabel spat out, "Ruth Troyer has told me all about your *mamm*. How she used to act when she was younger. How she was all crazy about Daniel Kauffman and haunted him right up to his wedding day. I wish *Daett* would have gotten married to Ruth before your *mamm* ever found out he existed."

Katie pressed her lips together. These were awful things that Ruth was spreading around the community, but it was to be expected. No doubt everyone would remember again what had happened. Hadn't *Mamm* told her much the same thing? But since her friendship with Margaret and Sharon, she wasn't quite Emma Raber's daughter anymore. At least she wasn't what that name used to mean. And *Mamm* was also changing in ways she couldn't even begin to understand.

"I think people change," Katie offered. "Don't you?"

Mabel looked up, but she didn't look convinced. "*Daett* is going to make us accept your *mamm* as our own whether we want to or not."

Katie slipped her arm around Mabel's shoulder, but Mabel pushed her away. "I can't help how you feel," Katie said, still touching Mabel's arm. "But perhaps if you came in and spoke with *Mamm* for a little bit, you would see that she really is in love with your *daett.*"

"Anyone can put on an act," Mabel muttered.

"May I help you finish?" Katie offered, ignoring Mabel's barb. "I've been standing here distracting you from your work when I came in to help."

"I'm done." Mabel washed her hands under the spigot. "The dishes can dry on the drainer by themselves."

Katie shrugged as Mabel marched into the living room. She followed, sitting beside Mabel on the couch. The three boys and Carolyn were sitting on chairs across from Jesse and *Mamm,* who were sitting in rockers. Everyone looked grim, and the soft murmur of conversation died down now that they'd arrived.

"I think I'll head on up to bed," Leroy said into the silence.

When Jesse didn't object, Willis also jumped up and followed his brother. Mabel did the same thing without saying anything, and Jesse still didn't object. *Mamm* had tears in her eyes.

"I'm sorry about the evening," Jesse told them. "It's hard on Mabel, and the others are uncomfortable when Mabel's upset. But she'll come around soon. It'll just take a little time."

Mamm nodded but the tears were running

down her face now.

"Come!" *Mamm* said to Katie. "I think we'd better go."

Joel was smiling at them from his chair as they walked out the door. Katie smiled back at him. At least one of Jesse's children liked them. Jesse went along with them outside, holding *Mamm*'s hand as they walked across the yard. He untied their horse and held the bridle as *Mamm* climbed in. Katie got into the buggy on the other side. Jesse let go once *Mamm* had the reins. He waved as they drove past, but *Mamm* was looking straight ahead. Tears were still running down her cheeks.

"We'll make it somehow," *Mamm* murmured. "We have to."

Katie didn't say anything, but she reached out to take *Mamm*'s hand. They had survived this storm, but the winds were still raging.

CHAPTER FORTY-ONE

By the time Emma and Katie arrived home, *Mamm* had stopped crying but then started again. Her cheeks glistened in the buggy lights as Katie helped unhitch.

Katie followed her *mamm* into the barn, and *Mamm* held the flashlight while Katie pulled off the horse's harness and led the horse into his stall. *Mamm* paused outside the barn, standing in the darkness and looking up at the star-filled sky. It was a beautiful night, but both of them were too distracted to enjoy the view for long.

"Come on, Katie," *Mamm* said, walking toward the house. "It's high time we were in bed."

Katie followed *Mamm* across the lawn and into the house. At the kitchen doorway, she paused as her *mamm* sat down at the kitchen table and put her head between her hands. Katie sighed.

Mamm looked up, her eyes red and her

cheeks wet. "Katie," *Mamm* said quietly, "I need some time by myself."

"I think we'd better talk," Katie countered gently as she pulled out a chair to sit down.

"Mabel doesn't like me," *Mamm* said, clutching her handkerchief.

Katie reached for *Mamm*'s hand. "I know, but at least the rest of the children seem to get along okay with you. Maybe we shouldn't let Mabel bother us so much."

Mamm's hand trembled. "I don't know why she shakes me up the way she does. I know she shouldn't affect me this much."

"Jesse loves you, *Mamm.*" Katie glanced away as the image of Jesse holding *Mamm*'s hand as the two of them walked across the lawn flashed through her mind. "And I can tell you've opened your heart to him. That's a *wunderbah* thing. I despaired many times thinking you never would find love again."

A thin smile played on *Mamm*'s face. "Maybe this is why I didn't wish to be around a man again — the pain I'm feeling. And not knowing what's going to happen. I see Mabel and I think she'll never accept me as her *mamm.*"

Katie squeezed her *mamm*'s hand. "We can't change Mabel. She is what she is. And what is she going to do? Bite our heads off?"

403

Mamm managed to smile. "*Nee,* of course not."

"Then what have we to fear from her?"

Mamm's eyes sought Katie's face. "Are you trying to encourage yourself or do you really believe this? Jesse says some of the same things, but Mabel is his daughter. He wants to believe only the best of her."

Katie winced. "I'm just talking, I suppose. But I do believe this — in my heart at least. It's better than living like we used to. You have to admit that."

Tears sprang to *Mamm*'s eyes again. "*Yah,* you're right. It does come down to that question. Is the pain worth the man? Is the struggling worth the possible victory at the end — if *Da Hah* so allows it? Is seeing my daughter happy worth having her run around with the Mennonites?"

"*Mamm!*" Katie caught her breath.

Mamm's hand touched her at once. "I'm sorry, Katie. I shouldn't have said that. It wasn't fair."

Katie hung her head. "I'm sorry for my part in your pain. Should I promise to never see Margaret and Sharon again? Maybe if I stopped thinking about how I feel, I could stay away from them. Would that make you happy?"

Mamm didn't hesitate as she took Katie in

her arms. "Dear daughter. *Nee.* Difficult as it is for me to admit this, it was your running around with the Mennonites that pushed me out of my frozen world. I don't think *Da Hah* was able to get to me any other way. And it's your courage tonight that's keeping me going. I know I'd falter if I had to face Mabel's anger on my own. Even Jesse's love wouldn't be enough right now. That was quite a blow for me tonight. Jesse had been so certain everything would go well. And it's always been you, Katie, that *Da Hah* has used to bring *gut* things into my life. And it was your words through which your *daett* spoke to me again. Why should I tell you to stop doing what you think is right?"

"Oh, *Mamm!*" Katie clung to her *mamm*'s hand. "You shouldn't say things like that. I didn't do that much to make you happy."

A wry smile played on *Mamm*'s face. "You just being here is what makes me happy."

Katie squinted. "I did misbehave now and then, I suppose."

"*Yah,* that you did."

"Do I now have to worry that *you're* going Mennonite, *Mamm*? You sound right-out sympathetic to their ways."

Mamm laughed. "Me? Of course not! I'm an old Amish woman, and I'll always be one. But I'm sorry for how I used to speak to you, Katie. I'm sorry for all those years I sat here when I could have accepted the love of a *gut* man and given you the *daett* you longed for, when I could have reached out to people so both of us would have been more accepted."

"But Jesse wasn't available." Katie eyed her *mamm.* "Unless there was someone else I wasn't aware of."

Mamm shook her head. "There was no one, Katie. But I suppose there would have been one if . . . well, you know, if I hadn't been the way I was. But I do wish this could all have happened before I lost you."

"But you haven't lost me!" Katie leaped to her feet. "I'm still here!"

"You've traveled far, Katie." *Mamm* tried to smile. "But *Da Hah* will bring *gut* out of this situation. He has so far. I will trust Him. And in my heart I believe you'll always be one of us. But it's best that you come home when your heart draws you, not because of some promise you would have to struggle to keep."

"Then you too have made peace with what I'm doing?" Katie stepped closer to *Mamm.*

Mamm met Katie's gaze with a soft smile. "I'm trying. But I also make no promises.

406

You can see how quickly I get blown around like a leaf in the wind. I listen to Jesse, and I stand strong for awhile. Then Mabel shows up and away I go."

"That's understandable." Katie gave *Mamm* a tight hug. "You'll have to live in the same house all day with Mabel. I can get out to Byler's and to visit Margaret and . . ." Katie let the sentence hang.

Mamm's face had already fallen even as she tried to smile.

"Sorry, *Mamm,* I shouldn't have reminded you . . ."

"It's okay, Katie," *Mamm* cut in. Her smile was back now. "How are we little people who run around on this earth ever going to understand *Da Hah*'s ways? I'm content with how you are, Katie. And Jesse seems to have no problem with you either. We love you, Katie. Just keep on following *Da Hah* even if we don't understand exactly what's happening."

"Mamm!" Katie squeezed back the tears. "You say such *wunderbah* things."

"It's high time I said them," *Mamm* told her. "Tomorrow I might be back to complaining again, and you'll have to forgive me all over again."

"Just don't say *gut* things about me and the Mennonites in public," Katie cautioned.

"You'll have Ruth's tongue wagging even more for sure."

Mamm's face fell again. "Let's not talk about that woman."

"You shouldn't be afraid of her either," Katie said. "She's not the one Jesse asked to wed."

Mamm sighed. "*Yah,* Katie. You're right. I should count my blessings instead of worrying about dark things. So, shall we plan the wedding? Jesse hasn't set a final date yet, but it will be soon."

A vision of *Mamm* with her head buried in Jesse's beard flashed through Katie's mind, and she turned red again.

Mamm was looking at her. She smiled, seeming to understand. "I know, Katie. Jesse is a man and I am a woman — deep down. And that's another place I've failed you. There are things that happen between the hearts of a man and a woman that are so *wunderbah.* I shouldn't have let my pain allow me to say some of the things I did. I do hope you find someone special someday. I don't think it will be Ben Stoll. *Yah,* I've noticed you watching him. I hope it will be an Amish boy. I'll pray for you, Katie, that *Da Hah* leads and you follow Him with joy."

"Thanks," Katie whispered. "I'm not in love with a Mennonite boy, *Mamm.*"

Mamm looked hopeful. "Perhaps this marriage between Jesse and me can be the healing of your heart too. That would be a small payment for all the *wunderbah* things you've done for me."

Katie smiled. "I love you, *Mamm*. And thank you for always loving me. Even when I . . ."

"Oh, you're such a darling!" *Mamm* wrapped Katie in another hug. "Let's not speak of this anymore. You'll get your problems worked out someday. And we have more than enough work ahead of us getting ready for the wedding. Now, don't you think it's time we both went to bed?"

Katie nodded, glancing toward *Mamm*'s bedroom. "Will you be okay? I can sleep on the couch to be nearer if that will help."

"Oh, Katie!" *Mamm* beamed. "That's so *wunderbah* for you to offer. I can see now that nothing has really changed between us — even with all these changes happening so fast. I'll comfort myself with that thought tonight. You go on upstairs to your own bed. I'll fall asleep before I know it, especially after this talk with you."

Katie slipped into the stairwell, pausing to listen until *Mamm*'s footsteps had faded toward her bedroom. Not that long ago *Mamm* would have been listening to her as she went up upstairs. Now *Da Hah* was ministering grace and healing between them, and *Mamm* was moving into a brave new world filled with new love.

All of their problems weren't solved. For one, Mabel hadn't changed her mind. And Katie was still Emma Raber's daughter to the community. *Mamm* still had to face Ruth Troyer's wagging tongue. But love was growing in the hearts of those who allowed it. Jesse and *Mamm;* Margaret, Sharon, and herself; and maybe it could even happen between all of Jesse's children and *Mamm* . . . if enough time passed. *Mamm* would try hard on her part, that much was certain. And maybe Mabel would one day even open her heart to Katie. Such a thing would be a great miracle, but was *Da Hah* not able to perform miracles, even in this day and age?

Mamm's bedroom door clicked shut, and Katie went up the stairs to her room. Getting ready for bed in the darkness, she slipped under the covers. She lay there with her eyes open. *Mamm* might be downstairs fast asleep by now, but sleep eluded Katie. Too many things were whirling through her mind. The bishop would soon be announcing the news of *Mamm*'s wedding to Jesse, and there would be astonished looks on many faces. "Jesse Mast picked Emma Raber as his new *frau?*" they would whisper to each other — all spoken well out of earshot of Jesse and *Mamm* and the church leaders, of course.

Ruth probably had let enough slip by now that everyone would know she'd set her *kapp* for Jesse, and that Emma had won out. That would remain the mystery of this year's wedding season, Katie was sure. The controversy would blow over eventually, especially after *Mamm* and Jesse said the vows. That was the way of the Amish. Promises made and kept changed everything. The people would look differently at *Mamm* after that. The women would gather for the monthly sewings knowing she was now Jesse's *frau* and one of them again. And *Mamm* would begin to see herself in the same way. This didn't answer the question of what would happen with their vision of Katie though. That part of the future remained uncertain. But wasn't that the way things often went when people opened their hearts? You never knew how the world would turn out or where the road would lead.

Ben Stoll's face floated in front of Katie's mind, and the accompanying thought made her face burn in the darkness. Would she one day bury her face in Ben's beard? After

411

they'd said wedding vows, of course, she mentally added. What a shameful and yet *wunderbah* thought to have. To have two conflicting thoughts was hard to understand, but so it was in her life right now. Who would have thought so much *gut* could come out of her attending Mennonite youth gatherings? Who'd have thought that *Mamm* would ever admit it? How amazing was that?

For now it was enough that *Da Hah* was with them. And that He was still blessing and giving His aid. And Ben Stoll was a little scary underneath all of his charm. She hadn't forgotten *Mamm*'s warnings and stories about how she'd fallen for Daniel Kauffman. But whatever happened, Katie wasn't going to follow in *Mamm*'s footsteps and spend her time mooning over a boy who wasn't interested in her. She wasn't going to waste time waiting for someone to open his eyes and see the longing in hers. She wasn't going to watch him take another girl home and keep on hoping he'd love her someday. *Nee. Mamm*'s warnings hadn't been in vain, just as hers hadn't been to *Mamm*, even when she didn't know they were having an effect. The two of them were closer now than they had ever been. In sharing their hearts with others, more room had been formed for the love they had between them. It was *wunderbah* indeed, and *Da Hah*'s way of doing things. You gave and then you received more back. That was the way of the Amish, and she'd now experienced it firsthand.

There would be plenty of work ahead even with the small wedding *Mamm* would plan. Their family would be coming in from Lancaster to visit. Some of them were people Katie hadn't seen in years. Katie would let Margaret, Sharon, and Esther know soon what was going on. Surely they would understand if she didn't show up as often for the youth gatherings since she would be helping *Mamm* with the wedding preparations. Their hearts would still be bound together in love as the hearts of true friends are, no matter what road they chose to travel in the years ahead.

Yes, *Da Hah* would always be with her. Katie stared out of the bedroom window at the dark sky lit by stars until sleep crept over her body.

CHAPTER FORTY-TWO

Ruth closed the schoolhouse early on Friday night. The day of her visit to Emma Raber had arrived. Ruth harnessed her horse and drove quickly toward the Raber farm. She needed to arrive before Katie arrived home from work. There was no sense involving the innocent daughter, Ruth had decided. Katie couldn't help it that her mother was who she was. And what Ruth had to say wasn't for young ears. But still it must be said. Ruth slapped the reins, urging her horse on. Ten minutes later she pulled into the Raber lane just as lather began gathering under her horse's harness.

Ruth pulled up to the hitching post, got out, tied her horse up, and went up the porch steps at a fast clip. She was ready to knock when the door opened.

"Ruth! Is something wrong?" Emma said quickly.

"You ought to know the answer to that!"

Ruth snapped.

"I suppose you mean Jesse and me." Emma's voice revealed a tremor of hesitation.

"Of course I do." Ruth took a step forward, and Emma stood aside, allowing her to enter.

Ruth marched right into the living room and plopped on the couch. "I should have come sooner, Emma. I admit it, but there's still time to remedy this horrible situation since the wedding hasn't been formally announced. I want you to call this nonsense with Jesse off right away."

"Nonsense?" Emma said. "I suppose you think yourself a better *frau* for Jesse?" Emma remained standing near the front door.

"Sit down!" Ruth commanded and motioned with her hand. She waited until Emma had seated herself on a rocker. "We're past that point now, Emma. I don't even know if I'd take the man as my husband, as stubborn as he's being. Right now I'm thinking only of Jesse's children. They're the most important issue."

"Not Jesse's feelings on the matter?" Emma interrupted.

"Jesse doesn't know his own feelings." Ruth dismissed the thought with a quick wave of her hand.

"Jesse thinks he knows them well enough," Emma ventured.

Ruth eyed Emma for a long moment. "You've always thought highly of yourself, Emma, pursuing Daniel Kauffman right up to his wedding day. Well, you're doing the same thing now — running after a man. Throwing yourself at him when you have no business doing so. Of course he looks your way, but do you think that's going to last?" Ruth gave a loud laugh. "You're pretty enough, but how long will that last. And why should Jesse's children have their future destroyed because of you, Emma? Look what your own daughter already deals with. What chance does Katie have in the community with a mother like you? No boy's going to ask her home from the hymn singing. You know that. You've made yourself and your daughter outcasts of a sort in the community. You surely don't want that for Jesse and his children, do you? No, I'm sure even you wouldn't want that. So I want you to tell Jesse you won't see him anymore because his children's welfare must be considered first."

Ruth stopped for a long moment as she glared at Emma. The woman appeared appropriately chastened, so her words must be taking effect. Ruth charged ahead. "Sure,

Emma, I admit that you're a little better looking than I am. And you've taken better care of yourself over the years. But you've had the time, what with your solitary ways and all. But beauty only on the outside is a dangerous thing. You know that. You've lived a life of seclusion away from the eyes of the community. How dare you act as if you are . . . well, worthy of someone like Jesse."

Emma seemed to take Ruth's words in. Then she said, "Perhaps it's because of Katie — why I even dare believe things can be different, why I even want them to change." Emma stared out the window. "Katie has always brought love into my life, and why should I deny her the privilege to do so again?"

"Have you lost your mind, Emma?" Ruth sat straighter on the couch.

"I suppose you might think so." A slight smile played on Emma's face. "I haven't done anything to attract Jesse's attention, Ruth. There are reasons for all this that, in your small mind, you probably can't begin to comprehend. You thought pecan pies, of all things, would result in a new husband. Any woman can bake pies."

Ruth huffed, "And I suppose you're the expert on catching men. That really worked out with Daniel Kauffman, didn't it? Or are you more experienced now?"

"I seem to be doing just fine," Emma said, meeting Ruth's baleful glare head-on.

"You don't know anything about pecan pies," Ruth snapped. "At least it's *gut* to see you're admitting your sins."

"Catching a man? That's a sin now?"

Ruth glared.

Emma tapped the edge of one of the rocker's arms. "I know my sins, Ruth. But they aren't what you think they are. I did wrong with Daniel Kauffman, and I've repented of that. I haven't forgotten my actions that day. They weren't appropriate, *yah.* But *Da Hah* sent me Ezra . . . and then Katie. I didn't deserve either of them or their love. Now He's sending me Jesse and his love. I won't turn him away or go against *Da Hah*'s will. As for my sins, *yah,* they are many perhaps. But *Da Hah* knows I'm sorry for what I have done."

"And you should be." Ruth was huffing and puffing again. "Why, the way you've raised that girl is sin in itself. Drawing her into your little world and away from the community. I'm surprised the ministers haven't done something about you and your situation a long time ago. It's a scandal, I tell you. And now you have Jesse and his children in your clutches. How can you raise his children? You couldn't even raise Katie right. The last I heard, she's running with the Mennonites! Think sensibly, Emma! You are not right for Jesse, and you are certainly not right for his children."

Emma rose. "You don't understand me at all, Ruth. If you did, perhaps I'd listen. I just told you I haven't done things right in my life. I was wrong in keeping myself and Katie away from the community after Ezra's death. I've worked it out with *Da Hah,* and I'm bound to changing now, Ruth. That's what you're not seeing."

"So that's why you cast your net for Jesse?" Ruth looked triumphant. "You want your marriage to him to redeem you in the eyes of the community? You see him as your way out of your . . . isolation."

"*Nee,* Ruth. If I'd gone after Jesse, I'd say you might be right in your accusation. But I did not. Katie wanted a *daett,* and Jesse wants a *frau.* I wasn't the one who went looking for anything. Jesse came to me with *Da Hah*'s blessing. Now that it's happened, I can also see *Da Hah*'s hand in this situation. He means it for my good too, not just Katie's and not just Jesse's and not just Jesse's children. And, *yah,* Jesse is a decent catch. Too decent for me to think I could have snagged him on my own. Daniel Kauff-

419

man at least taught me that much."

Ruth snorted. "You didn't think yourself too *gut* for Daniel, Emma. Don't tell me you've changed since those days. You're still the same person you've always been."

"Perhaps we will leave that to *Da Hah* then." Emma pointed toward the door. "Katie's coming home soon, and you really should be going. I don't want her or anyone else to know you've come here. Think how it's going to look once I've said the vows with Jesse if it gets out how desperate you were."

Ruth leaped to her feet. "I only have the best interest of Jesse's children in mind. I have thought little of how I would benefit from this situation. Thinking of others is one lesson I'm sure you aren't paying much attention to."

Emma sighed. "If Jesse wanted your hand in marriage, Ruth, I wouldn't blame him one bit. But he wants mine, so why shouldn't I accept? *Yah,* marriage to Jesse will improve my life and certainly will improve Katie's. It will also improve Jesse's and his children's. Do you blame me for that? With Jesse's help, we will raise all six children in the fear of *Da Hah.* I can do that as well as the next woman. Now, I think you'd better go."

Ruth stalked out the door, slamming it behind her. She should never have come, she told herself. It was only the softness of her heart and concern for Jesse's children that had led her here. Some things simply couldn't be helped. She'd done all she could do now, and she would wash her hands of the matter. She untied her horse and climbed into the buggy. She drove out the lane without a backward glance.

CHAPTER FORTY-THREE

Katie watched through the living room window as Jesse's buggy came down the lane. *Mamm* rushed around the kitchen before making a quick dash toward her bedroom. She came out with a new apron on, brushing out any imaginary wrinkles.

"You can finish the last of the dishes," *Mamm* told her before she went outside. "We'll be out on the porch."

"Okay," Katie agreed, watching *Mamm* go down the front steps and run toward Jesse's buggy. For a moment Katie thought the two love birds would give each other a hug right there in plain sight. Jesse had gotten out of the buggy with his arms wide open. Instead, *Mamm* stopped just before she got to him. Her arms were clasped in front of her, but she was leaning forward. Jesse came close enough to touch *Mamm*'s face with both hands.

Katie knew she shouldn't be watching, but

she couldn't help herself. Was Jesse going to kiss *Mamm*? *Mamm* was laughing now, and Jesse dropped his head closer, evidently to whisper something. There was no kiss.

Jesse turned around moments later to tie Lucy to the hitching post. Then *Mamm* and Jesse walked together toward the house. Katie rushed away from the window. It wasn't likely they would see her watching them, but she didn't wish to take the chance either. Spying on them was embarrassing enough without getting caught at it. Katie busied herself in the kitchen as she listened to the sounds of the two of them taking their seats on the porch swing. She could hear the low murmur of their voices rising and falling but couldn't make out the words.

Katie let her thoughts drift. *Mamm* had told her about Ruth's visit a few days ago. *Mamm* had also told Jesse. The result was that Jesse determined their wedding date should be set as soon as possible to stop anymore interfering by that woman — and to stop tongues from wagging about something that was no one's business but theirs.

On the very next Sunday, to the surprise of most in the community, Bishop Jonas gave the announcement of the upcoming wedding. It produced every bit the shock Jesse and Emma had expected it would.

Ruth had looked quite pale afterward, as if she'd still entertained hopes that the marriage wouldn't occur. Talk about the tables being turned! Ruth had accused *Mamm* of not being able to let go of her old flame, and here she was doing the same thing.

Katie had attended another Mennonite youth gathering, but this time she told her new friends that she was going to stay home for awhile to help prepare for her *mamm*'s wedding. They all understood and were excited for her.

The preparations were in full swing. *Mamm* was so lost in the details that it was like she came up only for brief gulps of air. Katie smiled as she glanced at the letters lying on the kitchen counter. *Mamm* had written to her brothers, enclosing personal notes with the wedding invitations. They should have been mailed out yesterday, but they would probably still get there in time if mailed today. The news of *Mamm*'s wedding would have reached the families by now anyway, the word being passed through the Amish grapevine after Bishop Jonas's announcement in the church service.

Aunt Betsy would be arriving a few days before the wedding, *Mamm* had said last night. She was *Mamm*'s sister-in-law with the fewest children, so she was the one most able to leave her family in someone else's charge for a few days. *Mamm*'s youngest brother, Darrell, would arrive the day before the wedding, along with the rest of *Mamm*'s brothers and their families.

Mamm was still on *gut* terms with her brothers, even if they hadn't seen her in several years. That's the way Amish families were. They'd all grown up together so the ties were close. That was an experience Katie would never have, even if Mabel changed her attitude — which didn't seem likely at this point. Katie refused to entertain any regrets. It did bother her that her *daett*'s side of the family hadn't been invited to the wedding. They couldn't be, *Mamm* said. It wasn't proper. Katie understood that, but the connection with her *daett*'s family was still strong inside her heart. Katie would always be her *daett*'s daughter. She consoled herself with the fact that she would surely get to see all of them at a family reunion sometime in the near future.

Katie brushed away the tears as *Mamm* and Jesse's laughter reached clear through the house. They must be having a grand time together. And *Mamm* should have a grand time, Katie decided. Unlike Mabel, Katie had no negative or hard feelings about the upcoming marriage.

Katie stopped washing dishes moments later when the sound of the front door opening reached her.

"Katie!" *Mamm* called. "Will you come out here for a minute?"

Katie peeked around the kitchen doorway. "I'm coming. I'll be there in a minute." She went back to the sink to return the dishcloth. Then she wiped her hands on her apron. *Mamm* had waited for her at the front door. When Katie got there, *Mamm* led the way outside. Jesse was still sitting on the porch swing with a big smile on his face. He folded his arms casually as *Mamm* sat down beside him.

"Ah, Katie." Jesse looked at her with joy in his face. "I asked your *mamm* if I could speak with you." Jesse paused and shifted his weight on the swing.

Katie tilted her head and waited.

Jesse cleared his throat. "Perhaps you will want to sit. What I have to say may take some time."

"Oh! Of course!" *Mamm* jumped to her feet. "I'll go get a chair for her."

Katie stopped her. "I'll sit on the porch rail, *Mamm*. It's plenty comfortable."

Jesse smiled as *Mamm* sat down again. "Your *mamm* has been telling me how well you've been taking all the changes coming your way. I wish my children were doing as well. I've noticed Mabel hasn't been very nice to you at church."

Katie shrugged. "I understand her point of view. She still misses her *mamm.* This has to be hard for her."

Jesse nodded. "*Yah,* but it still isn't right for Mabel to act this way. Much is going to change once you and your *mamm* arrive at our house. We will begin anew as a family. Neither your *mamm* nor I have wished things to be unsettled as they are. In our thinking, Millie and your *daett* should never have passed away. But *Da Hah* didn't ask us what our thinking was. And He knows the whys of His decisions. We can only trust that *Da Hah*'s choices were — and are — always for the best."

Katie didn't offer any comment when Jesse paused.

"I believe that the love your *mamm* and I have for each other is a sign of *Da Hah*'s grace and favor. He wants us to go on with life and live in acceptance of His will. With that in mind, Katie, I want to tell you what a great delight it will be for me to have you living at my house. Not only living at my house, but living there as my daughter. I will love you, Katie, just as much as I love Mabel and Carolyn and my boys."

Katie lowered her eyes, grateful to hear such words from a man who desired to fill the empty hole in her heart. "Thank you for that," she whispered.

"I know not much has changed yet," Jesse continued. "Mabel, and even Carolyn, still struggle with accepting Emma as their *mamm.* Such things take time. I'm confident that once they see the love your *mamm* and I have for each other, they will also be much affected. That is the way love works, Katie. And I hope that someday an Amish boy will ask to bring you home to our house. That will be a great day for me, Katie. I will rejoice because much joy will come into your *mamm*'s and my hearts. It will be a day of great honor, for me equal to the honor when an Amish boy brings Mabel home for the first time."

Mamm had tears in her eyes, and Katie caught her breath, sliding down the side of the rail to sit on the floor of the porch.

Jesse continued. "Our faith is a great one, Katie. It goes back hundreds of years to a time of persecution and testing. Over the years our faith has been tried against the world and the devil and the weaknesses of our own flesh. It has stood the test of time. I will count it a great joy to raise and protect you in our faith. Someday I will joyfully give your hand in marriage to a young man who shares our faith and who is worthy of you."

Mamm held on to Jesse's arm. Tears sprang to Katie's eyes.

"I'm sorry," Jesse said. "I didn't mean to make you cry, Katie."

"Her tears aren't from sorrow, Jesse. You've touched her heart. Isn't that right, Katie?"

"*Yah, Mamm.* Jesse, I don't know what to say. My heart is overflowing. I have much to think about." Katie's mind raced as she thought of her love for her Mennonite friends and, at the same time, her lack of Amish friends her own age. Would Jesse's words ever come true? Would a young Amish man ever come to love her? Would Ben Stoll be the one?

Jesse stood and offered his hand to help Katie to her feet. As she stood, he gave her a hug.

"Thank you," Katie said. That was all she could muster as she returned his hug.

Mamm looked to Jesse and then to Katie. "Katie, you can go in now. And don't worry about the rest of the dishes. I'll finish them later. Jesse and I have more to talk about."

Katie nodded and went into the house and up to her room. She walked over to the window as she wiped away tears. *Mamm* and

Jesse's voices rose and fell in the air below her. They were so happy, Katie thought. And Jesse spoke of such happiness for herself. He spoke words that had gripped her heart. Could he be right? It was almost too much to even hear, let alone believe. If it were true, living with Jesse as her *daett* would really be like heaven on earth. Maybe *Da Hah* had greater miracles than she knew planned for her.

CHAPTER FORTY-FOUR

Katie worked at the kitchen sink as the house lay silent around her. This was *Mamm*'s wedding day. The early morning darkness still covered the fields. Aunt Betsy and Darrell, as well as *Mamm*'s two oldest brothers and their wives, were asleep upstairs with their smaller children. A bunch of their boys were sleeping in the barn loft, and their girls were set up in the basement. From behind her, *Mamm*'s footsteps came out of the bedroom. When Katie turned around, the light from the kerosene lamp flickered on *Mamm*'s face.

"You shouldn't be here in your chore clothes," Katie said, surprised. "It's your wedding day. There are plenty of people for doing chores . . ."

"*Yah*, there are," *Mamm* agreed, as if she'd just realized that fact.

Katie stepped closer and took one of *Mamm*'s hands in hers. "Are you sick?"

431

Mamm shook her head. "It's nothing to worry about. I'm just a little nervous."

When Katie didn't move away, *Mamm* continued. "I think it's a *gut* sign. With your *daett* I was so worried on the morning of our wedding I couldn't see straight."

Katie squeezed her *Mamm*'s hand. "Oh, *Mamm* . . ."

"Don't worry," *Mamm* assured her daughter and smiled. "I'll be okay. I'll be as calm as a cucumber by the time the service arrives."

Katie took a deep breath. By noon today she would have a new *daett* and *Mamm* would have her new husband.

Footsteps came down the stairs behind them. Katie returned to her work at the sink, and *Mamm* sat down at the kitchen table. Aunt Betsy stepped into the kitchen moments later, her hair askew under her *kapp.*

"My, you two are up early for a wedding day!" Betsy exclaimed.

Katie smiled as Betsy clucked her tongue. "I know this is probably hard for you, Katie. But look at how much better life will be for both you and your *mamm.* No more living with just the two of you for company. And you'll have a *daett* and brothers and sisters."

Katie smiled. "I'm not worried really. It's

a *wunderbah* day! I'm very happy for *Mamm* . . . and for me."

Betsy was still smiling. "Why, before you know it, you'll be part of a great big, *wunderbah* family. You'll have forgotten all about living as an only child."

"Yah," Katie said hesitantly.

Betsy turned to *Mamm.* "And now you, Emma. You're not going out to chore on the morning of your wedding. I don't care what you say about it. I'll go with Katie and help like I did last night."

"But . . ."

Betsy silenced *Mamm* with a shake of her finger.

Katie almost laughed aloud. Betsy had been a delight to have around ever since she'd arrived last week. She took charge when necessary and ran the household without hurting *Mamm*'s feelings. They would never have finished the wedding preparations — small though it was to be — without her.

"Come now," Betsy was saying. "You just sit here and wait. The others will be up shortly, and they can make breakfast."

"But there are so many people. We need to start right now," *Mamm* declared and then set her mouth in a thin, determined line.

"Then I'm getting the others up to help!" Betsy headed toward the stair door. Before she got there, Clara, the wife of *Mamm*'s oldest brother, Lonnie, stepped out, looking chirpy and fresh for this time of the morning.

"We're going out to chore," Betsy told her without even saying *gut* morning. "And don't let Emma work herself half to death on her wedding day. The woman needs at least one day off."

"Okay," Clara agreed. "But the boys can do the chores for you. There's no sense in them lying around doing nothing."

"It would take longer to explain what to do than to just do the chores myself," Katie said. "In fact, I can handle them by myself, Aunt Betsy."

"You will do nothing of the sort!" Betsy pointed toward the washroom. "Let's go. We'll see about getting the boys up once we get out there."

The first streaks of dawn were on the horizon as Betsy and Katie walked across the front yard. Katie pushed open the barn door and felt around until she found the lantern. The matches she discovered on the bench close to the front door. Moments later light flooded the barn.

Molly and Bossy were standing by the

back barn door. When she let them in, they almost ran to the stanchions where Betsy had already poured their feed and was ready with the milk buckets.

This will be Molly and Bossy's last day in this barn, Katie thought. Jesse's two boys were coming to take all the animals over to their place this afternoon. *Mamm* had insisted the marriage vows be said before anything changed on the farm. That wasn't because she had doubts about the marriage. *Mamm* was just being her usual stubborn self. Some things would never change. Any other widow who was getting married would have moved the livestock a week ago.

Katie closed the outside barn door, and joined Betsy by the two cows. She closed the stanchions.

Leather boots and denim pant legs appeared on the wooden ladder coming from the hay loft, followed by the rest of a boy. James, Clara's oldest boy, climbed down and moments later his brother Carl appeared. Both paused at the bottom of the chute to brush straw out of their clothing.

"*Gut* morning!" Katie greeted them, smiling.

They'd arrived last night after supper with Darrell and his vanload of visitors. There had been no room left in the house, so the

435

boys ended up in the haymow with blankets. It had been so *gut* to see everyone again.

"*Gut* morning!" they said together.

"Is there anything we can do to help?" James asked.

"We like to work up an appetite before breakfast," Carl added. "Traveling sure leaves the muscles out of shape."

"There aren't that many chores," Katie told them.

Betsy interrupted her. "Go ahead and show them what needs to be done, Katie. I can milk both cows if I need to."

"Okay." Katie led the two boys around to the horse stalls. They didn't ask many questions, but they did pay attention to what she told them. Betsy was just completing milking Bossy when Katie got back.

"I'll finish," Katie said. She grabbed the other bucket before Betsy could and waved her hand toward the barn door. "*Mamm* doesn't have family around that often. Why not go in and talk with her?"

"You're as stubborn as your *mamm*," Betsy said with a laugh, giving in at once.

When her aunt had left, an image of Mabel's disgruntled face rose in Katie's mind. She shivered. *Mamm* and Jesse would have several days alone, until after Thanksgiving, but then she would be living in the same house with Mabel. Would this really work? No doubts on *Mamm*'s wedding day! Katie reminded herself. She would think only about her *mamm* and Jesse and how much they loved each other. And she would concentrate on the words of support Jesse had spoken to her. That had been *wunderbah* to hear and filled her with hope. *Da Hah* had not forsaken them.

Katie concentrated on milking as fast as she could. Margaret and Sharon were coming today. She'd seen to it that they were invited even though *Mamm* had raised her eyebrows. Esther was also coming. It was *gut* of all three of them to attend. They surely had to go out of their way to find time for an Amish wedding. If she had any doubts before, she knew for sure now that these girls were her friends indeed. She would always hold them close to her heart.

Behind her James and Carl came out of the horse stalls, laughing as their flashlight beams bounced around the barn walls. Katie stood up with her bucket of milk. She called to them, "You should get the rest of the boys up now. I'm sure breakfast is about ready."

That produced a yelp from Carl and a rush up the haymow ladder. Shouts from above were soon followed by loud groans.

"The washbasin is in the washroom at the house," Katie hollered up to the boys as she went out the door. She walked across the lawn. The sun's first rays were peeking above the horizon; dawn was well on the way. It would be a perfect day from the looks of things. Only thin clouds hung in the sky, but they should melt away soon. Mamm *deserves this kind of day after all she's gone through,* Katie thought. This was no doubt another sign of *Da Hah*'s approval.

Katie hugged herself in the chill of the morning air. She stepped inside the washroom and washed her face and hands in the basin before drying herself with a towel. She heard loud voices coming from the lawn behind her, and she hurriedly disappeared into the kitchen before the boys arrived. Katie paused just inside the kitchen door. Women were rushing all over the place. Breakfast was spread on the table — fried eggs, hash browns, ham, bacon, and a big bowl of steaming oatmeal.

"When will breakfast be ready?" one of the men shouted from the living room.

"Always hungry!" Betsy said with a laugh as she counted the places available at the table. Then she closed her eyes and reviewed the number of people in the house.

"There won't be enough room," Clara announced before Betsy was done figuring. "The adults can eat in here, and the children can eat in the living room. That's what I say, anyway."

"Sounds good to me," Betsy agreed, abandoning her counting.

Katie looked around for *Mamm* and found her standing by the stove, her face glowing. *It must be coming from joy and the temperature in the room,* Katie figured. The heat was rising steadily to the ceiling from all the cooking.

Katie gave *Mamm* a smile before stepping over to the kitchen window to push it open. Betsy grunted her approval as she rushed past. Katie went to stand beside *Mamm,* staying there until the aunts had brought order out of the chaos. Then Katie joined the children in the living room, taking a place on the couch. The adults filled the kitchen table, and Lonnie led out in prayer. After the amen, the children waited for Betsy to call them into the kitchen to fill their plates.

Mary, Lonnie's oldest girl, was around sixteen, Katie remembered. She was a quiet one and hadn't said much since they'd arrived last night. At least she smiled and offered a few comments now and then. The children ate their meal in silence. Then Lonnie announced the closing prayer from the kitchen. When they finished praying, the children scattered. The boys had the first use of the limited number of bedrooms upstairs to change, after which the girls had their turn. The men came next. By that time, the women were done with the dishes and took their turn to change.

Katie changed in *Mamm*'s bedroom. This was her special privilege of the day as daughter of the bride. *Mamm* slipped in after Katie was finished and it was a long time before *Mamm* came out.

Betsy saw *Mamm* first and gasped in delight.

Katie jumped to her feet to look. She'd seen *Mamm*'s wedding dress hanging in the closet, but not on *Mamm*. The dark-blue material glowed in the soft, morning sunlight pouring through the hall window.

"Oh, you're beautiful, Emma!" Betsy gushed. "Oh my! I shouldn't be making such a fuss, but this is simply *wunderbah.*"

"It's really nothing," *Mamm* said, but her face was beaming.

Katie didn't dare breathe for a moment as the reality hit her. *Mamm* really was going to marry Jesse Mast, and they really were going to be one big family. Even Mabel couldn't stop it now.

Betsy grabbed *Mamm*'s hand. "Come! We have to get to the wedding right away before very many people see you. It's late enough already. Quick, James, hitch up the buggy. I'm driving Emma over, and the others can come later."

James smiled as if he were pleased with himself. "I harnessed the horse before I came in for breakfast, so it won't be long." He disappeared out the door.

Mamm grabbed her shawl and bonnet, and Katie did the same, following *Mamm* and Betsy outside. James had the buggy ready and stood waiting by the horse's head, his hand on the bridle and his smile wide.

Katie climbed in the back, and Emma and Betsy climbed into the front seat. James slapped the horse on the neck, and they were off, heading to Bishop Miller's place where the ceremony would be held and the noon meal served. *Mamm* had debated long and hard about having the wedding ceremony at the home place. But everything would have been cramped in either the barn or the house, so she had finally decided against the plan. There would simply not be enough room even though it was to be a small wedding.

Mamm didn't say anything on the drive over, and Betsy concentrated on driving.

When they arrived at Bishop Miller's place, *Mamm* said, "I'm going to faint, I think."

"No you're not!" Betsy asserted, patting *Mamm*'s arm. Betsy smiled as heads turned toward them. She continued to drive past the sidewalk and out to the barn. There one of the boys came running.

"*Gut* morning!" he greeted them.

"*Gut* morning," Katie and *Mamm* replied together as they climbed out of the buggy. The boy took the horse's reins and motioned toward the house. "Go on in. I'll take care of your horse and buggy."

"Thank you!" Betsy said climbing down. *Mamm,* Betsy, and Katie walked to the house. *Mamm* immediately disappeared upstairs. Ten minutes later Jesse arrived in a new black suit. He too vanished up the stairs. Katie kept watch by the kitchen window, and when Margaret and Sharon arrived with Esther, she met them at the front door to make sure they felt welcome.

The line of men beside the barn moved toward the bishop's pole barn a few minutes before nine, when the service was scheduled to begin. Katie followed the women when they filed out. She was just sitting down when *Mamm* and Jesse walked out of the house. Katie held her breath for a moment, soaking in the sight of *Mamm* and Jesse coming toward them. Even Mabel, seated in the second row of girls, watched the couple with a hint of a smile on her face.

Mamm and Jesse moved with slow steps and took their seats in chairs up front. The singing began. At the second line of the first stanza, the ministers all stood. Bishop Miller led the way to the house. *Mamm* and Jesse followed them to receive their last-minute marriage instructions. What instructions *Mamm* and Jesse needed was hard to imagine since they'd both been happily married. But perhaps the ministers would offer advice on how to help all the children get along.

Katie closed her eyes and sang along with the rest as they waited for *Mamm* and Jesse's return. When they came back, Katie kept her eyes glued on *Mamm* and Jesse for a long time, and then she turned her attention to the preacher as the service progressed. The minutes ticked past, the hands seeming to turn slowly on the face of the clock hung on the pole barn wall. Suddenly ten minutes of twelve arrived! *Mamm* and Jesse stood up and answered *yah* to the marriage vows when Bishop Miller indicated.

Katie pressed back her tears as the bishop joined the newlyweds' hands and said they were now husband and wife before the eyes of God and man. Katie glanced down the row of girls and caught a glimpse of Mabel's face. She was actually smiling! What a miracle! Katie bowed her head and whispered a quick prayer. "Thank You, dear *Hah,* for this moment. Thank You for being so *gut* to us. I want to trust You for what lies ahead — even with Mabel and her feelings about *Mamm* and me."

When Katie opened her eyes, *Mamm* and Jesse were seated again. *Mamm*'s face was glowing and Jesse beamed. Katie clasped her hands and allowed the joy of the moment to fill her. Opening one's heart to love had, so far, been worth the cost.

DISCUSSION QUESTIONS

1. Is Katie justified in feeling unaccepted by the Amish youth?

2. Katie is known to others as "Emma Raber's daughter." Have you ever had a label attached to you that affected the way you thought about yourself?

3. Why do you think *Mamm* is so anxious about Katie? Is she justified in her feelings?

4. Why is Emma so unwilling to think about marriage again?

5. What do you think about Jesse? Why is he so persistent in pursing Emma when Ruth Troyer so obviously is interested in him — and in being a *mamm* to his children?

6. If you could offer advice to Emma Raber

about dealing with her past and with the present feelings she has as a result of that past, what would you tell her?

7. Have you done something in your past that still bothers you? How do you deal with the memory?

8. What do you think of Mabel? Are you sympathetic to her feelings or unsympathetic?

9. Was Katie right in continuing to attend the Mennonite youth meetings, knowing how her *mamm* felt?

10. What problems do you foresee for Jesse and Emma as they combine their households?

ABOUT THE AUTHOR

Jerry Eicher's bestselling Amish fiction (more than 400,000 in combined sales) includes The Adams County Trilogy, the Hannah's Heart books, The Fields of Home, and The Little Valley Series. After a traditional Amish childhood, Jerry taught for two terms in Amish and Mennonite schools in Ohio and Illinois. Since then he's been involved in church renewal, preaching, and teaching Bible studies.

Visit Jerry's website!

www.eicherjerry.com

The employees of Thorndike Press hope you have enjoyed this Large Print book. All our Thorndike, Wheeler, and Kennebec Large Print titles are designed for easy reading, and all our books are made to last. Other Thorndike Press Large Print books are available at your library, through selected bookstores, or directly from us.

For information about titles, please call:
  (800) 223-1244

or visit our Web site at:
  http://gale.cengage.com/thorndike

To share your comments, please write:
Publisher
Thorndike Press
10 Water St., Suite 310
Waterville, ME 04901